THE NORTH

THE FIFTH JON AND TERESA ZACHERY STORY

THE NORTH

THE FIFTH JON AND TERESA ZACHERY STORY

A NOVEL BY

J. J. ZERR

PRIMIX
PUBLISHING
THE WRITE CHOICE

Primix Publishing
11620 Wilshire Blvd
Suite 900, West Wilshire Center, Los Angeles, CA, 90025
www.primixpublishing.com
Phone: 1-800-538-5788

This is a work of fiction. Character names and the names of US Navy vessels are products of the author's imagination.

Lists of principal characters, acronyms, and US Navy ranks are included in the end matter.

Published by Primix Publishing   07/08/2022

ISBN: 978-1-957676-23-4(sc)
ISBN: 978-1-957676-25-8(hc)
ISBN: 978-1-957676-24-1(e)

Library of Congress Control Number: 2022908070

As always, God bless editors and the bubbettes and bubbas of my Coffee and Critique group.

1

Teresa Zachery stood and stared at the calendar. At January 9, 1972. The all-important calendar, pinned to the corkboard above the dryer in her kitchen, in on-base housing, on Naval Air Station Lemoore, California. A robe covered her nightgown. She'd brushed her hair, though. With her hair brushed, a woman can face anything. Something Mother often said as Teresa grew up.

Her husband, US Navy Lieutenant Jon Zachery, was aboard aircraft carrier USS *Solomons* as it approached the Hawaiian Islands. Two hours behind California time, he could still be asleep. The ship would conduct training operations there before entering port. She picked up the pen from atop the dryer and X-ed off the eighth. Five days X-ed off in what might be an eight- or nine-month deployment. As long as a pregnancy. And like a pregnancy, the last days of a deployment inched by at an excruciatingly slow pace. For that matter, the ones at the front end weren't passing all that fast either. And the end lay out there, months ahead yet. Months filled with worry for Jon. He and the other pilots took off and landed from their carrier. Carrier flying was twice as dangerous as flying from shore bases. Somewhere during flight training, she'd heard that. As if she needed to be aware that navy wives needed to worry about their husbands twice as much as air force wives. On top of that, as if carrier flying weren't enough of a worry, when she turned the calendar to February, the ship would be in the Tonkin Gulf, and Jon and the others would be flying combat missions.

From behind her, at the dining room table, three-year-old EJ, Edgar Jon, said, "Juice."

From five-year-old Jennifer, "Juice, please."

"Juice."

"Say please," Teresa insisted.

"Pweze."

"In a minute." The calendar held Teresa as if it connected her spiritually with her husband.

"Juice, pweze!"

Boys. Jennifer and two-month-old Ruthanne were sugar and spice next to Mr. Puppy-dog-tails.

Teresa sighed and poured orange juice for her son.

Two-month-old Ruthanne sat in her infant seat on the table, fascinated with her hands. She'd been fed. She was dry. She was quiet for the moment.

"Children are a nest full of baby robins cheeping feed me, feed me all day long." Naomi Engel, the wife of one of the pilots in her husband's squadron, said that at a wives' group function one day last year. The other wives had laughed. Teresa, however, hadn't considered it funny at all. At the time she'd been pregnant with Ruth, and two years prior, she'd delivered their third child, Daniel. Prematurely. The baby did not survive.

Last year, Naomi had NOT been funny. Now, though, Teresa found truth in what she'd said, and something to smile at, too.

Naomi, Harvey Engel's spouse. Supposedly, Engel in German meant angel. The squadron pilots decided Harvey was not an angel, so his call sign became Not.

Back to the calendar. *Solomons* would conduct two days of operations near Hawaii, spend two days in Pearl Harbor, then depart for the two-week trip across the Pacific to Subic Bay on Luzon. Then two days in Subic Bay and two days of transit to the Tonkin Gulf. January, and its twos, was known, but once she turned the page to February, nothing was certain. There wasn't even a projected end date for the cruise. This was Jon's third deployment, and all the previous ones had had at least a tentative return-home date. But not this one. Having a projected end to the separation gave her something to cling to, something to look forward to, but this time, the navy denied even that wisp of comfort.

The wives had talked about that. Something unusual was going on with the war in Vietnam. First, the *Solomons* and the embarked squadrons had been scheduled to decommission after the previous cruise. But, surprise! They hadn't disbanded and scrambled frantically to get ready for the current deployment in half the usual time the navy gave units to train. For sure something was going on. If the guys knew, they couldn't share what was probably classified info with their spouses. Even Sarah Fant, the squadron CO's wife, said she didn't know.

To Teresa, not having a projected end date of the deployment bothered her more than the notion that something was going on.

The things that niggled at her as she stood in front of her calendar on the cork board above the dryer were, in a way, complaints. Oh-woe-is-mes.

During grade school, Sister Mary Martin told the class, "Begin each day with a Thank You, God, for … . And look for something. There is always a blessing there if you just take the time to look for it."

Teresa thought: *Thank You, Father God, that I live on base, and that the Warhorse wives are here, too.*

For Jon's first deployment, in 1966, he had been assigned to a destroyer based in San Diego. Teresa had lived in an apartment in Chula Vista and had never felt safe the whole time Jon had been gone. She went to bed each night with the notion that the flimsy front door was nowhere near enough protection for baby Jennifer and her. Living on the naval air station provided a sense of safety and security she'd never felt in '66. And the members of the wives' group, for the most part, lived right there on base with her. However, the destroyer wives' group had been scattered widely around the greater San Diego area.

There were blessings in the morning if you but looked for them.

Then it was time to feed herself before she had to launch Jennifer off to kindergarten.

She prayed: Father God, watch over Jon. Please.

Then she fed herself breftus, as EJ called it.

2

NAVY LIEUTENANT JON ZACHERY, CALL sign Stretch, flew as flight lead with Mudder and Alice that night. Alice would deploy flares for them. Then he and Mudder would drop bombs on a radio-controlled boat off the southeast corner of Kauai.

After completing the flight-brief checklist, they left the ready room for the head. You always hit the head—visited the bathroom—before suiting up. Another rule on a carrier: never pass a drinking fountain without seeing if it worked, and if it did, you took a drink. Coming back aboard the ship at night, you didn't want to be thirsty, need to urinate, or have any other distractions. Night carrier landings demanded everything a pilot had to give.

Stretch considered the night landing aboard the aircraft carrier the worst thing he'd face on his upcoming hop.

And, as happened on all his night flights from a carrier, the notion persisted until he stepped out of the island onto the flight deck, which wasn't bathed in red light. It was barely moistened with red light. In the dark and dim, pandemonium. Sailors towed planes aft. Other planes were towed forward, and they passed at a goodly clip with inches of wingtip clearance. Bombs and missiles on carts trundled toward planes needing them. In daylight, the flight deck activity looked practiced, Holy-crap-those-guys-are-good professional. At night, pandemonium.

So, make it to your aircraft without getting run over, preflight, climb in the cockpit, start the engine, then taxi forward when signaled to do so. And you think: *It's too dad-burned dark. Turn on the fribble frapping lights.* Even in moments of terror, Jon would not let himself swear. Onboard the carrier USS *Solomons*, on the base at Naval Air Station Lemoore, cussing was all around him. It would be so easy to give in to it and swear like a sailor himself. But he could not swear at home, not in front of Teresa and the three children. If he did, Teresa would wash his mouth out with soap. Actually, his wife would be hurt, and that would be worse.

Get your head out of your butt!

He allowed himself the head out of your butt. It was so much more effective than Pay Attention.

He made it to the catapult without the brakes failing, and he and his plane going over the side. The cat shot. Plenty to worry about there. Sometimes it failed. Not often, but it happened. Sometimes a part on the plane broke. Not often, but it, too, happened. And you'd dribble off the bow with insufficient speed, and instead of having your butt strapped to a plane, you were strapped to a brick, and you were destined to get wet, and you had a second to react, or you'd be wet and dead.

That night, he and his plane, side number 510, received a good shot, and he felt when the wings grabbed air. Raise landing gear and flaps. Climb. Then he allowed himself: *Flying!* This smeared a grin under his oxygen mask. For a moment.

Watch out for other planes. Climbing and turning into the night sky filled with anti-collision lights—mega-watt fireflies flashing their don't-run-into-me warning—except fireflies'd be signaling: *Girls, I'm over here.*

Overhead the carrier, he set up a counterclockwise orbit at 22,000 feet, speed 250 knots. Level at 22K, since the altitude belonged to Stretch, he permitted himself a glance up at the starry, starry night. Solomons operated one hundred miles south of Oahu. No competition from any sort of civilized light from earth four miles below. Above, no moon, no clouds, just a bazillion dots of light, and it was as if in all the universe, only he could see the sight, sitting on his ejection seat, right after God, after having created the sun, had just now finished creating the lights of night.

Stretch! He scolded himself to get his mind back to the business at hand. The sky was big, but there were nineteen other planes aloft. One of them might contain a pilot lollygagging around, not paying attention, and run into him. And killing one or both of them.

Troll had been killed at the end of training for this deployment.

He chided himself yet again about keeping his mind on flying. His usual ritual was to approach his plane on deck and say to himself, "Hello, 510." And from that point on, nothing mattered but flying. He even put Teresa and the kids in a box and stashed it in the attic of his brain until after he landed.

He said it again, out loud, "Hello 510."

Off to his left, he spotted two anti-collision lights, one in trail of the other, climbing toward him. Mudder and Alice, his wingmen for the flight. After rendezvousing, they'd proceed northwest to south of Kauai. There, Stretch would contact range control, and he and Mudder would practice bombing a radio-controlled boat. Under flares. Alice carried flares on his plane. His job: illuminate the target.

Night flying, bombing at night, bombing under flares, in order, each of those ratcheted the pucker factor higher. Vertigo was the enemy. Day flying was a piece of cake. A pilot didn't have to think about it any more than a bird did. Night flying was work. Bombing at night was harder work. Rolling, diving, pulling Gs, all a piece-of-cake in the daylight where the brain received all kinds of cues as to where up and down really were. At night, with fewer visual cues, the rolling and Gs could confuse the brain as to where those two vital commodities, up and down, actually were. Flares made it even worse.

Flares had, in the past, turned Stretch's night world, not upside down, but on its side. His brain became absolutely convinced that the bright magnesium fire was the sun and that it defined "UP."

Fighting that sensation required him to concentrate with all his might on his instruments, to believe them, not the vertigo-induced sensation that screamed, *Don't look at your stupid instruments. Listen to me or we're going to die!*

During the preflight brief, he'd had warned Mudder about vertigo, "Believe your instruments and be prepared for a fight. I had it once, and it was like my left hand fought with my right to control the stick. Like one hand believed what my vertigo messed up brain was screaming, and the other believed what my flight instruments whispered. That's one of the dangers of vertigo. It screams. Reality whispers."

As the first aircraft closed on him, he turned off his anti-collision light. A major distracter when flying in formation, and only one plane in a flight had to have his on. Mudder took position on his right wing. As Alice joined on the left, Mudder turned off his collision light.

He rolled out of the turn, heading northwest, and switched the flight to Kauai Range Control radio frequency. After checking in with the range, Stretch turned on his anti-collision light. That signaled Alice to detach and drop his flares over the target boat and Mudder to drop back in trail on his flight lead. Each of the bomber planes carried six practice bombs.

Alice did a good job with the placement of his first flares. Stretch rolled in to fly up the wake of the target boat. He had to continually shallow his dive, and recalculate his bomb release point, as his target scooted away from him. Pickling off his first bomb at three thousand feet had been his intention. As it turned out, he couldn't drop his bomb until two thousand.

Stretch radioed, "Bomb," pulled up and rolled left to climb back to roll-in altitude. A minute later, Mudder called, "Bomb." As flight lead, he worried about his newbie wingman, but then it was time to call rolling in again.

On the second run, he set up at a right angle to the track of the boat. Once again, Alice had done a good job placing the flare. They dropped their second bombs and had gas for two more runs. On the third run, he set up with the boat heading for him. Stretch rolled in and set a steep dive angle, and it worked out. He'd anticipated, pretty well, the amount of lead he had to pull.

During the last run, the target boat would take evasive measures. Stretch set up a shallow dive, intending to release his bomb at about fifteen hundred feet above the water. He hoped it would minimize the boat's chance to escape with a last-second maneuver. He rolled in and tracked the target boat through a zig left, then a zig right.

What would the target do next? Another zig right or back to the left? Fifty fifty. Left.

Stretch made a last correction and hit the pickle and called, "Bomb." The boat zigged left. He pulled up, feeling the closeness of the water.

"Good hit," the range called.

Then the vertigo monster bit. As he pulled up and rolled into a left turn to climb, with the flare in front and above, his brain became convinced he had rolled too far and that he was diving for the water. The sensation was so powerful his hand on the stick almost jerked the plane into a hard right bank. But he looked at his attitude gyro. *Those stupid things screw up!* his brain shouted at him. It took all his discipline, all his mental strength to fight the voice and keep himself climbing and turning left.

He should look outside to make sure he wouldn't run into another plane, but he did not allow his eyes to let go of the flight instruments. Those competing, powerful and urgent drives filled his stomach with churning vinegary nausea. He was mastering—no, managing it, but barely.

All the way to twenty-five thousand feet, he fought himself for control of the where-is-up question. As he leveled off, the power of the false sense diminished. He was breathing hard, like after sprinting. Taking a deep breath of oxygen, he huffed it out. The vertigo monster let go. But once the monster bit you, even if you managed to exert control, it hovered near, like a dog that charged out of the bushes while you jogged and bit you on the butt, and it backed away when you faced it. But it hovered close, anxious for another tasty nip of bobbing buttock.

Huh! Fear of dying almost killed me.

That thought pushed the vertigo monster further into the background.

Mudder joined on him and radioed that Stretch had no hung bombs. His wingman's bomb racks were empty also. Alice joined the flight.

Stretch assumed the lead again and felt that up was up and down was down. His flight instruments agreed with him. But, man, the vertigo monster had grabbed him hard. And it was still near. There was no letting down his guard.

He switched the flight to the frequency for check-in with the ship. The air traffic controller assigned them 17,000 feet holding altitude. Flashing lights announced the presence of aircraft already in their orbits. Over the radio, others from the launch began checking in.

The air traffic controller issued approach times to all the aircraft.

Oh yeah. The carrier landing. The worst thing about night flying.

He remembered thinking that.

Tonight, God, can we have the vertigo monster be the worst thing on this hop?

Please?

Then it was time for his brain to work on the problem at hand. Hit the pushover point at precisely his approach time. His wingmen had taken up trail positions behind him. They would work to be precisely one and two minutes behind him.

Stretch hit his point five seconds early and started his descent. He waited to make the radio call until the second hand pointed straight up, then pressed the mike button and said, "510 commencing."

Five seconds off, he fussed at himself. Then he concentrated on controlling his rate of descent and holding his airspeed to 250 knots. That ensured the one-minute interval between him and the plane behind him, and the one in front, was maintained. Behind the carrier, minutes and fuel became sacred commodities. Maintain the one-minute interval, or you could screw yourself up by being too close to the guy in front, which could get you waved off or ordered to abort your attempt to land. And set up for another approach, if you had the fuel to do so. Otherwise, you'd be invited to bingo, head for, in this case, Barbers Point Naval Air Station, on Oahu, where if you flew the profile precisely, you'd arrive with the barest of fuel-remaining margin.

Stretch leveled at 1200 feet, slowed, and dropped his landing gear and flaps. It was a see-forever night. The flashers of the planes in front of him led him to the splop of light that was *Solomons*. CAVU to the moon, they called it. Ceiling and Visibility Unlimited all the way to the moon. Even on moonless nights, it could be CAVU to the moon.

A sudden, yellow-orange ball of fire burst from the carrier, brighter than a dozen flares all popped at once. He knew what it had to be. An airplane, an F-8 fighter, probably, had crashed on deck and the fuel in his tanks had exploded.

"Shit!" someone said over the radio.

Stretch jammed the throttle to full power and raised the landing gear as he climbed and turned toward Barbers Point. He was 500 pounds above bingo fuel state, and whatever caused the fireball, it would take some minutes to clear up.

"All aircraft return to holding," the air controller radioed.

"This is 510," Stretch said. "I'll be at bingo before I get there. I'm heading for Barbers."

"Negative, 510. Head for holding."

"This is 510. Three Warhorse aircraft are bingoing. Warhorses, switch to Barbers approach control."

THE PHONE RANG AND KICKED Teresa's heart … and Ruth awake.

0100!

Please, God!

She cupped a hand over one ear to block the baby's yowl and answered.

"Will you accept a collect call from Jon Zachery?"

"What? Uh, yes. Yes, I'll accept."

"Teresa?"

"Jon. What is it? What happened?"

"Oh," he said. "Ruth."

"Just tell me what happened."

"I flew tonight with Alice and Mudder. Before we landed, a plane crashed on the *Solomons*. We diverted to Barbers Point. I wanted you to know it wasn't me. It was probably an F-8. Not sure, though. We just landed here at Barbers. I wanted you to know it wasn't me."

Jennifer and EJ appeared in the doorway.

"I scared," EJ said and stuck his thumb in his mouth. Jennifer looked scared, too. Ruth was beyond scared. Way beyond.

"Jennifer. Take the phone and talk to Daddy. Hold it so you and EJ can both hear him. You talk first, then give EJ a turn."

Teresa got herself and Ruth out of bed. She cooed and patted the baby and brought her back over the precipice of terror. She continued to baby whisper as she changed her. Jennifer and EJ shared the phone.

Without fighting. *Thank you, God.*

Ruth was dry and calming down.

"Jennifer, you and EJ go back to bed. It's Mommy's turn to talk to Daddy."

Jennifer handed over the phone and started herding her brother to their own room.

EJ declared, "No. I do it me own self."

Jennifer looked back at her mother. Commiseration over having to deal with males passed between them. Her oldest was so grown up already.

Before this cruise is over, I'll probably appreciate that.

She sat in the chair and gave a breast to Ruth. The baby searched frantically for the nipple and latched on and began sucking nourishment for her body, but more importantly, security and serenity for her tiny soul.

Teresa put the handset to her ear. "Where were we?"

⸻⬤⸻⬤⸻

Jon hadn't given her many details, except the most important one. He was okay. Collect calls from Hawaii were expensive, and they didn't talk long.

After they hung up, Teresa put the baby down, climbed into bed, pulled the covers up, and wondered if she'd be able to fall asleep again. Her husband was safe, but, at the moment, the fright embedded in the phone ringing at that time of morning had held so much promise of disaster, comfort wouldn't be able to elbow its way in for some time.

She remembered Jon said he'd been flying with Mike Allison. The Allisons lived next door, their navy housing units joined at the carport. Amy had a baby the same age as Ruth. Both infants had been conceived during a visit to Hong Kong the previous deployment. Several squadron wives had traveled to meet their husbands there during *Solomon's* week-long visit. Teresa and Amy among them.

From the back door came a tap, tap, tap. Amy. Mike must have called her. Without bothering to grab her robe, she threw back the covers and hurried, barefoot, to open the door for her neighbor.

Amy wore a robe over a nightgown and carried her sound asleep baby in an infant seat.

"Come in, Amy. I'm glad you and Amelia are here."

"These things are hard enough to bear when we can be together. They are just godawful alone."

Amy placed the infant seat atop the dryer, and the two navy wives engaged in an embrace of commiseration. A type of hug they'd had occasion to practice a few times the previous cruise.

"Can I make coffee?" Amy said.

Amy knew where the Zacherys kept the pot and the fixings and helped herself.

Twenty minutes later, the women sat across from each other, with Amelia in her seat at an end of the dining room table, when the phone rang.

"The calling tree." Teresa hurried to the wall phone over the washing machine. Before she got there, it rang twice more. The one in the bedroom woke Ruth again, and she responded with her startled-awake-air-raid-siren cry, as Jon called it.

Tara Wisdom—her calling-tree contact—had more details. An F-8 had crashed during a landing attempt on *Solomons.* The crash killed the pilot, an experienced guy with over a thousand hours of flight time. He'd been considered a good stick.

After they hung up, Teresa gave the news to her contact, Amy. Amy dialed Monica Newsome's number. Teresa, meanwhile, went to calm her little air-raid siren. Patting, cooing, rocking and a pacifier ganged up on the little one, and Ruth slipped back into dreamland.

As she put the baby back in her cradle, she recalled when Jon had passed the one thousand hours of flight-time mark. He'd been excited, pleased with himself. "It means," he said, "now I know some stuff. Now you don't have to worry about me so much."

Right!

Nothing had the power to lessen the worry about her naval aviator husband. That worry infused all her days. Prayer didn't reduce the size of it, only caged it for a time. She'd learned over the last four years, since Jon started flight training, that it was not a good thing to latch onto something like a thousand flight hours as a reason to worry less. It was as if fate held it out with, See, a thousand hours in his logbook. You don't have to worry so much now, and as soon as she reached for it, Wham! An F-8 pilot with a thousand hours was killed.

Lord, please watch over Jon, and comfort the family of the poor man who was killed.

She found Amy in the kitchen, rinsing out her coffee cup. She smiled, "Your little noise maker woke Jennifer and EJ, but I got them back down again. Teresa, thank you for letting me be here, but I think Amelia and I need to get some sleep. God only knows what tomorrow will bring."

The next day, Teresa learned a few more details. After the crash on the flight deck killed the pilot, the burning carcass of the F-8 slid into and destroyed the lens, the landing aid on the port side of the flight deck.

The carrier had been scheduled to be in port for two days. Now she would stay a week to allow shipyard workers time to cut away misshapen steel and install a new platform and lens. Then the ship would have to operate for a day or two off Oahu to test the new landing aid.

During that week in port, every day he bought a roll of quarters to feed into a pay phone. Those daily calls, unexpected blessings, unexpected reassurance that, Jon, during those precious moments they spoke, was alive and well. During his first cruise, 1966, he'd been aboard a destroyer, and she had missed him much more than she'd worried about him. She just hadn't known enough about being a navy wife to realize what there was to worry about. Now she knew. Some. But there was always a new reason to worry popping up.

In one of his calls, Jon said, "Often, the US Navy finds reasons to shorten a stay in a liberty port. But a planned two days in Hawaii blowing up into seven! I heard a chief petty officer say, 'Twenty-plus years in this canoe club and I never had this happen before.'

"Most of the crew think it's a blessing to get extra time here, but I hate it. We are a five-hour plane ride apart, but if I spend the money on a ticket, you and the babies won't be able to buy groceries the rest of the month."

During his calls, she learned how he spent his awake hours. He ran three miles, read his flight and tactics manuals, and wrote to her. Before, when he was on deployment, it was never clear what he was doing. His letters were filled with … love. Love of her and the children. He rarely mentioned work. When he did, it was to report something funny someone did or said.

Several times, he told her how he hated being stuck in Hawaii. For two reasons. One, in 1970, before Jon reported to his squadron the Warhorses, he and Teresa had visited the islands. It had been a wonderful time for them. Now he did not like being there without her. Now it was just Limbo. It wasn't even right to say we're just marking time. "On cruises before, I always felt like every passing day meant one closer to the end and being with you again. It feels like they are not bringing me closer to being with you."

Another quarter clinked in. "Last one," he said. "Supposedly, money can't buy you happiness, can't buy you love, but these rolls of quarters I spend buy me an awful lot of both."

"For me too. And for the children. They love getting a few minutes with Daddy."

⸻◦⸺◦⸺◦⸻

When the repairs to *Solomons* were completed, Jon was happy. Teresa sighed, resigned to her days hinging on her calendar and, each morning, X-ing off yesterday.

After the carrier departed Pearl Harbor, Oahu, there would be fourteen Xs before *Solomons* entered Subic Bay in the Philippine Islands. The PI, the guys called it. Fortunately, during the two-week transit, mail departed the ship via COD (Carrier Onboard Delivery), propellor planes rigged to transport cargo and people between shore and aircraft carriers. She received three letters the day she X'ed off the first week of the transit.

In one of them, he wrote about playing volleyball. When she read that, a twinge of jealousy sparked. With three little ones to care for, she needed a forty-eight-hour day to get everything done.

And you are playing volleyball?

But her conscience gigged her. *Thank You, Father, for giving Jon something* normal *to do.*

During the rest of the transit, however, no more mail. A few days after the ship arrived in the PI, she'd get four, five, or more letters a day until she caught up. Jon wrote every night. The Warhorse wives knew, and some were envious. Some just wanted to know, "What's going? That's all. I don't want to know the juicy stuff." But, of course, someone always piped in, "Well, I want to hear the juicy stuff. Spill it, Teresa."

She didn't share the juicy stuff, and she'd learned when Jon deployed on the destroyer in 1966, she had to be careful about sharing the other things. Some of the wives of his shipmates wrote to their husbands words to the effect: "Zachery writes every night. You write once a week. He wrote about … . Why don't you write about those things?"

With the Warhorse wives' group, Teresa told them she would share some things with them from *her* husband's letters but only if they wouldn't use the information to rub *their husbands'* noses in it.

Jon's letters were precious, and not only to her, but to the other wives as well. Teresa liked to be able to share some of what was in the letters. It was a way to pay back for some of the support the wives had given her during the last months of her pregnancy.

But as precious as the letters were, the phone calls were priceless. They were brief touches of here-and-now contact, not reports on the state of things a week and a half ago. Priceless, and the one from the PI was just like that.

The bad thing was, it would be almost two months before there'd be another. And most of those two months, Jon would be flying combat missions again.

THE NIGHT BEFORE *SOLOMONS* DEPARTED the vicinity of Oahu for the Philippines, Lieutenant Zachery wrote about crossing the Pacific Ocean.

> This is my third trip across the biggest water puddle on earth. I remember the first time. My destroyer spent a couple of days to reach Hawaii, spent a couple more days conducting exercises, then spent a couple of days in port before departing for for the PI, Philippine Islands. The crossing took two weeks. We stayed in port a week loading supplies and ammo and having shipyard workers repair whatever was broken or worn out. On a ship, you never run out of things to work on to hold a ship together.

When he'd written that last line, he'd considered writing, "keep a ship in fighting trim," but he'd thought better of it. No need to give Teresa more reason to worry about him.

> Finally, we departed the PI, and, after two more days of travel, the ship arrived in the Tonkin Gulf. In position to do what we'd left home to do. A full month away from you and the babies before we start doing our job. It seemed so

deplorably wasteful, the first time, the second time, and seems so again this time. Thirty days away from home to accomplish not one meaningful task. And of course, at the other end of the deployment, there's another wasted chunk of time spent getting back home again.

At the end of last deployment, departing the Tonkin Gulf to return home, the feeling was, "Okay already! We did what we came to do, now I want to be home with Teresa and our babies. You know, like NOW. As it is, there's the wasted month to get to the Tonkin Gulf, and another wasted coming home. Out of an eight-month deployment, you only spend six months doing what you came to do. Only 75% percent efficient.

See? Deplorably wasteful.

I will admit that maybe we just have too much time on our hands during the crossing. Too much time to think about missing you, about not being where I am meant to be at night. In your bed beside you.

Mail closed out at 0600 the next morning. The postal clerk bagged up the mail and a COD, Carrier Onboard Delivery plane, delivered it, including Jon's letter, to Barbers Point.

During the following week, days for the Warhorses pilots followed the same routine. 0800 to 1100, briefings in the Ready Room. The Intel Officers reported on the state of affairs in North and South Vietnam, Laos, and Cambodia. Also covered: the support the Russians and Chinese offered the North Viets.

Not, the Admin Officer, and Nose, the Personnel Officer, identified those pilots whose Next Of Kin Notification Forms and other paperwork needed to be completed. For Stretch, he owed the US Navy's paper mill a Preference Sheet. Before he received orders to his next duty station, the navy would pull out his Preference Sheet, on which were listed his preferences for both shore and sea duty assignments. The navy would consider those preferences, and then send him to wherever in Sam Hill they wanted to send him. Navy officers had plenty of reason to call Preference Sheets Dream Sheets.

Of course, the prospects of LT Zachery having a future in the US Navy were pretty slim. The last two deployments of USS *Solomons* were expected to be the last. This current one, again, expected to be the last. When they got back home, the ship and the embarked squadrons were expected to decommission. If that happened, a lot of officers and enlisted men would be just as surplus as the old ship and the old airplanes. And what was the possibility the carrier would receive a third reprieve? Slim to none. Didn't seem worthwhile to fill out the Dream Sheet, but he did. Otherwise Not would bug him.

Stretch kept a calendar. He'd gotten the idea from Teresa. Instead of X-ing off days, however, he made small notes in the box around each day short-handing the most significant events of the day. Such as "IWB, VB PM." Meaning: Intel Wienie Brief, played volleyball in the afternoon.

A week into the transit, the arrival of mail busted up the monotony of the déjà vu all over again days. He received three letters from Teresa. One answered his last letter mailed the morning the Solomons departed Hawaii.

> Maybe, Jon Zachery, that month it takes to cross your big puddle isn't deplorably wasteful. I know you, Husband, as a kind, caring, loving, tender—most of the time— soulmate and father. I do not know you as a warrior. As much as I try to picture you as such, I fall short. And maybe that's the way it should be.
>
> You have written to me, that I have a sort of mother gear, and when I shift into it, there is a whole different Teresa you see. If that is true, it doesn't come from me. It can only come from the Father.
>
> I suspect, Jon Zachery, you have a navy pilot mode you shift into. You've written how you walk up to your plane

and say, "Hello, Five Oh One." You wrote that shifts you
into flying mode and puts everything else aside while you
and 501 defy gravity and soar with the eagles.

I've been thinking about this ever since I got your
deplorably wasteful letter. I think there is one gear for
flying and another for flying in combat. I think that time
it takes to get where you have to engage that particular
gear, maybe you need that to get yourself ready for it.

I take exception to one other thing you wrote. You said
that the wasted months going and coming made the whole
deployment only 75% efficient, and that was like a D
grade. Barely passing.

I will have you know Jon Zachery, the grade in high school
I am proudest of is the D I got in Physics, physics with a
capital P.

Jon smiled. Teresa had not wanted to take *Physics*, but her father
insisted. The only girl in the class, she'd worked harder than anyone else,
got extra help every day from the teacher, and squeezed that blessed D
out of the system with sweat, tears, and prayer. They had not been dating
yet, but he admired her grit, her determination.

The other thing, God created the earth. It is a beautiful
place to live. And maybe the size of it is to make it hard
to get to people with whom we go to war.

He read her letter and agreed. Earth was a beautiful place to live. For
many people, but not all of them. For those living under Communism,
the earth wasn't such a beautiful place to live.

Going to war wasn't a lightweight thing. Maybe that month to get
there gave him time to get it into perspective. The month coming home

after war, maybe he needed that as well to get himself out of being Stretch and into being Daddy, and Jon dear.

Teresa! When his thoughts puddled vinegar in the belly of his soul, he'd get a letter from her that was like a spiritual Tums.

That afternoon, Stretch skipped volleyball and went to the ship's chapel. As usual, he had the place to himself. He sat in his usual back row.

One other thing in Teresa's letter demanded some attention. She'd written that the circumstances that led up to him staying in the military and applying for flight training were parts of God's plan for "You and for us, your family."

The notion that God had a plan for each and every living thing always gave him pause. Teresa believed it, but he always bumped into a stone wall of disbelief. If everything was driven by this Divine Plan, then the plan included Adam and Eve eating the apple. Why would God plan for the human race to fail at the first test they confronted? It made no sense.

Jon looked at the folding table altar at the front of the space. The crucifix on the bulkhead behind the altar. The stark, navy grey bulkheads and overheads, the steel girder braces forming part of the carrier. The solid, sturdy, ship. Able to take a licking and keep on ticking, to borrow a phrase from a commercial. But the appearance of the place did not make the space a chapel. God's presence there made it such. Jon felt Him, as he always did when he sat and quieted all the stuff roiling around in the box of rocks that passed for his brain.

After he'd been there a while, the Render to Caesar thought crawled into the middle of his brain. "Oh," he whispered. *Render to God what is God's.*

Plan, no plan. That was definitely His business. *My worrying about it accomplishes not one useful thing.*

It was like flying in a two-seater and passing control. You say, "You got it." The other pilot says, "I got it," and he grabs the stick, and first guy lets go.

"Let it go, Jon. Let it go and give it to the Lord." Teresa had told him that many times in the past when something was troubling him. He'd never been able to do that before, let go. Relinquish control. But that afternoon, in the chapel, as to the matter of life plans or no plans, that did not matter to him. It mattered to God, and it was His business alone.

Some of the solemn silence in the chapel seemed, by osmosis, to penetrate and take up residence in his soul, and he saw somethings with rare clarity.

He, Jon Zachery, was where he should be. It was his duty to be there, to be on the way to the Tonkin Gulf.

He hadn't felt that way since the end of last cruise. The last hop of last cruise. When all hell broke loose.

Stretch had flown on the 1030 launch. When they landed back aboard, the ship would head east, start the month-long journey to home.

That last hop wasn't expected to be exciting. It was over North Vietnam, but it was just a photo reconnaissance flight. If the North Vietnamese didn't shoot at them, they wouldn't drop bombs on them. Usually, the North Viets didn't seem to care if the US took pictures or not. That day they cared. They fired SAMs and AAA. Two Warhorse planes were lost. Two Warhorse pilots were KIA.

Stretch had flown on that photo recce flight. He had SAMs fired at him, but his warning systems had not functioned. After the mission, he checked his aircraft and discovered his warning system had been sabotaged.

With an operating warning system, a pilot stood a good chance of evading a SAM. Without a warning, the missile could kill you and you wouldn't even know it was coming. So, AB and Skunk had been killed by the saboteur.

It turned out a Warhorse maintenance officer named Amos Kane had anti-war sympathies. He lived in the Junior Officer Bunkroom with four squadron pilots, none of whom cared for Amos' hippie, Commie views.

After Stretch reported the sabotage, the squadron launched an investigation. It became apparent that Amos Kane was a person of interest, a suspect. While the investigation proceeded with deliberation, one of the JOB residents, call sign Tuesday, leapt to the conclusion: Amos Goddamned Kane was the guilty bastard.

Tuesday and another pilot, Botch, found Amos stuffing clothes into a bag. It was apparent he intended to hide out on the ship until it arrived in the PI. An aircraft carrier had all kinds of places a person could hide.

Earlier that cruise, a sailor had hidden in a void, a space designed to absorb the explosion from a torpedo while protecting the vital interior of the vessel. He remained hidden for over a month. It had been presumed he'd fallen overboard.

All squadron pilots carried a survival pistol while flying in combat. Tuesday carried an extra weapon, a derringer. He used the derringer to shoot Amos. Then he and Botch rolled the body in a rug, carried it aft, and dumped it over the side. Stretch entered the JOB as Tuesday and Botch were cleaning up after they had dispensed their justice on the murdering saboteur. When challenged, Botch admitted what they had done.

Stretch thought about what he should do. Tuesday and Botch had committed murder, just as Amos had done. Finally, he decided, he would not rat on Tuesday and Botch, even though he was convinced that made him a party to the murder of Amos.

Thinking about it now, a year later, he recalled how much he needed that month of transit back to the US to deal with the notion that Jon Zachery, husband of Teresa, father of Jennifer, EJ, and Daniel their lost baby, was also Jon Zachery, murderer. During that homebound transit, he wrestled daily with the moral murder monster. What wound up saving him from his daily damning of himself, was the ship entered Pearl Harbor for two days before proceeding on to California. There they learned the ship and airwing would not decommission. Rather it would return to Vietnam for one more tour of combat duty. Not only that, the Warhorses would be assigned the responsibility of mastering the anti-SAM mission. And Stretch would be the squadron expert. He flew from Pearl Harbor to Las Vegas and met with US Air Force intelligence officers. There he began the process of becoming an expert.

Stretch had something to do. It was important. He'd been selected to do it. He would not screw it up and let the squadron down. Looking back on it, he could see how important it had been to get that assignment, to get that mission which forced him put aside so many things and focus on SAMs and Shrike missiles.

The anti-SAM mission, in no small way, saved his soul. But Teresa owned the largest chunk of his salvation. She'd embraced him and said, "It is so good to have you home, Jon Zachery."

And it had been so good to be home, and so dad-burned hard to leave again. But just then, it was good to find that sense of duty rekindled. It had been lost to him since the murder of Amos Kane.

And just in the nick of time.

Solomons would enter Subic Bay in the Philippines, spend two days, transit to the Tonkin Gulf, and be flying combat missions again. On the sixth of February.

The sixth. Happy birthday, Jennifer.

PLEASE, GOD, KEEP JON SAFE.

Teresa's morning calendar prayer. She prayed the same words each morning, but that morning, February 6, those words were packed with pleading. Today, people would shoot at her husband, the father of their children.

Jon had written to her about his sense of duty, that it was his duty to be where he was. He said he'd lost that sense of duty after the last deployment. During those six months of combat, all their bombing missions seemed to accomplish nothing useful. They blew up jungle trees and turned them into toothpicks. But now, his sense of duty had been restored. Her letters helped him get there, he'd written.

She hadn't wanted to help with … that. What she wanted was for him to not want to be there as much as she wanted him to not be there. But his sense of duty called him. And she was sure that meant he did want to be there, and not here with her and their babies. His duty felt like a betrayal to her.

Oh, for pity sakes, Teresa.

The voice of her mother counseling her teen-aged daughter to, in effect, *Get over it, move on. Grow up.*

"Mother, I'm flunking physics. Daddy will be mad."

"Oh, for pity sakes, Teresa."

"Mother, no one asked me to the sock hop."

"Oh, for pity sakes." But that time, Mother appended, "You're looking for sympathy. In this world, the harder you look for sympathy, the less likely you are to find it. Everybody has troubles, and for most of them, dealing with their own is all they can handle. Sympathy is for sissies."

God won't give us anything we can't handle.

Jon echoed the article of faith which she had first voiced to him.

"Breftus," EJ demanded from the dining room.

"Breakfast, please," Jennifer counseled.

"Breftus!"

Breftus! With an exclamation point! Now there's the sound of sympathy.

———◆━◼◉◼━◆———

Before the F-8 crash off Pearl Harbor, the ship expected to launch the first combat hops of the deployment on February first, EJ's birthday. But now the first combat flights would be flown on the sixth, Jennifer's birthday.

Happy birthday to your kid, Lieutenant Zachery, from the US Navy.

Snotty, snooty, self-centered sarcasm. So easy to slip into it. Every morning, as soon as his eyes popped open, it pounced. The luminous face of his alarm clock said 0540.

He said the prayer to St. Michael the Archangel. Defend us in battle. Not the battle against the North Vietnamese, but against the devil, who was there during a man's every waking moment with poisonous thoughts polished to gleam like golden treasure. Thrust into Hell, Satan and all the evil spirits who prowl about the world seeking the ruin of souls. Amen. Then he prayed for Teresa and the babies.

At 0541, he threw back the covers and climbed down from his top bunk. His roommate, Lieutenant White, Blackey, breathed softly, slowly in and out. Jon grabbed his Dopp kit and a towel and left the stateroom for the head.

Since his first days in the navy, Stretch rose early to use the facilities before reveille rousted the hordes out of their bunks to line up behind the sinks, commodes, urinals, and shower stalls with, "Hurry the hell up;" "Don't take all goddamned day;" "My grandpa is faster than you, and he's older than dirt."

Ten minutes later, he returned to the room. His roommate gathered his things for the head and departed without uttering a word. It had been this way since the end of pre-deployment training in December. When Troll was killed. Since then, Blackey didn't talk to him. A blessing, that. Prior to the death of his friend Troll, his motor-mouth roommate took great delight in antagonizing Stretch by spewing endless profanity in the room. He also delighted in recounting flying incidents that he had done better, like carrier landing grades.

This 1972 silence was so much better than the 1971 non-stop vile, vicious vituperation. Still, Stretch kept his guard up around the man. The man was capable of—murder?

Troll, LT Robert Stoll, and Blackey, LT Rob White, were called the Robsey Twins. They had been best buds. In December, the Robsey Twins had flown together. During the flight, there'd been a collision between their planes. Blackey had had to eject. After a helo recovered him, he said he hadn't seen a parachute from his wingman. The helo crew reported they'd searched but found no sign of Troll.

Back on the ship, Blackey said Troll had tried to thump him. Thumping meant to sneak up behind another plane with considerable overtake speed and fly very close to the target. As the thumper zipped past, the target felt a sudden thump and his jet lurched. Generally, it scared the thumped pilot, which was the point. Some pilots had peed their flight suits after a thump. According to the sole survivor, Troll tried to thump him, screwed it up, and killed himself.

Stretch had doubts. He'd had to collect information for the accident investigation. There'd been no proof things happened other than how the only witness reported. Still, knowing him, knowing Troll, and knowing something else, he believed Blackey lied. If anyone was inclined to thump, it wasn't steady, not-given-to-try-crazy-stunts Troll. You could count on him. The other twin, however, you never knew what the guy would do. He was a good stick, maybe even the best pilot in the squadron, but you just couldn't count on him to do what was expected—required. Rather, he delighted in doing the unexpected, in flaunting requirements.

In the air, the right way to join on a flight lead was to close on him with a controlled rate of speed, to slide under lead's aircraft and join on his right wing. Smooth, controlled, orderly. Instead of doing it the proper way, Blackey was likely to come roaring into the rendezvous, do a canopy roll over the flight lead's aircraft, and drop into position on the right wing. It was as if he had to continuously prove he was the best pilot in the squadron. Of course, he never did anything of the kind when he flew with L'il Lord, Commander Fant, Leroy, the squadron commanding officer.

At squadron parties, when L'il Lord couldn't hear, he'd lace his speech with casual profanity and discussion of sex as if he were describing how he chose the shirt to wear that night. Last November, the XO and his pious wife hosted a squadron party. Blackey knew St. Laura abhorred profanity, so he cranked out an especially odious spiel in front of her.

Carolyn White also heard it, and that was the straw that broke the back of their six-month marriage. Carolyn told one of the squadron wives at the party that she'd been so smitten by the dashing fighter pilot whose name was White but called Blackey, but the longer she was married to him, the more she saw of the vicious side of his nature. What he'd said in front of Laura was cruel and meant only to hurt her. She left the party alone after announcing she was divorcing her husband.

Shortly after that, Troll began spending time in LA, where Carolyn worked as a flight attendant. Stretch wondered if Rob White felt betrayed by his twin and thumped him to get even.

If anyone thumped anyone, it was *not* Troll doing the thumping.

But there was nothing to prove Blackey did it. Something had changed his behavior, though. Caused by the loss of his erstwhile best bud? Stretch couldn't buy it. This new Blackey personality had been spray-painted over the old, and it was onion skin thin. He was narcissism personified. He wouldn't mourn the loss of his mother because it would make her the center of attention.

Judge not. Sorry, God.

The new, subdued Blackey seemed like a new man. He showed up after the crash that killed Troll and remained through January and the transit to the Tonkin Gulf. That morning, Jennifer's birthday, *Solomons* would begin launching combat sorties. Would that lead to the resurrection of the old manifestation, the perpetual horse's behind?

The official weather report for six February: over Vietnam, totally crappy. Clobbered. Solid clouds from the surface to 25,000 feet. Over the Tonkin Gulf: only partly crappy.

Jon's first combat hop of the 1972 cruise was a sky spot. Sky spot: a radar controller directed his flight of four to an area over South Vietnam and told them when to pickle their bombs. From close to five miles up. Probability of inflicting any damage, or even inconvenience, to the enemy: one in a gazillion.

LT(jg) Nat Newsome—Nose, because he had a nose for news— pontificated, "Sky spot. It's supposed to be a tactic of area denial. If bombs go off at random throughout the area, day and night, it will discourage them from using it for their nefarious purposes. The only problem is, the North Viets can calculate odds as well as we can. Odds of one in a gazillion wouldn't keep my grandmother from going in there."

Making toothpicks out of jungle trees. Just like we did last year, Stretch thought. Flying combat missions that didn't accomplish any useful purpose. That's what they were doing. Everybody knew it, but only Nose had to mouth it. Of course, after puking your bombs, you still had to land aboard a carrier. Even in daytime, that was an evolution NOT to be taken lightly. The ceiling at the ship was five hundred feet, which dictated an instrument approach, like they flew at night.

To Stretch, breaking out of the clouds at 500 feet wasn't bad. There were seconds to adjust from trusting your flight instruments to trusting your eyeballs. To him, that transition from trusting instruments to trusting his eyes took a couple of tick-tocks. The minimum ceiling for landing aboard a carrier was half that 500 feet. Breaking out of the clouds there, it was sort of like vertigo. After flying on instruments for a long time, His brain grew comfortable with his flight instruments. His brain believed what they told him about up and down and sideways. And listening to the radar controller going, "On glide slope, oooonnnn glide slope. Come right one degree. On glide slope. Now left one degree," it was comfortable, reliable, trustworthy.

When he busted out of the clouds at minimums, though, it was as if his brain said, "Wait. I need a second here." But of course, there wasn't a second.

After a landing like that, he thought of Blackey. Blackey got his highest landing grades at night and in bad weather. For that matter, he always knocked down the highest, or second-highest, landing grade of all the pilots in the wing for a particular at-sea period.

Stretch felt that part of Blackey's brain, the flying part, the bird-brain part, was tougher, stronger, and better than his bird brain. He admired that part.

———◦━━◦━━◦━━◦———

The next several days, the weather remained totally crappy. Nothing but Sky spots over the beach and instrument approaches to the ship.

On the whiteboard in the ready room, Nose posted The Fighter/bomber Pilot's Prayer to the Weather God:

> Dear god,
>
> Remember me? I'm Studly. Yeah, that's my call sign. Anyway, You know I went to church every Sunday until I graduated from high school. Now, You know the weather's been really, really crappy out here, and we can't fly our bomber missions. That means the godless Commies are sneaking tons and tons and tons of bullets and rice into South Vietnam. Do You want these heathens to win the war? So, how about clearing up the crappy weather so we can get after them? Uh, please. If the weather does clear up, I will go to church this Sunday. I'll even ask the scheduling officer to put it on the flight schedule. So how about it, god? Please. And thank you.
>
> Studly

Nose had attributed the prayer to Studly. Nobody in the airwing was called Studly, but studly was how fighter pilots thought of themselves. Whether anybody else did or not.

The next day, the weather cleared, and Stretch flew with the skipper into Laos and bombed a suspected truck park under FAC (Forward Air Controller) control. Their bombs triggered no secondary explosions from under the dense leafy canopy. Bombing trees. Last cruise, ninety-nine times out of a hundred, a pilot got no secondaries. All they did was make toothpicks. Was this cruise going to be just like the last one?

Still, it beat crappy-weather flying.

Another aspect of the flight pleased Stretch. The bombing computers of the four Warhorse aircraft functioned properly. When the A-4 aircraft computers worked, they improved a pilot's bombing accuracy considerably. However, the computers were notoriously unreliable.

During pre-deployment workups, Stretch, as Weapons Training Officer, had emphasized using the bombing computer in the A-4. With the Operations Officer's help, he'd arranged for a technical representative from the computer manufacturer to work with Warhorse maintenance personnel. During training, thanks to the tech rep, and his factory equipment, the computers functioned reliably day after day.

And now, in the bombing computers' first test in combat, it passed with flying colors. For the remainder of the day and night, squadron pilots achieved excellent bomb hits.

⸺⸺◦▬◉▬◦⸺⸺

The intel guys briefed the pilots on their understanding of North Vietnamese intentions. The Viets, they said, were preparing to mount a major offensive. Bigger than Tet had been in '68.

But after forty days on the line, *Solomons* saw no indications of such a buildup. Stretch figured he had re-bombed every place he'd bombed in Laos and South Vietnam the previous cruise. With pretty much the same results. Out of 850 Warhorse bombing sorties, only three pilots inflicted any significant damage on the enemy.

Blackey killed a truck. Not destroyed a stack of supplies. Alice silenced a AAA gun firing at his flight during a night mission in Laos.

All three were put in for Navy Commendation Medals. The rest of the pilots logged flight time and carrier landings.

On the Ides of March, *Solomons* experienced a failure limiting its ability to distill seawater. Limited water for drinking, cooking, showers, and laundry were minor matters. The ship needed to distill thousands of gallons of seawater to make steam to spin the propellors, to generate electricity, to power the catapults. Loss of that capability cut short Solomons' stint in the Gulf, and she limped to the PI for repairs. Over the two days en route, the carrier scraped up enough steam to launch all its planes, except those undergoing heavy maintenance. While the ship was being repaired, the pilots would fly training missions from Naval Air Station Cubi Point, located at one end of Subic Bay. Docks and repair facilities for surface warships, destroyers and cruisers, occupied the other side of Subic Bay.

As lieutenants, Stretch and Blackey could have flown off the ship and gotten an extra day of liberty in the PI, however, both gave up their spots on the flight schedule to junior pilots.

Stretch didn't fly off because he was worried about himself. Three notions weighed him down: the making toothpicks missions served no useful purpose; being away from Teresa and the children accomplished not one useful thing; and, his decision in 1966 to stay in the navy and apply for aviation had not been answering a call to duty. Rather, it had been a colossal mistake.

Stretch sat at his fold-down desk, a pad of paper in front of him, waiting for words to come to him. Next to his desk, Blackey's. Although it was against US Navy regulations, Blackey kept a bottle of whiskey in his desk safe. Stretch wished he had one in his safe. Whiskey-wanting weighed on him as well.

A couple of years ago, he'd wallowed into the habit of two snorts a night, when the US Navy began reducing its effort in Vietnam. The squadron he'd been assigned to decommissioned, as did the carrier on which it had been based. He'd made what to him had been a noble sacrifice, to put aside his dream for himself and his family to serve his country. Only the country said, "Oh, Lieutenant Zachery, we don't need you or your sacrifice after all, but thanks, you know? Really appreciate it, but don't let the doorknob hit you on the butt on your way out."

Teresa disapproved of his drinking. He told himself, though, real men drink. Real naval aviators drink.

Only he hadn't felt like a real man, or a real pilot either. He felt like the navy fed him into a threshing machine to find out he was not grain but chaff. He was not a real man and drinking hadn't made him feel like one. For a time, though, he'd latched onto a smidgeon of self-delusion in the whiskey. See! You're drinking, therefore you're a real man.

If he hadn't applied for aviation, he could have left the service in 1969. They'd have a house with a white picket fence. He'd have a job as an electrical engineer, and he would be home every night with his wife and children. Instead, he was on the other side of the world, as far away from Teresa as he could get. And it was all for nothing. He'd applied for aviation because he became convinced the "Hell No We Won't Go" crowd were anti-America more than anti-war, and he believed in the country. He believed Communism indeed wanted to bury the US. It had been his duty to say, "Well, heck, I'll go."

He fought in the war, but the US wasn't trying to win it. The bombing halt back in '68 was supposed to encourage the North Viets to come to the negotiating table. Which they did, but in four years, what had happened? Not even one tiny concession from them. Back in Vietnam, the bombing halt made it easy for them to continue to slip supplies and troops into the South. Nighttime and triple canopy jungle—meaning little, medium-sized, and huge trees comprised it—provided all the cover they needed.

And what did the US do? Bombed trees into toothpicks.

A cloud of pessimism filled his soul from its foundation to halfway to heaven. And booze stuck up its hand again and said, "Hey, Stretch, I'm here to help you."

Back in 1970, he managed to see how he'd surrendered to pessimism, let it beat him. He drank whiskey to dull the pessimism. Only the booze hadn't dulled anything. It dumped him into a pit of despair and put distance between him and Teresa. He'd pushed God and Teresa away while both held salvation out to him. A combination of spending time in the chapel on base, and writing to Teresa, even though they were together and not apart, helped him pull himself out of that funk.

During the two days traveling to the PI, Stretch visited the chapel for an hour at 1600. He sat on a hard, cold, folding metal chair, as his soul drank in the weighty and solemn silence residing there; then he ate dinner; and then he wrote to Teresa. In his letters, there was no hint of darkness and despair over crushed and lost dreams. There was only love for Teresa.

She had told him how some of the wives wanted her to share "The Juicy Stuff" from the letters he wrote. There was plenty of that in those en route-to-the-PI letters. Time in the chapel and writing to Teresa, once again, saved his soul, saved him from the bottle, even more than not having one did. Plus, he had work to do.

Prior to flying off the ship, the Ops O had instructed Zachery to work up a training plan for the squadron pilots. The ship anticipated being in the PI for three weeks, and the Ops O did not want the Warhorse pilots' skills to rust. He wanted the pilots to fly once a day, Monday through Friday, and to log one night hop each week. "And," he said. "get each pilot scheduled for two mine-drop training missions."

Dropping mines was one of the missions for which A-4 pilots were required to train, however, during two stints of pre-deployment training, practice mining missions were considered to be putting an X in a box on a check-off list of A-4 pilot annual training requirements. No one expected to do an actual mining mission in Vietnam.

What the heck's going on?

He wondered if the Ops O knew. Perhaps he was told to "Have the guys do mine training." To which he replied, "Aye, aye, sir."

During pre-deployment training, Zachery had been briefed into a number of highly classified programs. Now, though, he was just like the rest of the junior pilots. In the words of Nose, "The heavies treat us like mushrooms. They feed us crap and keep us in the dark."

6

S TRETCH HAD GONE UP TO the flight deck to watch the carrier enter port. He hadn't been outside for two days and seeing the sky and how *Solomons* tied herself to a pier were worth the trip topside. Plus, seeing big things happening in the world also made the trip worthwhile. The universe did not revolve around Jon Zachery's interior, puny, personal problems.

For all the crappy weather when they'd arrived in the Tonkin Gulf, entering-port-in-the-PI day sported a don-your-sunglasses sun set in a blue, blue sky. Seagulls squawked and swooped over the ship's wake. The flag flapped and fluttered from the mast. A brisk breeze kicked up whitecaps on the sky-blue water in Subic Bay. When he'd been aboard a destroyer, Ensign Zachery's entering-port station was on the bridge. He always observed his destroyer enter port, but he'd never seen his carrier berth.

When he'd come out onto the flight deck, *Solomons* was still several hundred yards from the pier. Behind the pier, he saw the runway at Cubi Point Naval Air Station. Behind the airfield, the terrain rose a couple of hundred feet to where the administrative area of the air station was located. The most important building in the admin area? The Officer's Club, the O Club, of course.

Relative size-wise, the destroyer was a mosquito, and the carrier was a jumbo jet.

His destroyer had never used tugboats to dock itself. *Solomons,* however, used two. The destroyer USS *Manfred* approached a pier with a controlled, deliberate, regal pace and nudged to a sudden stop against the pier with a jostle you could feel throughout the mosquito-sized ship. Jumbo-jet Solomons, however, inched like a glacier toward the pier. Which Zachery thought made sense. His puny destroyer displaced 2,000 tons of seawater. His giant carrier displaced 50,000 tons. And the side of the carrier extended from the water fifty feet to the flight deck, and was, in effect, a giant sail. Even ten knots of wind could exert a lot of push. Thus, the carrier had to be careful. Fifty thousand tons moving at even one knot was a boatload of momentum. Enough to damage the ship and destroy a pier.

Solomons sidled against the dock without even a shiver rippling through the hull. Then the Boatswain Mate of the Watch blew his whistle over the announcing system, reported the ship was moored, and the Officer of the Deck was shifting his watch from the bridge to the quarterdeck—the same docking ritual that played out on tugboats to carriers across the US Navy.

Trucks, cranes, and a horde of Filipino workers wearing hard hats jammed the pier.

A mobile crane cranked up its engine and lifted a cargo container from a truck up onto the after-aircraft elevator—used to move planes between the hangar bay and the flight deck at sea. Forklifts then moved the containers inside.

Another crane eased into place a gangway from the shore to the ship, and as soon as it was secured, the Hard Hats swarmed aboard.

Zachery decided he'd seen enough and went below. At the main deck, he stepped out onto the hangar bay. Parked aircraft filled the forward third of the bay. Those would be undergoing heavy maintenance. Stacked containers already filled the rest of the hangar. A steady stream of workers filed from the after brow, crossed the hangar bay, and almost certainly, descended to the damaged distilling system.

Watching the parade of workers, Zachery thought it was strange. Out at sea, the ship was home, his home. Now seeing all the Filipinos swarm aboard, it seemed like *Solomons* belonged to them.

Teresa sat at the dining room table, her letter-writing material in front of her. She stared through the kitchen to the far wall, to the calendar hanging on the cork board above the dryer. The calendar ruled so much of her life, it was only right to acknowledge it before taking herself to her writing place, her writing-to-Jon place. For the moment, she put aside the children, the Warhorse Wives' Group, Lemoore Naval Air Station, and transported to where only she and Jon abided.

She smiled.

That's what I'll write about.

She picked up her pen and wrote "Dearest Jon," and stopped and stared again. *Jon does the same thing.* He'd never said, or written he, too, had such a place. But she knew he did. She just knew.

Her pen started to write as if it had a mind of its own, but it wasn't that exactly. Once she got herself into her letter-writing place, her spirit was freed of clutter and concerns. And then the words flowed, almost flew onto the pages of her stationery. But it wasn't her mind that wrote. It was her soul.

Three pages front and back, filled with words about her writing-to-Jon place.

Jon had written to her once,

In your row upon row, neat, precise, beautiful handwriting,

Well, she allowed herself, *my penmanship isn't all bad.*

Which brought to mind how navy pilots talked at a party. One of them would recount, "Herb, remember the time that F-8 got behind you and you—" And the rest of it was unretainable pilot jargon, gobbledegook, until, "It was the coolest thing I ever saw in the air."

And Herb replied, "Ah, it wasn't bad."

That *ah.* Dismissive. It wasn't that big a deal. At least not for a superhuman naval aviator.

Ah: modesty personified and braggadocio, all rolled into one syllable.

Ah, my penmanship isn't all bad.

Teresa smiled and considered she'd backed out of her writing place with some of that navy-pilot ability to brag with superior modesty stuck to her.

Then Ruth woke—herself, and everybody else in the house—and wiped the smile from her mother's face.

"Ah," Teresa said, and went to do her duty.

At the mandatory all Warhorse officers party in the Cubi Point O Club, Stretch sat at a small round table, in a corner, by himself. A waitress brought a double Jack Daniels and an ice cube in a separate shot glass. Just the way he'd ordered it. The Filipina, clad in a very short skirt and very low-cut top, bent over to lay his change on the table.

He looked up. At her face. Above the cleavage. She was a nice-looking young woman, except for her eyes. They would have been right at home in the head of a meat-eating bird. Her boobs pimped for a big tip. He picked up a nickel from the table and handed it to her.

Anger flashed over her face. She hissed at him and walked away without the coin.

"Guess she don't like you after all." Blackey watched the waitress return to the bar. "You mind?" He pointed to a chair.

Stretch shrugged.

His roommate sat, took a long drink from the tall glass in his hand, and plunked it almost empty on the table.

Nose walked over, and without asking, took another chair.

"Nose," Blackey said, "this table is reserved for asocial misfits. Amscray!"

Nose ignored him. "I want to know what you guys think about the mine training mission."

Stretch sipped. Blackey drained his drink.

"Did you hear what I said?"

Blackey replied, "Sure."

Nose turned toward Stretch. "Listen. This is what we talked about in the JOB."

"Great," from Blackey. "The Junior Officer Bunkroom. The fount of all wisdom and knowledge!"

"We figured the Chicoms and the Russcoms—"

"Russcoms?" Stretch said. "Like Chinese Communists are Chicoms, Russian Com—"

"Duh," Nose butted in. "So, the commies of all stripes, plus other nations, are shipping all kinds of material to the North Viets. Out in the Gulf, we don't see them because they hug the coast of Hainan Island, then skirt the northern edge of the Gulf. We figure most of North Vietnam's war-fighting supplies come by ship, just like we kept Britain in World War II. We figure we're practicing mining to drop real ones In Haiphong. What do you guys think?"

Blackey looked at Stretch. "He could be right."

"That's it?! I could be right?!"

Stretch thought Nose's sentences sounded as if they terminated not in one punctuation mark but two.

Nose let out a humph and rose.

Blackey watched him walk away. "He could be right."

"He could be."

"Junior officers can be right sometimes, but the worst thing that can happen is if a JO finds out he's been right." Blackey raised his glass. "To JOs."

Stretch clinked glasses with him. "Junior officers." He sipped the whiskey, felt it slide down his throat and puddle cold, and turn immediately to warmth.

That first sip, for all its harsh qualities, enticed powerfully for a second. Stretch poured a little whiskey into the shot glass with the half-melted ice cube. "I'm going to make sure the CO and XO see me, then I'm going back to the ship. Want to share a taxi?"

"Nope. I'm going to find that waitress you insulted and let her know I appreciate her assets."

⸺⸺◆⸺◆⸺◆⸺⸺

As Teresa changed Ruth's diaper, EJ said, "Roofann need a spanking."

"Why?"

"She wake up me and Jennifo. All the time."

"When you were her age, you used to wake Jennifer up all the time."

"I did?"

Teresa snapped together Ruth's one-piece and nodded.

"Oh."

"Do you think you should be spanked? Maybe you should say you're sorry to Jennifer for waking her up all the time?"

EJ looked up at her as if thinking that question would go away if he just stared at the questioner long enough. When it didn't, he turned around and faced his sister, who stood in the doorway. "I saw wee."

Jennifer stepped into the room and bent to give EJ a hug.

"No!" He ran out of his parents' room and into his.

"Well, at least you got a saw wee," Teresa said. "Go on now, get to back to sleep while you can."

As she passed the children's room, she said, "Nighty night, EJ."

His thumb muffled and jumbled his, "Nighty night, Mommy."

Four now. Going to have to work on that thumb sucking.

But that was for tomorrow. She nursed Ruth, put her back to bed, and returned to her letter on the table. It was late, but she had one more thing she wanted in that letter.

> In the place I go to when I write to you, time means something different than it does when I'm in the world.

She'd thought about writing "in the real world." But her write-to-Jon world was real, too, just as real as the … physical world.

> And this is how I know when you write to me, you go to the same place I do. When I read your letters, at least parts of them, it's not like you wrote the words on the date postmarked on the envelope. It's like you just said them to me and the ears of my soul heard you say them.

She filled one side of another page, and after putting on lipstick, planted a kiss on the blank side. Then she was ready for bed. More than ready. She fell asleep with her head still on the way to the pillow.

Back on the ship, in his and Blackey's, stateroom, sitting at his fold-down desk, inside the globe of dim light from the desk lamp, he reached for his pad of paper and wrote, "Dearest Teresa," but nothing else came. Two things refused to get out of the way.

Nose could be right. That would mean that the US really did have a plan to get serious about the war. Maybe the North Viets were getting ready to launch another Tet-like offensive. In '68, after the US and the South Viets beat it back, LBJ responded with the bombing halt and an offer, or maybe it was begging the North Viets to negotiate. And here we are four years later, and the North is getting ready to launch another one.

And, he thought, *our intel is good enough to figure out one is coming. It just couldn't nail down when. So, all the frantic effort to get ready to come back, and the rush to get here, they weren't wasted effort after all.*

Thank You, God. But then thanking Him for war didn't seem right at all. But with his rambling thoughts, he'd drifted into a measure of internal peace he hadn't felt since the ship left the States. He had to thank someone for that. God was the only One up there. Thank You, God, for this measure of peace in my tormented soul.

Then there was Blackey. What the heck? The guy acted … NORMAL. Normal and Blackey went together like a horse and carriage. Right. With a three-legged horse harnessed in backwards. Even if this evening was a precursor to the resurrection of the old Blackey, it was still good to know that the guy did have normalcy in the core of his being. Thank You, God, for that revelation.

Then every impediment was dealt with and out of the way. It was time to pay attention to Dearest Teresa. He wrote how he felt he was wasting time on this side of the world, while on her side, she had their little air-raid siren and the other two kids to deal with. He wrote he wished he could be there and spend his time usefully, like changing every diaper Ruth ever moistened or soiled.

But now, if Nose was right, Stretch wasn't wasting time. *Maybe I should write about something else.* He picked up his pen, and it did write about something else. He finished the letter. It was a long one. In the combat zone, postage was free, but this one would cost extra.

His conscience piped in: *Even with the extra postage, it'll cost less than the taxi-ride from the O Club.*

7

JUST NORTH OF THE ENTRANCE to Manila Bay and Corregidor, the US Navy operated a practice mining range. Zachery hadn't known the US Navy had a mining range in the PI. Of course, it could have been set up years ago, and he just hadn't learned of its existence. Also possible, because of the Vietnam War, the US needed a practice mining range and recently took it. The Philippine Islands were an independent nation, but they were such because the US helped them defeat the Spanish at the turn of the century and the Japanese near the middle of it. When the US needed a military facility in the Philippines, it apparently took it. He wondered if his country asked its ally first.

However, it wasn't a one-sided, benefit-only-the-US deal. Wherever the US plonked down a new base, there were jobs for the locals, to wit, the hordes of shipyard workers even now repairing Solomons.

Zachery. He chided himself back to work and bent over the chart of the waters off the coast of Luzon.

The problem for the mining mission flight lead would be to get his four-plane flying a heading of northeast aimed at a subtle geographic feature ashore and to drop the mines a half mile from the coast using radar ranging. Placing the mines precisely ensured two things. On an actual mission, if each plane dropped its weapons at the planned point, it ensured optimal coverage of the minefield. Also, knowing the location of each mine would make sweeping the mines after the conflict concluded easy, hopefully, in victory. Once two countries were done fighting, they'd be anxious to get back to selling stuff to each other. So, the mines would have to be removed.

Zachery flew number three on the XO's wing on the afternoon mission. Pilots called the mines trash cans. Both practice and real mines were blunt, high-drag-count weapons. Bombs, on the other hand, were sleek, pointy-nosed, designed to be low drag count.

The high drag from the two dummy mines was obvious during the takeoff roll. His plane needed three times the distance down the runway to reach takeoff airspeed. Once airborne, Stretch's plane handled like a truck rather than a sleek sports car.

On the training mission, during the run-in to the drop point, each of the wingmen would fly abeam the lead and separate, as best they could estimate, by five hundred feet from each other. The wingmen dumped their mines when Warhorse One dropped his. Stretch's trash cans fell away with a thump, thump. He rammed the throttle forward, snapped into ninety degrees of bank angle, and turned hard. G force pushed him against his seat. It was as if 507, his assigned side number, exulted at the sudden release of the ponderous weight and speed-sapping drag, exulted to be, once again, a sports car.

Stretch! No time to be lollygagging.

On an actual mission, the rocky terrain ahead of him would be North Vietnam, and they would be shooting at him. Furthermore, he was whistling along at four hundred knots, accelerating, a hundred feet above the white capped water, and turning hard. Furthermore, on a real mission, it wouldn't be just four aircraft. It would be twenty, and all of them driven by pilots being shot at and all of them intent on getting the crap out of there. Definitely not a time to be lollygagging. Even if he had been by himself, a hundred feet above the water and turning hard, he needed to have his mind on the business at hand.

Since Two was on the inside of the turn, he would assume flight lead and set the heading away from the beach, away from practice North Vietnam. Ahead, Stretch saw Two, then One roll out of the turn. Two would slow to 450 knots and remain at one hundred feet. They would not climb until they reached twenty miles from the beach. Twenty miles put them clear of SAM threats and MiGs. Friendly fighters ruled the sky over the water while the North Viets owned it over the beach.

The four-plane joined up and returned to Cubi Point. One led them down the runway at a thousand feet. He signaled Two to break away from the formation and set up to land. After five seconds, One broke away. By the time Stretch executed his turn, he was over *Solomons*.

Stretch felt good about the training mission. It was more rewarding than making toothpicks. Making toothpicks, though, at least you saw your bombs blow up. With mines, you never saw your weapons explode. Still, making toothpicks had such a stink attached to it, dropping mines smelled a lot better.

Following landing, parking, and post-flight inspection, the pilots assembled in the briefing room in the base operations building at the foot of the control tower. Their hits were waiting for them. The flight had missed the desired drop point by a half-mile. Missing the target by a thousand yards doused his warm feel-good with ice water. Still the Skipper, he knew, had missed the drop point by six hundred yards. He decided to put the warm feel-good aside until he saw how the other flight leads, including himself, did.

Over three days, the squadron flew seven mine training missions with a different flight lead each time. Stretch, as seventh senior, led the last one. His flight dumped their trash cans 800 yards from the desired drop point. The hits scored on all the training missions ranged from misses of 1700 yards to 300 yards. Blackey's flight scored the 300 yarder.

That afternoon, the Ops O called an APM, All Pilots Meeting, in the ready room on the ship.

"In the mining mission, like all ordnance delivery flights, precision is desired," the Ops O said. "Mines, however, can still do their job even if they are dumped a mile from the desired drop point. Merchant marine captains don't want to risk their vessels in a minefield. If we mine Haiphong Harbor, the navigation problem will be tougher than the one we practiced here. Geographic features will be tougher to find and aim at. But! As long as we get our weapons in the water off the North Vietnamese coast, anywhere near Haiphong, we will have done our job."

The Ops O wrapped up the debrief of the mine training and dismissed the APM.

Nose sat behind Stretch. He said to Skippy, "A buddy of mine, an A-7 driver, is on the USS *Constellation*. He was home on emergency leave and is now on the way back to his ship. Since we were in port here, he decided to drop by to see me before he catches a ride to Nam. The last time they were in port here, he told me, they did mine training drops. The A-7s all dropped their trash cans within 350 yards of their target drop points.

"A-7s, man!" Skippy said. "New airplanes with inertial navigation and *real* bombing computers that makes everybody Dead Eye Dick."

"You mean like Blackey?" Nose said.

"I do not mean like Blackey. I'd rather miss by a mile than have someone say, 'Skippy, you bombed as good as Blackey today.'"

"You hate him?"

"Pretty much."

"Why?"

"Because he's an ass."

Blackey's chair was on the opposite side of the aisle in the ready room. Stretch was sure he heard Skippy. Skippy hadn't lowered his voice.

Blackey stood. "Skippy, wanna' grab lunch?"

Skippy didn't respond, didn't even look at him.

The Ass stood in the aisle looking down on the JG, and it was as if Stretch was looking at the opposite of a kid at Halloween. The kid wore a scary mask, but innocent, I'm-having-a-lot-of-fun eyes peeked out the eyeholes. Blackey's face wore an innocent little-boy mask, while his dark eyes dumped unadulterated nastiness, from an unassailable height of superiority, onto his seated victim.

Oh yeah. Real Blackey's back.

⸺⫸⬥⫷⸺

Teresa was in the kitchen working on dinner. Jennifer sat at the table, drawing a picture for Daddy with her crayons. Ruthann, in her infant seat, gurgled and cooed next to Jennifer. EJ was quiet. Too quiet. She found him playing nicely with a truck on the rug in the living room.

She returned to the chicken enchilada casserole. A prayer came to mind. Father in heaven, if the person who invented the casserole is not already a saint, could You canonize her? Or him?

Fixing dinner took over an hour. Her family consumed it in about fifteen minutes. From a casserole, though, she and the children got four meals. Having the prep time equal to the eating time seemed like some sort of rare motherly justice. As she seasoned and stirred the sauce and shredded breast meat in the skillet, guilt seasoned her soul. Rare motherly justice. That thought had been selfish, and worse. It lamented the time it cost a woman and ignored the blessing inherent in being a mother. A matter for Saturday confession.

From the front door, the cover over the mail slot rattled. Jennifer jumped down from her seat and ran for the door with EJ right behind her.

"Jennifer, EJ. Stop. Stop." Teresa hurried through the kitchen and stood in the doorway into the hall.

The children could have hurt themselves fighting over who would pick up the mail and bring it to her. However, they had halted their headlong rush toward the door. They were, however, like dogs barely able to heed "Sit" and wait for the release command to get the anticipated treat.

"This is how you will pick up the mail. You will walk, not run, to the door. There will be no pushing, no shoving. Jennifer will pick up one piece of mail, then EJ picks one up, then Jennifer again. You understand?"

"Yes, Mommie."

"EJ?"

"Yeth."

"Take your thumb out of your mouth. Do you understand?"

"Yes, Mommie." And the thumb headed back for his mouth.

"Ahhhh!" Teresa warned.

The thumb stopped its ascent.

The angels proceeded as Mommie had instructed. Teresa could see at least two letters from Jon.

"Take the mail to the table. After I get dinner in the oven, we'll open the letters.

Teresa lined the base of the casserole dish with tortillas, spooned sauce over that, and covered the glop, Jon called it, with more tortillas.

From the dining room, Jennifer: "EJ, these letters are from Daddy. Can you count them?"

"One. Two. Fwee."

"Three. Say three."

"Thwee."

Teresa grated cheese over it all, slid the dish into the oven, and entered the dining room.

EJ tried again. "Thwee."

"That's better, EJ. Good job. And good job being a teacher, Jennifer."

The praise set Jennifer aglow as if her halo had disintegrated, and the fine fragments sifted down around her face like a snow of holiness.

EJ frowned and stuck his thumb in his mouth.

Jennifer was getting ready to fuss at him, but Teresa shook her head. Her daughter got the message and kept her mouth shut.

There were four envelopes in all. One was the phone bill. Hopefully, not as bad as the one with the collect call from Hawaii. Phone bill: later. Jon's letters, she slit them all open, and starting with the earliest postmark, she removed the contents. Each one contained pages for her and one for each child. He even included one for Ruth. Hers always read. "Baby Ruth, Daddy loves you. A bushel and a peck, and a smooch upon your neck."

"Jennifer, read Daddy's notes to EJ, please?"

Teresa looked at Jon's salutations to her. "Dearest Teresa" zipped her to her—their—writing place. She wallowed there for an instant. Then she kissed the letters, said, "Later," and stuck them back into their envelopes.

After dinner, after the cleanup, after the baths, after getting them all to bed, she pulled out her "Dearest Teresas".

One was postmarked four days ago. She'd written Jon that time did not matter when she went to their write/read letters place. But it did matter. Some. Four days vs. seven or ten, it mattered.

Reading the letters, she felt a subtle air of uplifted spirit. Jon didn't write that he'd been bothered by what seemed like a waste of time, like what the Warhorses were doing over there was not worth the price of separation from her and the children. One night last year, after making love, he'd talked to her about it. She smiled. Usually, after, he fell asleep. Holding her hand, or with his hand on her hip. But that night, he'd stayed awake and told her how it bothered him, to have stayed in the navy, following his sense of duty, only to discover they weren't doing anything worthwhile. The country did not seem to be interested in trying to win the war. Soldiers, sailors, marines, air force guys were dying, and what purpose did those deaths serve? "It was like we woke up one day," he'd said, "and discovered, holy crap, we're in a war. Anybody know how this happened? Anybody know how to get out of it?"

That was the only time he'd ever said, or written, anything like that. But she sensed it in his letters. Lately, however, the background flavor of his letters was more positive, had been written by a … happy, or at least satisfied, spirit, not one weighed down. She wondered what had happened, or was happening.

And she worried.

So many times, it seemed, what eased Jon's mind piled more worry on hers. Doing something useful meant more danger. The back of her mind formed a prayer for her consideration: Please, Father God in heaven, keep Jon doing USELESS things. The front of her mind rejected it, though. Instead: Father, please keep Jon safe. She carefully avoided appending a time to wish for him to come home. That was His business.

She took out her stationery to answer his letters. Before picking up her pen, she, as she did so often, looked out through the kitchen to the calendar. *Solomons* had one more week in the PI, then it would be back to the Tonkin Gulf. And combat missions. And combat missions of a kind that uplifted Jon's spirits?

The phone rang. Ruth Ann howled. Edgar Jon hollered, "Be quiet, Roofann."

Teresa hurried to the phone. It was Naomi Engel, with news from the phone tree. *Solomons* was getting underway immediately to return to the Tonkin Gulf. The North Vietnamese had launched a major offensive.

A knock sounded at the back door. Amy Allison? It was. With Amelia. In her infant seat.

"Take care of your air-raid siren. I'll see to EJ and Jennifer."

"God bless you, Amy Allison."

She set off for the bedroom.

Amy found out at the same time Teresa did because Nose Newsome had his wife set up a lieutenant (junior grade) wives' phone tree. Nose generally found out things the same time the heavies did, so he had called his wife Monica, and she'd called the other JG wives. Mike Allison was a new full lieutenant, but Nose asked Monica to keep Mike on the junior officer phone tree.

Poor Ruth. The phone always scared her, filled her little heart with terror. Truth be told, that phone ringing late at night set Teresa's heart to pounding, and dreading the terrible news waiting to pounce on her, "Hello."

But, she could not do without the phone near her bed.

STRETCH AND TINY, LIEUTENANT GREG Haywood, Lieutenant Zachery's best friend since days on the USS *Manfred*, stood on the flight deck of *Solomons* and watched the frantic activity on the pier below. Since the carrier received the order to "get underway ASAP!" it had been a mad scramble to wrap up the shipyard repair efforts in the engineering spaces and to load airplanes.

A stream of yellow aircraft tractors towed A-4s and F-8s from the airfield to the pier below. Cranes then lifted the jets onto the forward aircraft elevator, which raised them to the flight deck where they were parked. Simultaneously, equipment containers brought aboard by the shipyard workers were being craned off the after-aircraft elevator and loaded on trucks which conveyed them off the pier and around Subic Bay to the surface navy base opposite Cubi Point Naval Air Station.

"Looks like a Mongolian goat rope down there on the pier, doesn't it?" Tiny said.

"How about extremely well-organized pandemonium?"

"By definition, pandemonium can't be organized."

"They do it on the flight deck every day."

Tiny, a foot taller, snatched off Stretch's barracks cover and messed his hair. He did that when he conceded an argument.

Stretch grabbed his cover and put it back on.

"Remember the USAF guys we had aboard last cruise?" Tiny said.

"They were watching us launch and recover airplanes. One of them said it looked like chaos on the flight deck. 'How do you conduct flight ops on a floating postage stamp? We have ten thousand acres for our base in Thailand.'"

"Yeah. I pretty much wondered the same thing the first time I did carrier landings in the training command. A carrier flight deck is a long way from the DASH landing pad on the *Manfred*."

On the destroyer, Jon's duties included driving an anti-submarine torpedo-carrying drone helicopter. DASH: Drone Anti-Sub Helicopter.

"Flying machines are meant to have pilots inside, not outside wiggling a joystick on a control box," Tiny said.

"Based on how our machine worked on *Manfred*, you won't get an argument from me."

"I wasn't aboard when our DASH went berserk and nearly killed you and Almost. But I heard you would have bought it if you hadn't figured which switch to throw."

The DASH came equipped with counter rotating main rotor blades, obviating the need for a tail rotor. The drones were notoriously unreliable, and occasionally, the control signals to the aircraft got confused. Those counter-rotating blades could bash together and send flying blade-part shrapnel flying hundreds of yards.

"Ah. I didn't do much. Almost was controlling it. He started the engine and got the rotors turning. Then, as rotor RPM approached normal takeoff and flight RPM, the gust locks disengaged. That's when the blades started flailing."

"Yeah, and Almost told me you flipped the one switch that saved both of you."

"I was watching him. He tried everything. He flipped every switch on the control box except one. I was sure we were really close to the blades bashing together, and I flipped that switch. And the helo immediately settled into routine, ready-for-takeoff mode."

"Almost told me the problem was in shorted wires in the umbilical cable. Standard procedure was to control the helo through that cable until after start checks. Then you switch to radio control to do the mission."

"Yeah. Controlling DASH through the umbilical cable was thought to be safer than using radio signals."

"Heck of a thing when the safety features try to kill you, eh, Stretch?"

Tiny reached for his hat again but Stretch ducked.

"By the way," Tiny said, "I appropriated the Almost name for our newbie. It stands for Almost halfway worth a shit."

In Manfred's ensign locker, the Almost nickname meant Almost Normal.

"J'eat?"

"No. J'ou?"

"Let's gw'eat."

En route to the Tonkin Gulf, intel officers briefed the aircrew on the situation in South Vietnam.

North Vietnam had launched three attacks. One came through the DMZ. A second through Laos and into the central highlands of South Vietnam. The third staged in Cambodia and aimed itself at Saigon. All three prongs constituted major offensives, which included tanks and other armored vehicles. The South Vietnamese Army was hard-pressed. With the drawdown in US troops in-country, only aviation remained to save the day. Normal transit time to the Tonkin Gulf took forty-eight hours. This trip, *Solomons* arrived in the Gulf after thirty-couple hours underway.

The Tonkin Gulf Fleet Commander assigned *Solomons* to Dixie Station. The US Navy used two aircraft carrier stations in the Tonkin Gulf. Yankee Station was north of the DMZ and situated to attack both North and South Vietnam. Dixie Station sat off the coast of South Vietnam and served as a launch point for attacks against targets inside South Vietnam and Laos.

The first missions of the day catapulted off the ship at 0700. The Skipper led a Warhorse four-plane. Stretch flew number Three.

Their FAC worked in an area about halfway between Saigon and the western border of South Vietnam. Targets: troops and trucks in the open. Not like before when the jungle hid vehicles and the enemy. After dropping their bombs and strafing, the FAC credited them with destroying two trucks, a stack of supplies with secondary explosions, and ten KIA.

Back on the ship, in the ready room, Nose exulted, "Hell, man! We got more BDA (Bomb Damage Assessement) on our first hop here than the whole squadron did over all of last cruise."

Following a bombing mission, A FAC gave the flight their BDA. Last cruise it most often came as "One hundred percent of bombs within one hundred meters of the target." Which could have been stated as, "Made toothpicks."

Stretch looked at the Skipper. The Skipper rolled his eyes, probably thinking, as he was: junior officers!

Nose had, of course, exaggerated. But not by much. After last deployment, all the Warhorse pilots received at least one medal. To receive a medal, you had to achieve significant BDA on a mission while being shot at. Stretch flew more than a hundred combat missions that cruise and received a single medal. It wasn't hard to see why Nose was excited.

Finally, we're doing something useful. Stretch felt it, too. And he was sure even the Skipper did, but he and the CO were not JOs. They were, in fact, seasoned pilots. Calm, cool, collected, not given to juvenile displays of emotion. Ah, not that big a deal.

On his second hop that day, his flight's BDA included enemy supplies destroyed, with secondary explosions, and two KIA. Not quite as rewarding as the morning hop; still, it was not making toothpicks. Besides his two flights over Nam, Stretch also flew a tanker hop on the last go of the day. A couple of times last cruise, he logged three hops in a day. A couple of times. Three at most. But now, the first day back on the line, a three hopper.

This '72 cruise was looking like it might be worth a hoot.

Solomons launched not only her A-4 aircraft as bombers, but the F-8 fighters dropped bombs as well. In effect, the carrier was throwing all she had at the enemy.

This first day back on the line had finally-we're-doing-something-useful stamped all over it.

After he landed from his tanker hop, Stretch made his way to the ready room and filled out the paperwork on his aircraft. Then, the day caught up with him. Three hops. No time to think, just prepare to fly,

fly, debrief and prepare to fly again. Now, the flying was done. He visited the chapel and, with the place to himself, sat and soaked up the solemn silence and said a prayer.

> Father God, Who art in heaven. Hallowed be Thy name. Thank You for this feeling of accomplishment. That being over here and away from Teresa and our children is worth something.
>
> But, Father God, here's the kicker. I felt joy over blowing up those North Vietnamese trucks and killing those soldiers. It seems like a little satisfaction at having done my duty could have a place in my heart, but joy at killing? I ask Your help, Lord, in dealing with this.
>
> Please and thank You.
>
> I just needed to say that. Now, though, I need to grab some chow. I'm hungry enough to eat my flight boots, even though they stink of jet fuel and toe jam.

In the Dirty Shirt dining room, the air was redolent with mouthwatering aromas and alive with raucous banter, more at home in the Cubi Point O Club than aboard a US Navy ship at sea. Stretch's fellow diners did not seem to be bothered to feel joy over killing and destroying.

The place was packed. Most of the time, the Dirty Shirt was not a place where people dawdled after eating. Usually, diners there stuffed their food in their mouths and left. That night, however, dawdling and talking were the norm.

Stretch was behind Nose and both stood by a table filled with eight guys who had empty trays in front of them, and they all gabbled like a tableful of teenaged girls at a sock hop during a band intermission.

Nose said, "You guys know the Dirty Shirt has a new theme song? I'm going to sing it for you."

"Buzz off, Nose," a dawdler said.

"The Dirty Shirt theme song," Nose shouted. "Walk right in. Sit right down. Snarf your food." Then at the top of his lungs. "Then move your big butt along."

The dawdlers looked up at Nose.

"Second verse." Which he belted out at the threshold of pain decibel level. When he said, "Third verse," the dawdlers vacated their seats. Nose, Stretch, and six others took their places and began to eat.

As soon as the dawdlers placed their trays on the conveyor belt into the scullery, they returned to the table and hollered, "Fourth verse."

Stretch wadded up bits of paper napkin and stuffed them into his ears. It didn't help much. He sure didn't dawdle, though.

Most nights, when he didn't have work to do, he sat in his stateroom and wrote to Teresa. That night, however, he stayed in the ready room and watched the movie. A western. While it played, he flopped the swing up desktop of his chair into place, used his red lens flashlight to illuminate the paper, and wrote to his wife and children. That night, he was drawn to be with his squadron mates. Not exclusively. But with them. Among them.

⸻ ❖ ⸻

Teresa asked EJ to bring in the paper. Fetching The Fresno Bee made the boy happy. The deliveryman tossed it onto their driveway after Jennifer left for Kiddie Garden. He got to bring in the paper without having to compete to do so.

Normally, Teresa had no time to read the paper until the afternoon or evening. That morning, though, she noticed two front-page articles about the North Vietnamese Easter Offensive and invasion of South Vietnam. One above the fold, the other below. The children's needs and her shower filled the mornings. That morning, the newspaper shoved aside her sacred morning routine. Even Ruth's bath in the kitchen sink waited until after the paper.

As Teresa read, a sense of dread and worry for Jon mounted, but she also got a glimpse of understanding of what Jon had told her the year before. The country did not seem set on trying to win the war. For years, newspaper stories included statistics such as the number of American aircraft sorties flown, the number of tons of bombs dropped, the numbers of enemy soldiers killed. Recently, however, there had been stories about how many thousands of US soldiers had been pulled out of Vietnam.

That's how we got ready for the Easter Offensive! By pulling our troops out.

And who was left to deal with the invasion? Jon and the Warhorses. And the other squadrons aboard *Solomons*. And the other carriers. A story related that the US had deployed three aircraft carriers to the Tonkin Gulf. Usually, only a single flattop operated there.

That night last year, when Jon opened up to her about his frustrations with how the US conducted the war, she listened to his words, but hadn't understood them. Now she understood. A little.

Oh, foot!

Her window to get a shower had opened and closed while she read the darned paper. She sighed. Even if her mother were filthy, Ruth would be clean. Teresa folded the paper and filled the kitchen sink with baby bath water. As she bathed her infant, Teresa recalled the night of the dog poop.

1966. After Jon returned from a deployment on his destroyer, they visited Teresa's Uncle Theodore and Aunt Penelope Prescott north of Los Angeles. Their daughter Christine joined an anti-war protest at college. Some of her friends found out that Jon had been deployed to Vietnam, and they trashed the Zachery's car with dog poop and a garden hose.

"Before that," Jon said, "The protestors were people in newspaper stories, not real people. The night of the dog poop made them real. It made the protest real, and the protest was aimed at me."

The Prescott's local newspaper printed an article about the incident.

Uncle Theodore said, "It's better to read the news than be the news."

Besides being the news, the night of the dog poop changed Jon's intentions. Until then he'd intended leaving the service when his obligated time expired, but he'd decided he didn't agree with the protestors, and that it was his duty to stay in and serve.

Ruth liked her personal bathtub and having warm water sponged over her back.

Teresa didn't want to say the words out loud.

Oh, Ruth. Daddy is the news.

Again.

BLACKEY LED THE FOUR-PLANE ON the mid-morning go. He checked in with Covey Two One, a FAC, and reported the number of planes and bombs carried.

"Warhorses, this is Covey. I'm fifty miles west of Saigon. Need you to hustle. I got a tank in the open, but he's hotfooting for the trees."

"Warhorses, this is One." Blackie radioed. "I'm going to full power. Keep up if you can."

Stretch added full power. He flew Number Three. His wingman, Mudder, inched behind. To the left, Stump flew Two, and he fell behind at a good clip. Sometimes one plane put out less thrust than the others. Stump had drawn a dog to fly.

"Stump," Stretch radioed, "punch off your drop tank."

The three-hundred-gallon fuel tank didn't weigh much, but it added drag. By this time in a flight, it was empty. Getting rid of it might enable Two to keep up.

"Covey, Warhorse One. We'll give you three runs each."

Two dropped farther behind. He was about to tell him again to punch off his drop tank when it flew off his jet. *Crap. Newbies!* Not only the tank, but the bombs and bomb racks fell away, too. He'd set the ordnance switches wrong.

Now Two was catching up. He looked like he wanted to resume his position in trail of One.

"Stump, orbit above us," Stretch radioed.

"Three. Stay off the air." Blackey was torqued off.

Normally, as Number Three, he would have kept his mouth shut. But Stump had been dropping back at a good clip. Letting a new guy get lost over the beach was not a good idea. Blackie didn't see what was going on behind him, so, he tried to help. But giving the flight lead a big explanation as to what was going on, this was not the time for that either. So, sorry, Blackie, get over it.

"Covey, Warhorse. We should be one minute out."

"Roger, Warhorse. Covey is rolling in. I'll fire two smoke rockets. They'll point the way to the target. The tank is heading due west."

Hopefully, Four was doing what he should be doing. Checking ordnance switches.

"Rockets away. Covey will hold north of the target. The tank is really hauling ass, Warhorse."

"This is Warhorse One. Tally Ho on your smoke, and I see you. One's rolling in."

Stretch zigged left, then back to the right so he could see the ground past his nose. One looked to be in a thirty-degree dive. He adjusted his gunsight for the shallow dive. Almost at the roll-in point, he changed his ordnance switches to drop four bombs on the first run.

"This is Covey. The tank is about to enter the trees. If you don't stop him with your first run, we'll lose him."

"Four," Stretch radioed. "Master arm and thirty-degree dive." This to remind Four to turn on his armament switches and adjust his bomb sight for a shallow dive.

"One's off. Tank fired a machine gun at me."

"Nice hits, One. Just short," Covey radioed.

"Three's in."

As Stretch rolled into the bank angle, he picked up the tank spewing a trail of dust. A wall of jungle rose in front of it. The set up was much like the radio-controlled boat he'd bombed off Hawaii. He shallowed the dive, sensing the need for more lead. The gunsight helped, but it was still by-guess and by-god seat-of-the-pants flying.

Tracers rose from the tank as he hit the pickle. The bombs thump,

thump, thump, thumped as they fell away. He jerked the stick back and turned left hard.

Four called rolling in.

Covey radioed. "You got him, Three."

Stretch saw the tank stopped, dust roiling around it.

Four's bombs landed long.

Covey radioed, "Okay, Warhorses. Looks like Three blew the tread off the left side of the tank. Now see if you can kill it."

On the second bomb runs, the Warhorses missed by a little, a little more, and a lot more. However, on Blackey's third run, his bombs caused a series of secondary explosions and left the tank a burning hulk.

***

Ruth had been fed. Jennifer and EJ ate their cereal. Teresa looked at her calendar and X-ed off yesterday. Today—whenever today was on Jon's side of the world—*Solomons* would stand down. After two weeks of the pilots flying two or three hops each day, they, and the ship's flight deck crew, got a day off.

However much the pilots and flight deck crew appreciated that stand-down, Teresa appreciated it more. For twenty-four blessed hours she could lay aside the worry of him flying two combat hops. It was a blessed, Thank You, God, reprieve from that part of her wedding vows nobody told her about. Besides love, honor, and obey, there was that hidden, unspoken worry like crazy for you, Jon Zachery.

She touched the tip of her finger to her lips and transferred the kiss to her stand-down day.

***

Flight ops secured at 1900. Tomorrow, being a stand down, a party was called for. The JOB was the perfect venue, as it was one of the few staterooms on the entire ship to have its own stainless steel bathroom sink. Even squadron COs did not have such an amenity in their staterooms. Skipper Fant, Stretch knew, shared a bathroom with another squadron CO.

More important than the sink, though, the JOB was located port side forward and had a porthole, perfect for discarding post-party detritus. In addition, the double bunk beds arranged around the sides of the room acted like conversation group sofas in a living room. Each bottom bunk accommodated three butts.

The party would commence at 2100. The JGs who lived in the JOB— Nose, Nooner, Skippy, Mudder, Stump, and Bee— started celebrating a half-hour earlier. All the Warhorse lieutenants—except Not—arrived by 2105. Besides not being an angel, Not was not an on-time guy. What he was, though, as the Administrative Officer, was a department head, which put him in rank, importance, and responsibility, one notch below the CO and XO. As such, he was expected to ride herd on the junior, less mature, less responsible officers. If he did that, of course, he would be threatened with dismemberment and his body parts being tossed out the porthole. Still, he served as a visible reminder that the Skipper expected them to not get so rowdy, they would call attention to themselves. That worked to a certain extent after he arrived at 2110.

Not stepped into the JOB and closed the door. Nose said, "Let's say hello to the department head."

A lusty, "Hello, Asshole!" burst forth from the assembly.

Not winced. "You guys might want to hold it down a bit."

Nose said, "Let's say 'Aye, aye, to the department—"

The door to the JOB shoved open, the Skipper stepped in and closed the door. He glared at Nose. "You might want to hold it down a bit." The glare continued.

Stretch thought Nose's brain floated in enough alcohol to where it could not tell the difference between bold and brave and downright stupid. Then a commonsense lightbulb blinked on.

"Sorry, Skipper."

"Switch to soda for a while." The Skipper looked at Not, and he nodded.

Taking a paper cup from the fold down desk, the Skipper moistened the bottom with a drop of whiskey and added water from the tap on the sink. He raised the cup, and said, "To the *Solomons*, our airwing, and the Warhorses."

Not raised his glass and whispered, "The Warhorses," and the rest of the JOs whispered an echo.

The Skipper sipped. "After a couple of weeks of hot and heavy flying, this is what we think we've done. The North Viets launched an all-out offensive. They threw everything they had into their three-pronged attack. We've worked exclusively against their southern probe aimed at Saigon. They were bold and confident enough to work in daylight. A mistake on their part, and we knocked the snot out of them. But we haven't killed them. They've switched more of their effort to nighttime. So, when we start flying again, day after tomorrow, we'll be doing the noon to midnight schedule.

"We've done good work to this point, so a little celebrating is in order. The operative word being what, Nose?"

"Uh, little, Sir."

The Skipper nodded and departed.

Not sat next to Stretch on the bottom bunk against the aft bulkhead.

"This was your bunk last cruise, right?" Not said.

"It was."

"Bring back fond memories, being here again?"

Stretch sipped his watered-down whiskey and wished it was straight. "It brings back memories."

The memory that kicked down the back door into his brain was of Amos (gerund form of the F-word) Kane.

Last cruise. Last combat sorties of the deployment. Once the planes on the last launch landed, *Solomons* would depart the Tonkin Gulf and begin the journey home.

Among the twenty planes launched on that last go were an F-8 photo reconnaissance bird with an armed F-8 escort and four Warhorse A-4s to provide protection against SAMs (Surface to Air Missiles) and AAA (Anti-aircraft Artillery). The ship launched a photo recce mission twice a month while in the Gulf, and the unarmed photo bird and its escorts had never been fired on before. On that last launch of the '70/'71 cruise, however, all hell broke loose.

The photo bird called, "Commencing," as it started overflying the main route the North Viets used to truck supplies to their fighters in South Vietnam. At the same time, the North Viets fired SAMs at Stretch and his flight lead. Stretch saw them, and they evaded the missiles. There was a problem, however. All the Solomons' aircraft were equipped with electronic warning systems to warn a pilot a SAM had been fired at his aircraft. Neither Stretch nor his flight lead received a warning about the SAMs. It turned out that Amos Kane had sabotaged those warning systems in the Warhorse airplanes. The other two Warhorse pilots on the mission had been shot down and killed.

LT (JG) Amos Kane was not a pilot, but a ground pounder, a maintenance officer. In the past he'd worn wings, but turned them in after he met, and fell in love with, an anti-war protestor. Amos lived in the JOB with five pilots and their deep-seated animosity toward him—which he reciprocated in kind.

During the transit back to the US, an inquiry board determined that only Warhorse aircraft had been sabotaged. The board was unable to ascertain how long the planes had their warning systems disabled.

The board's major conclusions were: Amos Kane sabotaged the warning systems of the Warhorse aircraft; that he acted alone; that he had been overcome by remorse after the two squadron pilots had been killed; and he committed suicide by jumping overboard.

Stretch knew that two of the conclusions were wrong. Amos had not been overcome by remorse, and he had not committed suicide.

After the last launch recovered, Stretch discovered how the sabotage had been done. The connection between the warning system electronic box and the antenna had been severed. Clever, really. By pushing the BIT (built in test) button in the warning system, a pilot would still get an indication of proper operation. BIT did not check the connection to the antenna.

On the heels of discovering the "how" of the sabotage, it came to light that LT (jg) Kane recently began helping squadron technicians run tests and repair the A-4 warning systems. Amos Kane was a suspect.

Stretch surmised that Kane figured the others would suspect him because of his anti-war views, but he figured he'd just deny it. They wouldn't be able to prove it. But when the weight of the circumstantial evidence topped a ton, Amos decided he'd leave a fake suicide note and hide on the ship until it reached the PI. An aircraft carrier was big enough, with enough hard-to-get-to spaces where a person could hide. A sailor had done that earlier in the cruise. Only a fluke chance discovered the kid's hide away. Then Amos'd sneak off. He had plenty of money to buy new ID, a way back to the States, and to start a new life with his new name. The next part of the story was not speculation, and only three people knew of it. Stretch, Tuesday, and Botch.

Tuesday and Botch were JGs and residents of the JOB. As soon as they heard about the sabotage and that Amos Goddamned Kane, as Tuesday called him, was suspect number one, the two of them hustled to the JOB and found Kane stuffing things into a small travel bag. Tuesday carried a derringer in his flight suit as an extra survival weapon. He used the gun to shoot Amos; then, he and Botch rolled the body in a rug from the deck of the JOB and tossed the roll over the side.

Stretch, too, went to the JOB looking for Amos and found Tuesday and Botch. Tuesday tossed his derringer out the porthole. The rug from the deck of the JOB was missing, and by the behavior of the two JGs, he knew they'd done something, and he questioned them. Botch folded and spilled the story. Then they discovered the suicide note Amos had left.

He thought about reporting what he knew to the squadron CO but decided not to rat on the two, even if it meant he carried their murder on his soul.

That last launch of last cruise, a heck of a way to end ops in the Tonkin Gulf.

"Hey, Stretch. Earth to Stretch. Didn't you hear what Blackey said?" Not asked.

"I was—"

"Ah. He had his head up his ass. Like he did that day I killed the tank," Blackey said. "First, I was flight lead, and Stretch started telling my wingman what to do."

"Here's what really happened," Stump said. "I was number Two. When the FAC told us about the tank, and that we had to hustle or it would get away, Blackey went to full power. I was flying a dog airplane that day and started dropping behind. At a goodly clip. I … panicked. A little. Blackey didn't even notice me dropping back. Stretch did."

"I saw you dropping back," Blackey said. "But we had to hustle or the tank would get away."

"Stretch told me to jettison my drop tank," Stump said. "I thought that was a good suggestion, except, in my haste to do it, I screwed up the switches and dumped off not only the drop tank, but my bombs, too."

"And made yourself useless because you listened to him," Blackey pointed to Stretch, "instead of to your flight lead."

"Blackey, what are you doing? Skipper said this was supposed to be a celebration." EC, LCDR (Lieutenant Commander) Wakefield, the Maintenance Officer said.

Stretch hadn't even noticed him come in.

"The guys have a right to know what a dipwad Stretch is. He's always giving us lectures about systems on the airplane, how to shoot Shrike missiles, how to use," Blackey sneered, "the bombing computer. They might want to think about whether they should listen to him."

"Come with me," EC said.

"I'm not going anywhere with you." Another sneer. "East Coast puke."

Call sign EC for East Coast. He'd made two deployments to the Mediterranean Sea and had less combat experience than most of the Warhorse JGs.

Stretch watched EC, to see what he'd do.

EC walked across the deck to where Blackey sat on a bottom bunk, grabbed the front of his shirt, jerked him to his feet, and dragged him out the door.

"Well, that answers that question," Nose said.

From Stump: "Which question?"

"How far can you push EC?"

10

T HE WARHORSE WIVES CLUB HELD, not a potluck, rather a pot-organized supper on the *Solomons'* standdown day. The Skipper's wife Sarah hosted the event and assigned dishes for the attending wives to bring. Teresa and Amy Allison brought salad makings and their babies. While the two mothers chopped carrots, olives, and tomatoes, their infants passed from hand to hand as the club members took turns holding and cooing to the adorable bundles.

Teresa was surprised to find Blackey's former wife at the pot-organized. Carolyn had reassumed her maiden name, Masterson.

She'd returned to Lemoore because she had arranged for a memorial service in the base chapel for Robert Stoll. "I wanted to see all of you once more, and I wanted to invite you to the memorial service for Rob." Her face crinkled into a smile rouged over with loss and sadness. "For Troll."

Through the rest of the preparations and the dinner itself, Carolyn was the center of attention. Her story was riveting, and she needed to unburden herself of it.

"I'm sure you all remember the night I fell out of love with Blackey." Carolyn glanced at Laura Davison. "At the party at your house. he behaved terribly, swearing loudly, knowing it would upset you." She shook her head. "I am so sorry. Until that night, I guess I was smitten with his charm and what I viewed as an attractive iconoclastic behavior. I hadn't picked up on the cruelty."

Laura comforted Carolyn and said that was all in the past, and, "What I had to bear is nothing compared to how it hurt you."

Carolyn admitted the decision to divorce her husband had left her depressed. She'd committed herself not only to him, but to his way of life. Her own life as a stewardess might have to end. She'd considered doing just that so that she could be a full-time navy wife. But then she'd discovered the true base and cruel nature of her spouse. And just in time. Instead of resigning, she'd taken leave. Troll, aware of how distraught Carolyn was, drove down to LA from Lemoore to be with her, to help her pick up the pieces of a shattered dream.

"Rob," Carolyn smiled wistfully, "I mean Troll, told me Blackey had been his best friend for two years. He'd witnessed some of his harsh treatment of student aviators in the training command. But lots of instructor pilots were tough on the kids. A big part of navy flight training involved identifying and weeding out those men who *just didn't have what it takes*. The ability to suppress fear of death and to learn to operate their planes at the absolute edge of what aircraft and pilot could do without killing themselves.

"Rob said Blackey was the best pilot he'd ever seen or heard of. In a squadron, other pilots quickly learned he was the best. In a social setting, he seemed to think he had to be the best there too. Except he had no clue as to where the boundaries were. Not like he knew the boundaries in an airplane.

"I think Rob was right about him. He had to be the best, and he didn't care who he hurt to prove it."

"Deborah," Sarah Fant jumped in, "How do like being a West Coast puke?"

Deborah placed her fork on her plate. "The thing I like most is living on base here, and how close you are to each other in the Warhorses. In our last squadron, we lived off base and I was closer to people in our kids' school than I was to the other squadron wives."

Teresa noted Carolyn take a first bite of food, and after the first bite, a more enthusiastic second. As if she had just discovered how hungry she was.

Almost as hungry to eat as she had been to say what she did.

After the cleanup, and during the ride home in Amy's car, with their babies in infant seats in back, Teresa said, "Did you notice how Sarah shifted the attention from Carolyn halfway through dinner?"

"Yes. Poor Carolyn hadn't touched her food until that point."

Amy took a quick glance at Teresa, then turned back to the highway between the town of Lemoore and naval air station of the same name. "I think Sarah knew Carolyn needed to … unburden herself. Then when she'd done that, Sarah maneuvered the conversation away from her. So, she could eat."

"It was obvious Carolyn had lost weight since we saw her last." Teresa checked on the back seat. "Both sleeping."

"I am so glad the Fants came to the Warhorses," Amy said.

"Jon really admires Skipper Fant."

"Mike does, too, and I admire the Skipper's wife."

"Ditto."

A few seconds of silent driving followed.

Then, "Teresa, when I was drying dishes and you were checking on the babies, Carolyn said something … odd."

Teresa waited.

"She doesn't believe Troll's death was an accident. She thinks Blackey deliberately killed him."

"What?"

"Yes. She thought Blackey got mad at Troll for taking Carolyn's side after the divorce. And Troll had driven down to LA to support her."

Teresa put her hand over her heart. "He's Jon's roommate on the ship!"

———◆━■◆■━◆———

The guys at the party said Blackey was just an asshole and don't pay any attention to what he says. Stretch, however, found it hard to ignore being called incompetent, no matter the source. Despite entreaties to stay, he left and went to the chapel.

The chapel was for him, a compartment filled with solemn silence. Sounds from outside registered in his ears, but the carrier-at-sea sounds seemed to come from a mile away instead of just a few feet. To him, the chapel's weighty stillness shielded him from further intrusions while he dealt with what was bothering him. At the moment, two things topped the list: was he appropriately concerned over the lives he'd taken and what his roommate had said.

Blackey was definitely the south side of a horse headed north. He had a lot of practice sluffing off his roommate's spewing of profane and personal attacks. He shouldn't have let what he said in the JOB get to him, but it did.

The chapel contained five rows of six folding chairs each, with an aisle in the middle. In front of the room, a folding table with a white cloth served as the altar. In a Catholic church, behind the altar, there would be a tabernacle that contained consecrated hosts, the body of Christ. When consecrated hosts were present, a lit sanctuary candle signified God was home. In the Solomons' chapel, there was no tabernacle and no sanctuary candle. God was not at home.

Except He was. He was in the silence, and if you quieted yourself, you could hear Him there.

Out of the silence, a notion settled in Jon's brain. He had not followed his flight lead's orders. That upset him. But Stretch was sure that, in some corner of Blackey's self-centered brain, he understood he'd never have killed the tank unless his Number Three had stopped the target before it escaped into the trees. Instead of following orders, He had done what he considered to be the right thing to do.

Officers took an oath to obey the orders of the officers appointed over them. When he'd been in boot camp just after high school, an instructor had listed what should be a sailor's moral priorities: God, country, navy, family, self. The fact was, on the day Blackie killed the tank, he represented the third priority: navy. God and country before. By dropping four bombs, instead of the two his flight lead had ordered, he'd stopped the tank before it escaped into jungle trees. It was his fourth bomb that landed next to tank and blew the tread off.

It had been the right thing to do. What he had done was to enable Blackey to kill the tank and eliminate a significant threat to the army of America's ally.

And, he decided, even if the CO, or CAG, had been leading the flight, and the same thing happened with a new guy falling behind, he'd still get on the radio to try to help the Newbie keep up. It, too, was the right thing to do.

Stretch sat on his last row chair and leaned forward with elbows resting on knees. He huffed out a deep breath.

Then he thought about the lives he'd ended, and was he concerned enough with that?

Out of the silence came the thought: It's good that war is so terrible; otherwise, we would grow too fond of it.

He was fairly certain it was Robert E. Lee. Yes, Lee.

From his reading about the southern general, he considered the man to be driven to do the right thing, to pick the right thing from two hard choices.

Is that why You brought me here? To listen to the words of Robert E. Lee?

He felt as if the solemn silence smiled on him.

When he returned to his room, Blackey was asleep.

Thank You, God.

He wrote to Teresa from a heart cleansed and pure.

⬤

Standdown day or not, Stretch's eyes popped open at 0545. He climbed down from his bunk, grabbed a towel and his Dopp kit, and left for the head. Before closing the door, he checked for his room key on his dog tag chain. If he forgot the key, Blackey probably wouldn't let him in. He'd have to parade half the length of the ship wearing shower shoes and a towel to the Ready Room to call a steward to open the door for him.

When he returned to the room, Blackey was still zonked out. His roommate asleep, always a blessing. For the first time in weeks, Stretch donned khakis, not a flight suit.

When flying, the navy required its pilots to wear flame-retardant Nomex. There was a problem though. Flying over southeast Asia was a hot and sweaty business. Laundry was done once a week, and few airwing pilots owned enough Nomex to change every day. If a pilot did not change his flight suit every day, he would pay a price for stinking up the Ready

Room. He would be awarded the Moldy Jock Strap Award. The award was a high school kid's jock strap that hadn't been laundered for an entire school year, and if you received it, an actual jock strap, hardly moldy at all, hung from the hook above your Ready Room chair intended to hold a flight helmet. You retained the award until someone else stunk up the place. The solution: supplement authorized cockpit wear with unauthorized, non-flame-retardant cotton fatigues. Burning to death in a crash because you wore fatigues that day was considered a small price to pay compared to catching all the flack over smelling bad.

But today was a khaki day. His lieutenant bars went on the collar quickly. With the wings, he took the time to ensure the top of his aviator wings lined up perfectly horizontal with the top of his shirt pocket.

As he finished dressing, reveille sounded. Which meant the Dirty Shirt dining room was open. Outside the Dirty Shirt, he met Tiny. Tall Tiny and small Stretch grinned at each other, and both said, "Hey."

They grabbed aluminum trays and proceeded along the serving line. Bacon. Scrambled eggs. Sausage. Fried potatoes. Toast. Bacon. They put their loaded trays on a table and sat down.

The dining room accommodated fifty, and on a fly day, it would have been packed, but that day there were only a half dozen maintenance officers sitting at one table.

CAG busted into the room. His eyes locked onto Stretch.

"You two dipwads come to my office. Now." CAG spun on his heel and left.

Stretch guzzled his OJ and started to stand.

Tiny grabbed his arm. He mumbled through a mouth stuffed full of eggs and potato, "Make a bacon sandwich."

Stretch did and took his tray to the scullery window, and with his sandwich wrapped in a paper napkin, he left for CAG's office. Hustling down the passageway, he heard Tiny stomping after him.

In CAG's office, they found Skipper Fant and the OINC (Officer in Charge) of the photo recce (reconnaissance) detachment assigned to the airwing. CAG's Ops O was there as well.

The office bulkheads were bare, except for a map of northern South Vietnam taped next to the airwing commander's desk, which was pushed into one end of the narrow room. Folding metal chairs, enough to accommodate all the squadron COs plus a few others lined both sides of the space.

CAG spun around in his swivel chair. "Take a seat."

"CAG, can I grab a cup of coffee first?"

CAG glared up at Tiny. "Ops O, get Tiny a cup of coffee. Please."

"Little sugar. Little cream," Tiny said.

"Black," CAG snarled. "Sit. Down."

Stretch, with Tiny right behind him, slid between the knees of seated Skipper Fant and the OINC and sat.

The Ops O handed Tiny a mug and stepped next to the map. He pointed to a spot just south of the DMZ. "An A-7 from the *Constellation* was shot down here about half an hour ago. He was part of a four-plane. They'd been bombing North Vietnamese Army positions under FAC control when a SAM hit him in the middle of a bombing run. The pilot got out. He's on the ground and talking on his survival radio. He's a couple of miles from the nearest North Viets, but before they commit a full-blown rescue effort, they want to try to kill the SAM site. It's still active and has fired other missiles at early rescue attempts. They asked us to bring TIAS birds and a photo recce."

CAG jumped in. "Our crews are prepping two TIAS A-4s, two F-8s, and a photo bird. We should launch in about forty minutes. The TIAS birds will each have a Shrike and three bombs. Stretch, your CO will be your wingman. I'll fly fighter cover for you. Tiny will escort the photo bird."

"Can we put two Shrikes and two bombs on each A-4?" Stretch said.

CAG Ops said, "Shrikes are expensive, and we don't have that many aboard."

"Yeah," from CAG, "But if we need them, they sure as shit won't do us any good if they are sitting back here in the ship. How expensive is an airplane, Ops O? How much does a pilot cost?"

The Ops O shrugged. "Two it is. I'll make the call."

"Okay, Cal," CAG said to the photo bird OINC, "how do you want to do your piece of this business?"

"This is going to be different from our normal mission. Fly over a length of road. We have to find the proverbial needle in the haystack. A point target hidden in triple-canopy jungle. We'll have to make multiple runs back and forth over the suspected area."

Stretch: "East, west or north, south?"

"East, west," Cal said.

Stretch: "Okay. We'll set up on the southern edge of the DMZ. Skipper, we can fly an oval flight path with one of us pointing our nose north as the other heads south. That way, we should have a Shrike aimed at the suspected target site most of the time."

A few more details were ironed out, and CAG said, "Man up is in fifteen minutes."

Stretch ran through the passageway back to his room. Light traffic that morning because of the standdown day. He threw open the stateroom door, and it banged against the bulkhead.

Blackey leaned up on an elbow. "What the hell?"

Stretch didn't answer. He did take a big bite from his bacon sandwich, then tore off his khakis, zipped up his flight suit and boots, and hustled out of the room.

TERESA ZACHERY STOOD BY HER dryer looking at the calendar and the standdown day. She kissed the tip of her finger and touched it to the calendar. She did that when the calendar blessed her with less worry than normal. *Please give Jon a restful day today.*

She chided herself. *More like praying to the calendar than to God the Father.*

"More juice," Edgar Jon said from the dining room table, ending her morning prayer.

"More juice, please." Jennifer had become such a blessing, such a help with the other two.

"No. More juice." EJ. Willful, stubborn. He was four, and by all rights, his last birthday took him out of the terrible twos and threes. But the boy hung onto the attitude as if his life depended on it.

She walked through the kitchen and into the dining room. "EJ, tell your sister, 'More juice, please.' If you do, she will get you more juice. If you don't, you will leave the table."

EJ slipped off his chair and glared at his mother.

"Fine," Teresa said. "Wash your hands. With soap. And brush your teeth."

The boy stomped away. Jennifer looked at her with *Boys!* written on her face as clear and bright as a harvest moon. Teresa had to be careful with what she said. It was tempting to confide in her oldest daughter. But she had Amy Allison next door. Neighbor, friend. Blessing. She would tell Amy about EJ's behavior that morning and say, as she had before, "We've been blessed to have girl babies, and not a stinker like my son."

Ruth sat in her infant seat on the table, playing with her fingers. Angelic. As if to emphasize the difference in gender-based behavior.

Teresa sighed. There were reasons to sigh these days. In a way, it was as if she and her daughters ganged up on the boy. And, probably, EJ missed and needed his daddy. Still, he was a stinker. She almost sighed again, but it was time to get everyone ready to walk Jennifer to school.

Teresa dressed herself and checked the older children. EJ's ensemble required some adjustments. In the carport, she strapped Ruth's infant seat into the stroller. Amy strapped her baby into a stroller as well, and they walked together down the sidewalk.

"I wish I could ride in a helicopter over family housing on a school day," Amy said. "I think it would be interesting to see all of us like ants converging on the school as if it were a piece of candy a child dropped."

Teresa recalled one of Jon's letters. He wrote about having more than one mind. "My mind has a mind of its own." She remembered that one. He'd also written that he thought his mind had compartments with hard walls. One compartment shut out everything else the other compartments were involved with and dealt with one aspect of life around him. She sensed something akin to that in her own mind.

Teresa found walking and talking with Amy comforting, nourishing. One compartment in her mind recognized that. Another compartment listened to the words Amy spoke and responded. It didn't matter so much what they talked about. What mattered was one soul reaching out and embracing another. So, it wasn't just one woman facing the mysteries of the universe alone. It was two of them. And whether they understood those mysteries was not as important as they did not have to face them alone.

"Jon writes to you every day." That engaged all the compartments in Teresa's mind. "Does he write about what they are doing? Mike writes one page a week. Out of some sense of duty. Not because he wants to. He probably doesn't want to. He says every day is the same as the day before. What's to write about? Does Jon think every day is the same?"

Jon had written about that subject in the letter Teresa received yesterday. He'd commented that in some ways, each day was like the one before. In others, each day is unique "because I am so aware I long for you more than I did the day before." That would not be a thing to say to her friend. Besides, voicing a sentiment like that would water it down. Seeing it written, she could absorb the thought exclusively with her mind, or one of its compartments, and not have the purity of the thought adulterated by another opinion.

"He has written that in some ways, each day is like the one before. But he did write that the missions this deployment are different from last year. Last year, most of their flights were over Laos. This year, most of them are over South Vietnam."

"Mike wrote that he felt like they were doing something worthwhile this cruise. The last one they just blew up trees. Making toothpicks he called it."

"Jon said something similar, but he doesn't say much about his bombing missions. He writes about flying though. He likes flying with Mike."

"Mike likes flying with Jon, too. He lets Mike be the flight lead half the time."

"RT let Jon fly lead last cruise."

They arrived at the school with other mothers and children flowing to the point of assembly from every direction. Cars stopped in the circle, spewed out a child or three, and drove on.

Jennifer kissed each baby on the forehead, hugged Mrs. Allison and Mommy, and tried to hug EJ, but he pushed her away.

"EJ!" Teresa packed heavy admonishment into his initials and held his arm while his sister administered a hug.

With a big smile on her face, Jennifer ran toward the entrance, her bookbag swinging wildly and banging off her legs.

Teresa sucked in a breath. "I'm always afraid she'll trip on her bookbag. For children, uncontainable joy can change to tragedy in a heartbeat. But, thank you, God, not this time."

Jennifer joined the rear of the jam of children pressing and squeezing itself to fit through the door. She chatted and smiled with classmates—such an outgoing, happy girl. Teresa looked at EJ. Once he finally transitioned out of the Terrible Twos and Threes, he would fit in as his older sister did. Perhaps.

Please, God. Life will be so much easier for him.

EJ insisted on leading the walk back to their quarters. He knew the way and wanted to prove it.

When they arrived back at their quarters, Amy sang, "Hi ho, hi ho, it's back to work we go."

Inside, EJ established himself on the rug in the living room with some of his toys. Teresa bathed Ruth in the kitchen sink. Then, with the baby in her infant seat on the bathroom floor, Teresa got her shower. After she dressed again, she nursed Ruth and put her down for a nap. Today was clean-the-living-room day. One room every day of the week, except Sunday. Well, most Sundays.

Lunch, read a book to EJ, tend to Ruth, watch Amy's baby while her neighbor shopped at the commissary, drive to school to pick up Jennifer, dinner, baths for the older children, put them to bed. At last she could write to Jon. As she did, Ruth sat in her infant seat on the table.

Teresa began her letter by writing about walking to school with Amy. As she inked her thoughts to her husband, the subjects she discussed with her neighbor became more meaningful. It was as if Teresa would have missed most of the value in their discussion if she failed to write it down.

> I write these letters for you, Jon Zachery, but they are for me, too. I would not choose for us to be apart, ever, much less so very often and for so very long. But in our letters, I find new ways that I love you. With the children asleep, and the house steeped in silence, when I begin putting words on paper for you, I find these things. These blessings I would not find any other way.
>
> And I hope you had a peaceful, restful standdown day. I appreciated mine.

She wrote four pages on both sides, sealed and stamped the envelope, and climbed into bed, placed her hand on his side of the bed, and whispered,

"Good night, Jon Zachery." In two exhales, she dropped into sleep. Shallow sleep. On her side, her ear not pressed into the pillow listened. Like it always did when he was not there protecting her and the babies. There was no standdown day from that worry.

Stretch had the flight at thirty thousand feet head headed for a spot midway along the east-west southern boundary of the DMZ. The Skipper was off his right wing, CAG the left.

Kodak, the photo bird, and Tiny were to the east, speeding north along the coast. Once they reached the DMZ, they would turn west and set up for the first run over where they thought the SAM was located.

"Point One," Kodak reported crossing the beach and heading west.

Stretch radioed, "Freq. two." A signal for CAG and the Skipper to switch to the radio frequency being used by Sinbad, the on-scene commander of the attempt to rescue the downed A-7 pilot.

Stretch called Sinbad and reported in.

"Roger, Warhorse."

"Flight of three. Two birds with Shrikes. We are three minutes out."

"Roger, Warhorse. Situation here: We're in contact with the downed pilot; he's about a mile and a half from the closest North Viets, but they are closing on him. We bombed a bunch of trucks. Now we think they've sent foot soldiers after him. So, we are blanketing the area with cluster bombs. Air Force dropped some nape. But we're on borrowed time here. We got to get our guy out of there. The Air Force won't send in a helo until we get that SAM site."

A target blip blossomed on Stretch's TIAS scope. "Two! Up twenty-five." A call to the Skipper to pull his nose up twenty-five degrees and fire a Shrike.

The Skipper's plane shot skyward. Stretch banked hard to the left. CAG had anticipated the move. Stretch turned harder; then, he reversed and picked up the smoke trail of the Shrike streaking into the blue sky.

The Skipper rolled upside down and started pulling into a dive. He called, "Tally ho." He probably spotted CAG. The F-8 was a lot bigger than an A-4.

"Descending to ten," Stretch radioed, meaning ten thousand feet.

Sinbad called and wanted to know what was happening. Stretch replied he didn't have time just then, and he switched the flight back to Kodak's frequency. He had to know if Kodak saw any SAM radar indications.

Kodak replied, "Had a strobe, but it only lasted a couple of seconds." Huh!

Normally, SAM sites got rough target location from Early Warning radars. EWs could see a long way but could not pinpoint targets precisely enough to guide a SAM to a kill. The SAM operators had learned to minimize the time they operated their radars to limit their exposure to Shrike missiles. Maybe these guys had no EW support. This far south in North Vietnam, it made sense. Maybe.

And maybe they brought their radar up, figured out how far out Kodak was, then shut down. They could estimate their target was making eight miles a minute. If I have this worked out right, they'll bring up their radar about now. To fire at Kodak.

He had the flight at ten thousand, and they were less than ten miles to the target. Probably. Any second now.

"Two, up five," Stretch radioed.

The Skipper pulled up abruptly and parked the nose five degrees up. What the hell? The Skipper didn't fire a Shrike. He dropped a bomb!

Stretch pulled up five degrees and fired a Shrike. The missile streaked away. He pushed his nose back down into a dive. The Shrike missile abruptly pitched down and plunged toward the ground. There was a blip on his TIAS scope. He leveled out. The plane had to be in level flight to get the range to the SAM site. It was six or seven miles dead ahead.

"Kodak," Tiny radioed, "SAM strobe, twelve. J and C." Twelve o'clock, dead ahead. J and C meant switch your jammer on and dispense chaff. "Launch signal," Tiny again. "Hard left." A couple of seconds later, "Roll out."

Stretch knew Tiny had turned so he'd be better able to see the SAM missile. Coming right at him, it would have been a dot. Offset to the side though, it was a big missile, the size of a flying telephone pole.

From directly in front of him, Stretch saw a plume of dust rising from the jungle. Was it the Shrike hit? Or maybe the SAM launch dust?

Stretch was in a gradual descent, passing through eight thousand. "Two, stay at ten thousand. Three, you still with us?"

"Three."

Stretch told Two to take a trail position on him and Three to trail Two.

As he approached the dust plume rising out of the jungle, he turned off the ordnance switch for the remaining Shrike. Then, he turned on his bombing computer and reset the bomb aiming reticle. He'd have one chance to kill whatever was left of the SAM site, and maybe, just maybe, the computer would work.

Sunlight glinted off a windshield or metal surface. It was close. He rolled over, pulled his nose down, and set the aim point dot of light in his gunsight on the spot where he'd seen the glint. His dive was forty degrees, not the usual forty-five. Also, he was going faster than usual, but if the bombing computer worked, it would take care of all those off-optimum parameters. Tracers, a lot of them, 23 millimeter, rose from right where he was aiming and a cloud of sparks flashed past his cockpit. Had he seen a AAA site instead of the SAM? Well, no time to diddle with that question. At four thousand feet, he hit the bomb pickle and pulled hard on the stick. Once he got his nose pointed up, he turned hard left and climbed.

Secondaries were cooking off. "Two, see if you can spot another target nearby. I think I hit a AAA site, not the SAM."

"No, Lead. You got the SAM. After your bombs blew, I saw a rocket motor torch off and snake away under the trees."

"Roger, Three. Break, break. Two. Dump your bomb on the north edge of the dust cloud. Pickle at six thousand. Lots of triple A down there."

Stretch saw the Skipper, zoom up a couple of thousand feet, then roll upside down and pull into his bomb run.

Three, CAG, radioed, "Kodak, what's your status?"

"Kodak evaded a SAM, and we are commencing our run over the target area. I see dust. I assume that's you. We are a mile or so north of your position."

Stretch had one Shrike left. He decided to stay in the target area to provide coverage in case the North Viets had another SAM down there in the trees. But there were no indications on TIAS or warning systems of any SAM radar activity.

Stretch radioed Sinbad that they had located a SAM site and had killed it. They'd observed secondaries and had seen no indications of another site.

Sinbad thanked them and called Oscar, the call sign of US Air Force Search and Rescue. He informed Oscar that the SAM site had been killed and requested a rescue helicopter.

<hr>

Back on the ship, the flight debriefed in the Intel Center and then met in CAG's office. CAG first questioned Kodak flight as to what they saw and when they saw it. Tiny, as the photo escort, had the most information to report. The OINC of the photo detachment had been concerned with navigating and managing his cameras.

Tiny thought the first indication of a SAM meant the North Viets brought up their radar just long enough to get a range and bearing to Kodak flight. "Probably got our speed figured out, too. Then they shut down, and maybe forty-five seconds later, I got a SAM launch warning and a second later SAM radar warning."

"So it was like you've told us before, Stretch," CAG said. "They shoot the missile first but don't turn on their target tracking radar because, during the first handful of seconds inflight, the missile is incapable of receiving guidance signals. Once it can receive guidance, they bring up the radar and start directing it to the target airplane. In this case Kodak."

"Yes, Sir," from Stretch. "I had the same thought. I saw the SAM radar on TIAS and told the Skipper to fire a Shrike. Which he did. Then I had to maneuver to keep from getting too far in front of the Skipper. It was a long-range shot, so he had to pull up to twenty-five degrees to get enough lead angle on the target. By the time I got back in position on the Skipper, which took maybe seven seconds, the site had shut down. The TIAS screen was blank. And the target, I was sure, was looking at Kodak, not us, or we'd have seen a SAM radar warning."

Tiny said, "As we turned and dove, the SAM missile followed us. I planned to call for a hard pullup at the last minute to try and get the SAM to miss us, but the nose of the missile abruptly pitched up, like it wasn't guiding on us anymore."

"Right," the photo det OINC jumped in. "Then we picked up our route again and started snapping pics."

CAG brought the discussion back to the Warhorse flight. He wanted to know if the Skipper had possibly screwed up his cockpit switches when he, instead of firing a second Shrike, had dropped a bomb.

"No, Sir. I'm sure I did not screw up the switches. I had them set up in accordance with our SOP. All ordnance switches on. If we want to shoot a Shrike, all we do is push the bomb pickle. If we want to drop a bomb, we have to turn off the Shrike stations first. What happened is, I punched the pickle to fire the second Shrike, but nothing happened, so I punched it again, and a bomb came off."

Stretch intervened and said he'd radioed ahead to the ship to have ordnance men standing by to check out the Skipper's missile and that, hopefully, a report would be available soon.

The door to the outer office of CAG's space jerked open. The airwing maintenance officer charged in with a chief petty officer right behind him. The chief carried a manual with a yellow cover, the tactics manual for the A-4 aircraft.

"Sorry to interrupt, CAG," his Maintenance Officer said. "But the chief here, he works in the magazines where the Shrike are stored. He knows what happened to Skipper Fant's missile."

CAG's MO wasn't a runt. The chief was taller by a couple of inches. Broader across the shoulders too. A face that looked like it hadn't smiled since his last *kitchy-koo*. About four decades past.

"Tell 'em, Chief," the MO said.

"Dumb-ass pilots screwed up two Shrikes."

12

TERESA STOOD BY THE CALENDAR, pen poised to X off yesterday, the blessed day of standdown and peace, when *Bring, bring!* The wall phone jolted her heart. She snatched up the handset, listened for a moment to see if Ruth, in her seat on the dining room table, would cry.

"There, there, Ruth," Jennifer said.

"It's okay, Roof Ann," EJ said, "It's just the phone."

EJ acting the part of protective big brother? Will wonders never cease? As quick as she had the thought, she chided herself for being snotty with her son. Sins came in the form of words, deeds, and thoughts.

"Teresa?" came from the handset.

"Sorry. This is Teresa."

"And this is Tara with a phone tree call." Tara Wisdom. "There's a coffee this morning at ten at Sarah Fant's house."

"Do you know what this is about?"

"All I know is that Naomi Engel called me about the coffee. It's supposed to be important."

Teresa sighed.

Tara said, "Right. Not how I was expecting to spend my morning, either."

"Thanks, Tara." Teresa hung up, checked on the children at the table, took the baby from her seat, and walked the sidewalk behind the carports to Amy Allison's backdoor. Amy was Teressa's phone tree contact. A knock on the door at seven in the morning wasn't much better than the phone ringing, but it was some better.

The chief petty officer's name from the Shrike magazine was Rudy Pitts. Chief Pitts said to CAG, "Your pilots had both Shrike stations armed."

"Yes. We do that to minimize the need for fumbling with armament switches in the heat of battle with SAM sites."

"The problem is that with both Shrike stations armed, when you punch the pickle, you send a firing pulse to one missile, and you send another signal to ignite the battery in the second missile. The battery only lasts sixty seconds. Then a minute later when you punch the pickle a second time, the battery is dead and won't accept the fire signal."

"The Tactical Manual doesn't say that," Stretch jumped in.

"Hell it doesn't. Sir," Pitts said, and he opened the Tactical Manual and handed the book to CAG.

CAG pointed to Stretch, and the chief gave him the book and pointed to a paragraph halfway down the page.

"This pertains to firing Shrikes with the CP-741 computer. We don't use the computer," Stretch argued.

"Read the paragraph," Pitts growled. "Sir."

He read the paragraph. For the first time. He'd probably read every other paragraph in the whole blinking manual twenty times. That one he'd passed over because it dealt with firing Shrikes using the CP-741 computer. He'd discounted using the computer to fire anti-SAM missiles because it took a lot longer to fire using the computer than memorizing lead angles for certain ranges. They always flew their missions at ten thousand feet. Lead angles for ranges of ten, seven, and five miles covered the requirement. Three numbers to remember. Piece of cake.

"Uh, Skipper, CAG," Stretch confessed. "I never read this paragraph before." He explained why. "But it says it right here. It talks about using the computer to fire two Shrikes at one target. Improves the probability of kill from seventy percent to more than ninety. But, the way it's designed, when you have the switches set up to shoot a pair in that mode, when you pull up, you hit the pickle and hold it down. The plane sends a signal to both Shrikes to light off their batteries. You keep pulling on the stick and, at the right lead angle, the computer fires the first missile. You keep pulling until the computer fires off the second missile."

"Right," the magazine chief said. "You have two Shrikes selected, computer on or off, and you punch the pickle you light off the battery in both Shrikes. And if you don't fire the second missile pretty damn quick, the battery dies. And then you can't fire it." The chief shook his head. "Buy you guys books, and you dipshits eat the covers."

CAG jumped to his feet, startling his MO and the chief. "Chief," he said with a low, growly voice. "Listen. Listen good. Look at the lieutenant. Tell him precisely this. 'You are a dipshit, Sir.' Now do I need to repeat that for you?"

"Uh—"

"'You are a dipshit, Sir.' You got it this time, Chief?"

"Uh—"

"Say it."

The chief repeated it. Mumbled it rather. Not much above a whisper.

CAG sat back down, his pissed-off demeanor throttled back a bit. "You've seen this problem before, haven't you, Chief?"

"Yes, Sir. Coupla times."

"You didn't say anything, though, to warn us airwing pukes about this. How come?"

The chief looked down.

"I'll tell you why." CAG's torqued off demeanor blossomed new and full blown. "Because you enjoy climbing up out of your hole in the bowels of the ship and coming up here and telling an officer that he is a dipshit." The chief still had his eyes cast down.

"Look at me, Chief." The word called loathing upon itself. "Tell me, Chief," CAG said. "Who's the real dipshit here?"

"It's both of us," Stretch said. "I should have read that paragraph."

CAG spun his chair. He looked ready to bite a piece out of Zachery's hide. But the wall mounted phone sounded a bzzt, bzzt summons. He ripped it from its mounting. The airwing commander listened. "Yes, Sir."

Over the general announcing system came, "Man flight stations. Now man flight stations."

The wing commander spun his chair around. "Chief Pitts, wait in the outer office." Zachery felt the weight of the absence of please. "That was the Skipper."

Stretch knew he meant the commanding officer of the ship. The only man aboard to whom he'd say "Yes, Sir."

"After Lieutenant Dipshit here," CAG said, which caused Stretch to blush furiously, "killed the SAM site, the Air Force rescue helo was ordered in to pick up the A-7 pilot from Constellation. The Air Force had four A-1 s escorting the helo. Before the pickup could be attempted, one of the A-1s was shot down. The Air Force stopped worrying about the Navy puke on the ground and put all their attention on rescuing their own guy.

"Connie has launched their own rescue effort, but they are a little too far out for their own helos to play a part. Our Skipper promised two of ours. We are also launching a four-plane of bombers from each squadron. Plus two TIAS birds."

CAG looked at Stretch. "Can you handle this? Or are you worried about being a dipshit?"

"Lieutenant Dipshit can handle it, Sir."

"L'il Lord," CAG said. "Zachery said shit. You said he wouldn't say that word if he had a mouthful."

"Well, I got a mouthful right now."

CAG looked at Stretch for a long-drawn-out moment. Then he nodded. "Ops O, get this mission organized."

⸻ ◆━◉━◆ ⸻

Stretch asked for Alice to fly the other TIAS bird. After launching and crossing South Vietnam, they set up as they had on the first rescue attempt. At the southern edge of the DMZ, halfway between the South China Sea and the border with Laos. And flying opposite sides of a racetrack pattern. Altitude, ten thousand feet.

Listening to the chatter on the rescue radio channel, it sounded like the Connie had launched every bomber they had for the effort to recover the downed pilot. A-7s and A-6s checked in. Some carried regular bombs. Others were loaded with cluster bombs. Cluster bombs looked like regular bombs except the shells were white instead of drab green, and each contained two hundred fifty bomblets. When dropped properly, the bomblets carpeted an area two-hundred-fifty feet by fifty wide. Each bomblet spewed out a lethal dose of pellets capable of destroying trucks and damaging even a tank.

From the chatter on the radio, it sounded like the On-scene Commander had completed blanketing the area around the survivor. Now he was using the remaining bombers to precede the rescue helo. The rescue effort was eating up tons of ordnance.

And on the other side, the North Viets were committing a lot of resources to their side of the conflict. They wanted to shoot down airplanes, and they probably appreciated having such desirable bait as the downed pilot. They'd already knocked down an A-7 and an A-1.

Just before Stretch completed the north bound leg, his warning system showed a SAM strobe dead ahead. A blip appeared on his TIAS scope. Ten degrees down. He pulled the nose up ten degrees and punched the pickle. A Shrike whooshed off the rail. As he pushed the nose back down, the strobe and the blip disappeared.

He thought about flying north, descending, and trying to find the site, but thought better of it. He turned and explained what he'd seen and done to Alice. Alice rogered and reported nothing during his northbound run.

Then, just as Stretch started his next turn to the south, the blip and strobe appeared again. He decided to try something, switched off his remaining Shrike and selected a bomb, pulled his nose up, and punched the pickle. The bomb thumped away. The strobe and the blip disappeared as they had when he'd fired the Shrike. That meant the North Viets could see on their radars that something had separated from their target airplane, but they could not tell if it was a Shrike or a bomb. Probably.

Stretch called, "Rat lips," over the radio to Alice. A code phrase telling his wingman he was breaking out of the racetrack pattern and heading north to look for the SAM site. Alice was to go to full power and follow.

Stretch had set up a three thousand feet per minute descent. Passing seven thousand, he figured he was perhaps two miles from the SAM site.

Then his warning system alerted him. A AAA radar had locked onto him from ten degrees left of his nose. He switched on his jammer, punched out some chaff, turned toward where the strobe had indicated the radar was located. He had a blip on the TIAS scope. He fired his Shrike, pulled up hard, and rolled right. After a few seconds, he turned back left. From his target, secondaries cooked off. But all hell had broken loose below him. There was a carpet of flak puffs obscuring the jungle. Thirty-seven-millimeter shells that looked like tennis balls of fire floated past him.

"Shotgun," Mike radioed. Which meant he'd fired a Shrike.

Stretch turned hard back to the south and climbed back to nine thousand. He called his altitude to Mike. Running into each other out here would not be good.

Mike reported the blip disappeared. Stretch told him to reverse and head south.

Over the radio came the news that the downed A-7 pilot had been picked up by a helo from Solomons and it was taking him to Danang.

⸻⬥⬦⬥⸻

Back on the ship, Stretch was surprised to find CAG sitting in on the debriefs of the returning pilots.

"Any SAM activity this go?" CAG said.

"Sort of."

CAG frowned.

"What I mean, Sir, is that Alice and I both got SAM indications from our warning systems and on TIAS. They never fired a missile at us though. But we did fly into what I think is a flak-trap they'd set for us.

"It was close to the same place we had SAMs fired at us on that last mission of the '71 cruise. A boatload of AAA cut loose at us same as it did last year. I don't think they had a real SAM system down there. I think it was a dummy intended to draw us into their trap."

What do you think, Alice?" CAG said.

"Sir, when we went north, I was a good mile behind Stretch and at ten thousand, while he went considerably lower."

"How low?"

"Five thousand," Stretch replied.

"Speed and altitude are life. You heard that before?"

"Yes, Sir. From you. But we poke our nose over even South Vietnam, we are hanging it out some. Over Laos, we hang it out more. Over the highly militarized Dee Militarized Zone, we hang it out more."

"And when you go trolling at five thousand over the DMZ you are really hanging it out to the point of reckless stupidity."

"CAG, I knew what those guys were doing. They either had a dummy SAM radar down there, or an actual one. If it was actual, they either had no missiles to shoot at us, or what they had, they wanted to save, for maybe a chance at downing a helo."

"So now you're telling me you can get inside the head of the North Vietnamese? The admiral at Seventh Fleet would like to have you on his staff. I think I'll send you to him."

That hit Stretch like his heart just sucked an ice cube into a chamber.

Alice said, "I don't think he can get inside the heads of North Vietnamese in general, but, sure as shit, he can get inside the heads of the SAM operators."

"CAG," Skipper Fant said. "He got the job done. Not only once, but twice today."

"Well, yeah. There's that. And the Connie got their pilot back and so did the air force pukes. And Stretch had a big hand in making that happen." CAG winced like he had a headache. "Hell! This means we can't get rid of Stretch. We have to give him a medal."

"What? You can't give me a medal. I screwed up the ordnance switches this morning. I ruined two Shrikes. Each one cost two years pay for a lieutenant."

"You didn't ruin the Shrikes," the wing's Ops O said. "You only ruined the batteries. Those cost only $117.00. Each."

"I bet the Connie pilot and the air force A-1 puke would be happy to pick up the tab for those two batteries. Now," CAG said, "get the hell out of here. I've got work to do. You know, push papers. Important stuff like that."

Outside the office, Skipper Fant grabbed Stretch by the arm. "You've got a lot of credibility with the wing commander. The way you took charge of the mission this morning, and from the get-go, just assumed you should be flight lead and started briefing it that way. Never mind you put your CO and airwing commander as your wingmen without batting an eye or asking. And he knows you've got a handle on Shrikes and SAMs like nobody else."

"I should have known about those switches. I should have read that paragraph."

"You should have. But none of us is perfect. And we found out about that lapse in a way that did not keep you from getting the job done." The Skipper stared hard into Stretch's eyes. "So, this morning you got one little aw-shit and one big atta-boy. You killed a SAM site and saved an A-7 pilot's ass from the Commies."

"They say it takes a thousand atta boys to make up for one oh shoot."

"Stretch," the Skipper said, 'that is the saying except for the last word. If you don't say it properly, if you don't say shit, it takes five thousand atta boys to make up for one screw up."

Stretch looked down, away from that hard stare for a moment; then his eyes met the stare again. "Yes, sir. I owe you four thousand, nine-hundred ninety-nine atta-boys. Can we do an All Pilot's Meeting before the movie tonight. I need to amend our Shrike SOP, and I need to explain the switches to the guys."

The Skipper stepped back. "See the Ops O about the APM. Then he walked away.

Stretch went to the chapel. He had one thing niggling at him, other than the oh shoot.

He sat on one of the folding chairs in the last row, closed his eyes, and let the silence soak into him.

> Here's the thing, God. During the rescue of the A-7 pilot, we threw everything we had into trying to rescue the man who'd been shot down. For the rest of the day, we stopped fighting the war. The North Viets didn't stop fighting. They exploited the shoot down to try to shoot down more planes, and they spent a lot of equipment and probably soldiers' lives to knock down that A-1. They kept fighting. We went rescuing. I don't know, Lord. Would I

feel better if we'd just left the A-7 guy on the ground and spent all our effort on blowing up North Viet trucks and tanks and soldiers?

We're in this war, but we're not trying to win? What the heck are we doing here?

Stretch sat there in the silence, not expecting an answer to come, but one did.

Win your part of the war.

Stretch felt as if he had been wrapped in electrified barbed wire. But then, with the answer, the charge in the wire dissipated, and the coils disintegrated. He stood, made the sign of the cross, genuflected, and left. He had an SOP to revise.

13

SARAH FANT'S DINING ROOM TABLE accommodated ten, but necessity squeezed in an eleventh spot for Wanda Mason, the junior wife. As the wives scooted their chairs closer together, Teresa looked at Wanda and smiled. She remembered when she'd been the junior wife on USS Manfred, Jon's destroyer after college, and had to wrap her head around the notion that among the Manfred's wives, she wore Jon's ensign bars as much as he did. The notion no longer seemed strange, rather, it felt right and proper.

Sarah and Laura Davison each carried a coffee pot and a platter of pastries from the kitchen and placed them near the ends of the table.

"Help yourself to coffee and scones," Sarah said, then sat at the head of the table.

While pouring, passing cream and sugar and pastries, a subdued buzz of conversation, with a frantic edge to it, hovered over the assembly. As if they had to rush to get in words of normal socializing before Sarah brought up the business—the important business—at hand.

"Ladies!" Sarah's tone of voice stopped the chatter. "The reason I wanted to get us all together is I have some news. Today, planes from our carriers in the Tonkin Gulf are mining the harbor of Haiphong in North Vietnam."

Wanda Mason's coffee cup stopped short of her lips. "But today is a standdown day."

"Yes," Sarah replied. "It is. For *Solomons*. Not for the other carriers in the Tonkin Gulf, though. And right now, there are four carriers out there. Which is part of why I wanted to get us together. I thought you should know that the Vietnam War is heating up again. Back to what is was before the bombing halt in 1968."

The CO's wife was obviously plugged in to a good source of information. Teresa was grateful she shared so readily with the rest of the wives.

Laura jumped in, "The Warhorses will not participate in the mining Sarah mentioned, but tomorrow, our husbands will be engaged in a different kind of war than the one they had yesterday."

That statement sprinkled ice water over the warm social interchange. Conversation ceased. Silverware clinked on China, and eating, too, ceased.

"Skippy wrote that all they are doing is making toothpicks," Wanda Mason reported. "That they aren't doing anything worthwhile. It sounds like the guys will be doing something worthwhile now."

"Wanda," Naomi Engel said. "Trees don't shoot back at the guys when they drop their bombs. Doing something worthwhile means that what they are bombing will shoot back."

"Oh." Wanda sat back and raised her hand to cover her mouth. As if to keep it from talking Skippy into any more danger.

Teresa frowned. She'd thought she'd worried as much as was possible about Jon. But she'd been mistaken. Now a whole new level of worry stewed inside her.

And this worry pit had no bottom. *Father God, Who art—*

The phone rang.

Sarah rose to answer it.

Please, God—

Sarah picked up and answered, and they all watched her listen.

Sarah hung up, turned. "That was a friend. Her husband is CO of an A-7 squadron on the *Constellation*. The XO of another Lemoore squadron on the ship was shot down. But he was recovered. She said the Warhorses flew missions to support the rescue effort."

What? The Warhorses flew— Jon flew on their standdown day?

Teresa felt like she'd been betrayed. If the squadron flew, she knew Jon was one of the pilots who launched. She just knew. A standdown day had been promised. She could lay down heavy worry for one blessed day. But now that had been snatched away. And if something had happened to Jon, if he was shot down, she knew it would be because she hadn't worried and prayed him to safety. She'd been betrayed. By the United States Navy. And God.

Teresa did not drink coffee. Her hand shook, and the cubes rattled in her iced tea glass. She reached to set the glass on the table and dumped it over. A brown stain spread across the starched white tablecloth. Every woman at the table jumped to her feet and worked to corral the spill before it leaked onto the floor and stained the white carpeting.

⸺⬦⬩⬦⸺

As they drove back to the base from town, Teresa said to Amy, "I felt so stupid. I … I was so upset to find out they had to fly on their standdown day. And I know if that's the worst thing that happens with the war kicking into high gear, as Naomi put it, we'll be very lucky indeed. At the moment, though, it was too much."

The highway blurred. Teresa sucked in a big breath and swiped the back of her hand across her eyes. The car had drifted to the left, half occupying both lanes. She got herself squared away on her side of the road again.

Amy placed a hand on her neighbor's shoulder. "Maybe we should thank God for the four-lane highway."

She was right. The highway was four-lane between the base and the town of Lemoore. Most of Highway 198 was only two lane.

Amy sounded like one of the guys spouting something about the danger of flying. Acknowledge the danger, then make a joke about it.

Emotion welled up inside Teresa, and she didn't know if she'd laugh hysterically or cry her eyes out. What she did was turn on the blinker and pull off onto the shoulder. "Thank You, God, there is a shoulder here to cry on."

Both of them burst into laughter, intermixed with sobs. Amy undid her seat belt and scooted over next to her neighbor and hugged her.

"This would have been lots more awkward if we were still seven months pregnant," Amy said.

When that round of sob-punctuated guffaws wound down, both of them pulled tissues from the box of Kleenex between them on the seat.

A knock on the driver's window startled them. A highway patrolman stood beside the car. He signaled, roll down the window.

"You ladies all right?"

"Yes, Sir." Teresa and Amy suppressed giggles.

"Have you been drinking?"

"Not yet," Amy replied, which inspired yet another round of sobbing hilarity.

It took a while, but Teresa convinced the state trooper that neither she nor Amy had had any alcohol. And he finally accepted the reason for their behavior. He did, however, trail their car until Teresa turned off the highway for the back gate into family housing on the base.

After picking up EJ and the two babies from Child Care, Teresa drove them back to their quarters, parked in the carport, and turned off the engine.

"I've heard there's healing power in laughter," Amy said. "I think there's more healing power in laugh-tears."

Teresa smiled, reveling in the calm, the peace which now occupied the core of her, when but minutes ago, hysteria had raged there.

"Laugh-tears," Teresa said. Do you mind if I write to Jon about your word?"

"It's our word."

The friends embraced, and entered their respective quarters, with their children, and confronted the never-ending chores waiting there. Teresa had one bit of housekeeping she needed help with. She called the chaplain's office and made an appointment for that afternoon. She'd gotten angry with God, and that was a sin she could not abide dirtying her soul.

⸺◈⸺◉⸺◈⸺

During the night, *Solomons* returned to the southern carrier station she'd occupied previously. All daylight flying was the best schedule possible. But, now the airwing would fly noon to midnight. This was second best, and so much better than midnight to noon. But, Stretch knew exactly that loomed in the near future. After two weeks of the current schedule, they'd juxtapose two words and transition to the godawful midnight to noon.

Crawl into your bunk at 1600, exhausted, dead on your feet, your head hits the pillow, and your eyes would pop open. Then it was as if the eyes told the brain, "Why the crap did you bring us here at this time of day? It's not even suppertime, and you want us to sleep! Ain't gonna happen!" And sleep did not happen. Until what seemed like fifteen seconds before the stupid alarm went off at 2200. Then it was get up with what felt like an industrial-strength hangover, pull on flight suit and boots, snarf down chow in the dirty shirt, and sit in on the 2230 brief in the Intel spaces. And hope like hell your wingman, or flight lead, stayed awake and wrote down the important stuff. Then at the crack of midnight, the cat would fire, smash you back in your seat while your brain screams, "I'm not ready! We're going to die!"

At least if you do die, you'll be wide-the-crap awake. Which was good. Wouldn't want to miss any part of that dying business since a guy got to do that only once.

Stretch was in line behind the Skipper, EC, and Stump on the way to the Ready Room. The passageway was as jammed as an LA freeway with sailors going in both directions, as if the 1MC had ordered everybody aft to move forward, and everybody forward to move aft.

Sometimes, having time to think was a curse. He chided himself to get his head on straight. Midnight to noon was two weeks away. *And wouldn't that be ironic? Kill myself flying in daylight because I was so worried about flying at night on the Midnight to Noon.*

Stretch!

In the Ready Room, before starting on the pre-flight briefing, the Skipper handed the checklist to EC and told him to lead the flight, which moved Stretch to Number Two, the Skipper to Three, and Stump to Four.

EC briefed the flight, part of the 1330 launch. They manned up, took off, rendezvoused overhead, and headed for the beach. EC checked in with Labrador, the US Air Force agency assigning targets to bombers. The controller sent them farther south in South Vietnam than Stretch had ever been and told them to check in with Hawk Two One, a ground-to-air liaison.

Hawk 21 was an American, probably an advisor to the South Vietnamese Army. "I'm with a patrol of a dozen South Viets. We've run into a large force of VC. They outnumber us. We can use some help."

Below them, only unbroken jungle.

"Can you give us a range and bearing off the Tan Son Nhut TACAN?" EC radioed.

"I don't have time to screw with that. We need help. Now."

"This is L'il Lord. I've got the lead. Two, use your direction finder. Get us a bearing to Hawk. Hawk, I need you to give us a ten count."

Stretch separated from the formation and dropped a thousand feet. They'd been flying due south, but his direction-finding needle swung left. He banked in that direction and wound up heading east-southeast. He turned off the direction finder and radioed, "Hawk. We're a flight of four jets. Can you hear us?"

"Only goddamned thing I hear is automatic weapons and grenades."

"Okay. Give me another ten count."

Stretch turned his direction finder on again. The needle pointed behind them. He banked hard left and started a descent. He radioed, "L'il Lord. Hawk's below us. I recommend you guys take ten-thousand feet. I'm going lower. I'm not even seeing muzzle flashes."

The Skipper roger-ed.

Stretch descended to three-thousand and made a tight orbit of where he thought Hawk 21 was located. Below him, the jungle canopy was solid dark-green, lush carpeting in all directions. Hawk stopped responding to radio calls. He descended to one-thousand feet and made another circle. Still no response from Hawk.

"The bad guys got him," L'il Lord radioed. "Join up, Two."

"Shouldn't we drop our bombs on the spot?" EC suggested. "Maybe we'll get some of the gomers."

"Switch to Labrador frequency," L'il Lord replied.

The Skipper reported what had happened to Hawk 21 and asked for an area to dump their bombs. Labrador gave them a spot close to their present position. At the TACAN coordinates of the dump zone, the Warhorses pickled off their bombs from twenty-thousand feet. As soon as the bombs were gone, the CO climbed them to thirty-thousand feet. The whole flight was low on gas, but Stretch was lowest.

L'il Lord switched the flight to the Solomons' frequency and requested a tanker be sent toward Tan Son Nhut.

After the debrief in the Intel spaces, the Skipper kept the members of the flight at the table. "EC, you thought we should have dumped our bombs in the area where Hawk 21 went silent. You still think we should have?"

"Yes, Sir. We were there. We had bombs. Hawk went silent. It was obvious the gomers got him and the men he was with."

"Tell him, Stretch."

"Nothing was obvious. I couldn't see a thing under the jungle canopy even from a thousand feet. Hawk might have had his radio disabled. His patrol might have been hanging on. Other good guys might have been coming. For sure we didn't know, and it wasn't clear if Hawk knew what was going on."

"Hawk was a newbie" the Skipper cut in. "He was probably under training, only his trainer probably got morted."

"Right," Stretch inserted. "His number one job should have been to help us find him, but he said he didn't have time for that."

"Bottom line, EC," the Skipper said, "if we would've dropped our bombs through the trees, our chance of killing good guys was the same as us killing the bad guys."

"But then we just dumped our bombs in the jungle a few miles away from Hawk."

"Right. But it was in an area Labrador knew was clear of friendlies. A cardinal rule of Close Air Support. You have to know where the good guys are, and you have to know where the bad guys are. Do you understand, EC?" A note of threat tinged the CO's question.

"I got it, Skipper," EC replied, "but can I ask another question?"

"Shoot."

"How much gas did you have when you landed?"

"Eight hundred pounds."

"A thousand pounds below bingo fuel? You let Stump and me have five-hundred pounds from the tanker, and Stretch took a thousand. That's all the tanker had to give."

"What would you have done?"

"I'd have sent Stretch to Tan Son Nhut and split the tanker's gas between the three of us."

"I'd have done that, too. If it had been nighttime."

Flying a jet, fuel was always a matter of concern. At night, the fuel pucker factor was even higher. One of the lessons from RT. Last cruise, RT had been a Warhorse department head. He'd also been the pilot Stretch respected the most. *Huh!* He just had the thought that RT was as good as Blackie, but he wasn't It's-all-about-me, and he wasn't a horse's butt.

EC was a good guy but flying in combat taught you things. Some of those lessons you couldn't learn any other way.

Today, EC soaked up some of that wisdom. Hopefully.

EC said, "Sure wish we could've helped Hawk Two One."

"War is hell," the Skipper said. "It is super hell on new guys. You could hear it in his voice. He knew he was going to die, and he was going to die scared."

14

AFTER PICKING UP JENNIFER FROM kindergarten, Teresa drove to the Catholic chaplain's office. She left the two older children in the outer office with books and brought Ruth into the inner room.

"Will you hear my confession, Father?"

"Would you like to go to the chapel and use the confessional?"

Teresa shook her head. The confessional, Jon told her once, was like a double-wide coffin. A sinner carried in his soul dead from sin. After confessing, the priest absolved the sinner, and an Easter miracle occurred. The sin-dead soul resurrected. Teresa didn't quite see the confessional box that way. Confession was a mind-, body-, and soul-wrenching event. And the box cut off the world, the things of the body, so her mind and soul could better deal with the sins they committed. There was security of a sort in the box, but just then, she did not want to let herself off the hook for what she had done.

Father Randall opened a desk drawer, pulled out a stole, kissed it, and draped it around his neck.

Teresa knelt on the floor and said, "Bless me, Father, for I have sinned." She told him about the standdown day, and how much she appreciated being able to set aside worrying over her husband for one blessed day, but then she found out the ship did not get a standdown day. And she got mad at God for taking away that blessed day. And even though she knew that because *Solomons* flew on her day off, a pilot from another carrier, who'd been shot down had been rescued. She knew the wife of that pilot lived on base at Lemoore, but that hadn't made any difference to her. She had valued her standdown day more than she valued that woman's husband.

The empty shell of Teresa knelt there with her head bowed, her eyes brimmed with tears. A hand extended into her field of view. It held a Kleenex. She took, said, "Thank you," and dabbed at the puddles.

"Mrs. Zachery, why don't you sit?"

As she took her seat, she glanced at Ruth. Asleep. Peaceful. Innocent. She longed for a teaspoonful of that innocence in her own soul but could not pray for it. Not until Father gave her absolution.

"Mrs. Zachery, in our business, navy business, in even normal times, so many things are beyond our control. In times of war, that is truer still. War is hell, they say, and it is, not just for those fighting, but for those of us left behind.

"The men fighting in the war have to do things they would never do except in war. Thou shalt not kill. But they must kill the enemy. And they must try to find a way to live with it after. For you, when you said, 'For better or for worse,' you had no clue about this particular worse and how terrible it would be to bear."

Father handed her another Kleenex and nudged the trashcan toward her with his foot. "You have told me before, Mrs. Zachery, that a pillar of faith for you is that you believe God will not give you a challenge you cannot handle. Has something happened to that pillar of faith?"

Teresa looked at the priest. She didn't think so, but she also didn't know how to put an answer to his question.

"Your faith in God Our Father is strong as ever, but you latched onto this standdown day as a blessed reprieve from the daily, debilitating grind of worry. God promised that to you. Is that not how you looked at it?"

The second tissue was soggy. She dropped it in the trash. Father handed her the box, and after taking one, she placed it on her lap.

"Are you going to give me absolution, Father?"

"As it is within my power to discern the will of God, He wants you to absolve yourself."

Teresa sat back as if he'd slapped her.

Father Randall had black hair going to grey on the sides and a perpetual frown. She always thought the weight of all the sins he heard in confession caused the frown. A wistful smile suffused the worry etched into his face. "Absolve yourself. I know. What would the world come to if sinners could just commit the worst sins and then forgive themselves? In this case, in this one single case, that is what God would have you do. So, Mrs. Zachery, will you follow the will of the Creator? Will you forgive yourself for getting mad at Him?"

That night, Stretch flew on EC's wing. They were assigned a target at An Loc, a village sixty miles northwest of Saigon. There was no airborne FAC. Instead, EC checked in with a ground controller, an American advisor with South Vietnamese Army troops. When they arrived overhead, EC had them at ten thousand feet.

"I've got a big fire," EC radioed. "Where are the bad guys from that?"

"We are a couple of hundred yards south of the fire. The fire is the ville. The whole thing's burning. Now we got enemy troops coming at us from the south. There's a lot of them and they are getting close. Need you to run in from east to west and drop a thousand yards from the fire. Call bombs away and we'll duck."

EC radioed, "Roger. Two, take a trail on me, but give it a good interval, so you can correct off my hits."

EC wasn't descending. Was he going to bomb from ten thousand? You did not do Close Air Support from ten thousand.

"Warhorse One, this is Two. I recommend we descend to five and start bombing runs from there with a ten-degree dive."

"Hey, Warhorses, things are going to hell down here. Get your heads out of your respective asses and get down here and give us some help. The Gomers are so close, I can smell what they had for dinner."

"I'm taking the lead," Stretch radioed. He started descending and checked his ordnance switches. "We only have gas for one run."

Stretch turned off his external lights and called rolling in. A thousand yards from the fire. Hell of a thing to estimate on a black-assed night. He set up his ten-degree dive. *Hit the pickle the first time at sixteen hundred feet on his radar altimeter.* That should get the last bomb off before a thousand feet. *Please God, let me get it right and help these guys.*

A thousand yards from the fire. Hell of a thing to estimate. Stretch flicked on his lights. "How do I look?" he radioed to the ground controller. Tracers rose from in front of him. EC answered, "You're too close to the friendlies. Abort."

"Like hell. Keep it goddamned coming."

Lights off. Two thousand feet. Still got the tracers, but not so many. Nice steady descent. An Loc burning like a son of a gun off to his left. Sixteen hundred. He called, "Bombs away." To himself, *pickle, pickle.* He'd intended on saying pickle to himself every time he punched off a bomb, but he was hitting the bomb release faster than he could think the word. Nine hundred fifty feet on the altimeter. Full power and pull like hell.

The bombs would be sailing along under him. When they exploded, frags would rise to three thousand feet. He needed to be up there before the bombs went off down there. Sailing past three, he flicked his lights on and turned left over the blazing town.

"That was really close. I hope like hell you didn't hit the good guys," EC said.

"That was right where we needed it. Okay, Warhorse One, see if you can drop right on top of where those last bombs landed."

"One's in." EC.

At three thousand feet, Stretch banked hard left and flew over the burning town. The controller was right. The whole bloody ville was on fire.

EC had his lights on as he started his run.

"Bring it more north," the controller told EC.

From Stretch's view, it didn't look like EC had turned at all. He thought about reminding his flight lead to check his armament switches, but it was too late.

"Turn more to the north." The controller's voice dripped urgency.

A lot of tracers were rising toward EC.

"Lights out," Stretch called.

The lights stayed on and a lot of green tracer automatic weapon fire rose out of the dark. He expected, "I'm hit," at any second. But nothing, until, "Bombs away." Time of flight for the bombs should be between six and ten seconds. He started counting One potato, two potato. He got up to thirteen potato. Still no explosions.

"One, did your bombs come off?" Stretch radioed.

"Uh … yes."

"Warhorse Two, you got anything left?"

"Twenty-millimeter machine guns. I'm low on gas, but, if you need it, I can give you one strafing run."

"We need it."

"Roger. Setting up. Warhorse One. Climb to ten thousand and wait there. Warhorse Two rolling in."

Stretch armed his guns. A thunk vibrated through the aircraft as the machine gun charging mechanism rammed a round into the chamber. "Lights on." He checked that he had his Master Armament Switch on.

"Looking good, but come left a bit."

Stretch zigged left.

"Little more left."

He zigged again.

Tracers were flying up at him. He turned his lights off. Set his radar altimeter for seven hundred fifty feet. The machine guns in the A-4 were reliable if you were shore based. Carrier based, however, half the time, the force of the cat shot screwed up some of the bullet feeding mechanism, and the guns would not fire. Please, God, this time?

At fifteen hundred feet, he squeezed the trigger.

Brrrp.

He eased back gently on the stick to walk his bullets in a swatch, rather than concentrate them at a point.

Deedle, deedle.

The radar altimeter. Let off the trigger and pull like hell. Stretch got his nose up and climbing toward the ship. When he got to twenty thousand, he'd call the ship to get a tanker headed his way. Otherwise, he would have to land at Tan Son Nhut for gas. Ahead, he could see EC's lights and called tallyho.

Climbing away from An Loc, Stretch checked EC's heading. Good. At least East Coast knew how to get back home. Acknowledging that last thought to be confessable snarky-ness, and acknowledging that he was one rank senior and a department head, and deserving of respect, none-the-less, he wondered what was going on with the man. There were things a pilot counted on a wingman or a flight-lead to provide. That afternoon, and again this evening, LCDR Wakefield had not delivered the minimal expected performance.

What was going on with— Oh crap!

His flight lead should have been flying three hundred knots, but he was much slower than that. Stretch pulled his throttle to idle and deployed his speed brakes. He slowed and stopped off lead's left wing. Judas Priest. Two hundred fifty. At night, fifty knots was a lot of extra overtake speed.

"EC," Stretch radioed. "You alright?"

"Yeah."

"Okay, I'm checking underneath you." Normally, that would not have required a radio call, because you checked the other plane for hung bombs and combat damage every flight. But tonight, it seemed prudent to make sure. He passed slowly beneath his lead. No hung bombs and no signs of damage. Coming out on the right wing, he edged forward of the lead's plane and turned off his anti-collision light, a signal which meant he was assuming flight lead so the other pilot could check him for damage and hung bombs. Again, SOP, but he radioed the info. To make sure.

"You're clean," EC radioed.

Stretch expected him to edge forward and turn off his collision light, signaling he was assuming flight lead. But he didn't do that. "You want the lead?"

"No. Keep it."

Stretch kept the lead and landed back aboard Solomons at 2130. By the time he debriefed in Intel, and returned to the Ready Room, it was 2200. The pilots on the 2230 launch were leaving to man their airplanes. After they left, he completed the maintenance paperwork on his airplane and sat on his ready room chair.

LT Howie Wisdom occupied the duty officer desk.

"Wis," Stretch said, "I assume EC landed?"

"Yeah. A minute behind you."

"Funny. I didn't see him in debrief."

The phone rang and Wiz picked up, identified himself, and listened; then he replaced the handset in the cradle. "XO wants to see you in his room," Wiz said.

THE **XO** WANTED TO KNOW what had happened on the flight. Stretch gave him a summary; then asked what was going on with EC?

"He's with the Skipper. He turned in his wings." The XO shook his head. "Skipper wants to know what you think. You were with him twice today. If the man has lost his confidence, there's nothing else to do but take his wings. Otherwise, chances are he'll kill himself and a few others to boot. But the Skipper wonders if you think he might be worth a little effort to save him, to pump him up, boost his self-confidence?"

Stretch frowned.

"I know," the XO said. "It's asking a junior to write a performance appraisal on a senior officer. There's something wrong with that picture. Right? But this is about flying in combat. In a lot of ways, rank takes a backseat to ability to perform in combat."

Someone rapped on the XO's door.

"Come."

EC opened it. "Skipper wants to see you in his room, Stretch."

Outside the XO's room, he joined the flow of bodies moving forward, knocked on the CO's door, entered, and sat when told to do so.

"First thing," the CO said. "We got word from the South Vietnamese Army that you saved some guys' bacon tonight. The unit had been hit hard, and they were barely hanging on when you arrived. Your bombs and strafing run devastated the attackers, and they bugged out. Night strafing? How was that? I never did that before."

"It's like strafing while flying instruments," Stretch said. "The big thing going for me was the ville of An Loc was on fire. The good guys said where they were relative to the fire. In the run, I turned my lights on and the ground controller lined me up properly. And this guy was good. Not like–"

"Not like the newbie we had this morning," the Skipper said.

"Right. The strafing. It was just like I said. With the fire giving me orientation, I just flew instruments."

"That's what got EC. You took a set of unusual circumstances and adapted. You saved those guys. He didn't add anything to saving them. On his bomb run, he pickled too low, and his bombs didn't have time to arm. They all *dudded*." The Skipper looked at Stretch. "What do you think about him? I know you sized up all of us for doing the anti-SAM mission. This isn't much different. How do you size him up for general combat flying?"

Stretch looked away from the Skipper, stood up, decided there really wasn't room to pace, turned a circle, and sat back down.

The Skipper laughed. "You looked like a hound-dog on a bed and deciding it wasn't comfortable the way he was laying. So, he gets up, turns in a circle, and lays back down, just the way he was, and sighs, 'That's so much better,' and falls asleep."

A man's future was at stake. It didn't seem like a thing to joke about.

"Skipper, when I trained EC to fire Shrikes, he paid attention. But that was something new. My two cents? He probably figured he'd been training for combat his whole career. He expected to fly a few combat hops with us, and then he thought he had a handle on it. If JGs could be section leads and even division leads, he sure as shooting ought to be able to handle it. He has twice the flight time of the JGs. But there is pilot substance to the man. I'll work with him. If he'll let me."

The CO nodded, called the XO, ordered EC to come back to the Skipper's room, and hung up. "You got an idea as to how to work with him, or do you need to think about it?'

"I have an idea, Skipper." And he explained it.

At the knock on the door, Stretch opened it, let EC enter, then stepped into the passageway, and closed the door. For three minutes, he leaned against the bulkhead in the passageway. Then the CO told him to come back in. "Tell him about the program you'd work him through."

After the explanation, the Skipper said to EC, "Will you take your wings back and work with Stretch?"

EC leaned back in his chair, his head dropped so his chin rested on his chest, took in. a deep breath, huffed it out, and raised his head. "I feel like such a stupid damned newbie."

"Well," the CO said, "that's what you are."

EC frowned. His mouth dropped open.

"Will you take your wings back?" the Skipper asked again.

EC said, "Shit!"

"Answer the damned question."

EC shook his head and busted out laughing. "Shit yes, Sir, I'll take them back. And thanks."

The next day, EC flew two tanker hops.

Stretch also spent an hour with him before the first brief. Homework: read the entire Tactical Manual. Skip no paragraphs, as he himself had done. Together, they studied the bomb dropping section, paying a lot of attention to delivering bombs in ten, twenty, thirty, forty, and forty-five-degree dives. Stretch kept a card on his kneeboard with dive angles and bomb sight settings for each dive angle, and he listed the pickle altitude which would enable the bomb time to arm before it smacked into the earth. He told EC he had all those numbers memorized, but it was a comfort having that card on his kneeboard.

On the third day after taking his wings back, EC flew a combat hop as Stretch's wingman. Later he flew a night tanker hop.

⸻⚬⚬⚬⸻

Teresa stood in her kitchen. The calendar hung on the wall with the standdown day looking back at her.

This standdown day held no comfort at all. The previous one led her to get angry with God. *With God!* Besides that, once this one was over, *Solomons* would fly midnight to noon. Jon hated that schedule. She was pretty sure he thought it was a lot more dangerous than the noon to midnight. He'd never said, and she never asked.

Father God, Who art in heaven … .

The calendar had come to be an inspiration to pray, every bit as much as being in church. On the plus side, it did connect her to Jon, tenuously perhaps, but it still brought a sense of her husband, the father of their children, into the kitchen here and now.

She recalled Wanda Mason saying, "They'll be doing something worthwhile now."

Teresa Velmer Zachery, perhaps you should do something worthwhile. Fill your pit of worry with prayer for the safety of Jon and the other Warhorses.

Flying midnight to noon was godawful, but once he finished two weeks of that, the ship would head to Hong Kong for a week of R&R. Rest and Relaxation in Hong Kong. Everybody looked forward to the port visit.

Except Stretch. Some of the wives were coming, but not Teresa. She had come to Hong Kong the previous year, and it had been an extraordinary honeymoon for them. But Teresa was nursing Ruth. She did not want to leave the baby for so long. Furthermore, at the end of the cruise, there was the expectation that *Solomons* and the entire airwing would decommission. The US Navy might invite Jon to seek employment elsewhere. If Teresa came to Hong Kong, it would take every penny they had.

It appeared the navy was done with LT Zachery, and he would leave the service with no job prospects, one wife, three small children, and no money. Plus, the car was only half paid for. As glorious as it would be to see Teresa in Hong Kong, that could not happen. Zachery believed the surest way to allow disaster to overtake a person is to do nothing to prepare for a disaster you could see coming. They had to have as much money in the bank as they could.

Jon had written all this into a letter. Teresa responded that she agreed and leaving Ruth at this point would be agony for her.

Good. We have that settled.

Which was fortunate. Riding herd on EC on day and night hops for the next week was a full-time job. After each hop, they spent an hour going over every detail of the flight. When faced with the necessity to make a decision, what options had been available? Was the one chosen the best? If not, why not?

One morning on the 1030 to noon go, Stretch and EC were assigned to work with a ground controller operating near Pleiku. They had to descend through an overcast and broke out at three-thousand-five hundred feet. Beneath the clouds, Stretch saw two gunships, cargo planes equipped with rapid-fire, computer controlled cannons they fired through side cargo doors. The controller had the gunships operating a racetrack pattern east of Pleiku just under the overcast. When the gunships fired, way off in the distance, after a pause of a few seconds, something the size of a football field lit up with dancing twinkles, as if Tinker Bell had just dumped a big bucket of pixie dust on the area. It, of course, was cannon shells exploding.

By the Pleiku TACAN, Stretch and EC were fifteen miles south of the base. The two gunships, Gunslinger One and Two were off to the left. To the right, a pair of US Air Force F-4s orbited. The ground controller was Harlan One Seven.

Smoke belched from the side of a Gunslinger. When it ceased, the pilot called, One's off."

"Harlan, this is Devil Dog. You remember me? Flight of two F-4s, a dozen five-hundred-pound bombs each. You have to work us now, or we head back to base. We're running out of gas."

"This is Harlan. I don't have time for you. Head home. Break, break. Gunslinger Two, this is Harlan. Target a half a click farther west from One's hits."

Harlan One Seven just wasted twenty-four five-hundred-pound bombs! Those gunships probably had lots of gas. Harlan should have used the F-4s.

Stretch pumped his nose up and down, a signal to his wingman, EC, to fly close formation. When he flew into position, he passed him the lead.

Gunslinger Two fired. EC waited until twinkles erupted to the east; then, "Harlan, this is Warhorse. This is what we're going to do. After Gunslinger One fires again, me and my wingman are going to drop our bombs west of the twinkles. That's what you're doing, right? Working the cannon fire west?"

"What the hell do you think you're doing, Warhorse? You don't tell me what to do. I tell you."

"Which would be okay if you didn't have your head up your butt. Break, break, Gunslinger, Warhorse, do you have gas to give us five minutes to dump our bombs and get out of your way."

"No problem, Warhorse."

"So, this is what we're doing," EC said. "As soon as Gunslinger One calls off, Warhorses will roll in south to north and dropping a thousand yards west of the last twinkles. We'll be in and gone in less than five."

"Warhorses, this is Harlan—"

"This is Gunslinger One. You got your five minutes, Warhorses. Shame Harlan didn't use the Devil Dog's bombs."

EC dropped his bombs. They exploded. Stretch's bombs did too.

Back on the ship, during the debrief, Stretch didn't tell EC he had done well. He didn't have to.

⸺⸺◆⸺◈⸺◆⸺⸺

The day after the Pleiku incident, the Skipper flew with EC on a night and a day hop. Next day, EC showed up on the schedule as a section and a division lead. Also, that day, *Solomons* moved from the southern carrier station to north of the DMZ. The Intel guys said that the North Vietnamese and Viet Cong in southern part of South Vietnam were now considered to have been beaten up enough so that the South Vietnamese Army and Air Force could handle the situation there.

The biggest threat remaining from North Vietnam was considered to be the thrust through the DMZ. At the time, three US aircraft carriers operated in the Gulf of Tonkin. Two of them flew missions into North Vietnam. *Solomons* would operate around the DMZ.

It was 0530. Stretch and Stump had flown on the 0130 go. They'd bombed trucks under flares dropped by a US Air Force FAC. The FAC credited them with three trucks destroyed. After they debriefed the hop, Stump went to the JOB to sleep before his daylight hop. Stretch took his seat on the left side of the room and wrote up a Navy Commendation Medal recommendation for his wingman. Then he got out his letter writing material.

Besides the Squadron Duty Officer, Wiz, five pilots had their chairs circled up on the right side. They were briefing for a four-plane and a spare had been laid on in case one of the primary airplanes developed a downing discrepancy prior to launch.

A petty officer was behind the maintenance counter at the rear. The only other occupant of Ready Room Five was Midnight to Noon. A palpable entity. A strength and energy sapping ghost. You felt the Midnight to Noon Ghost as deep exhaustion, as part gloom, part anguish, part something to be unavoidably suffered and endured. Almost evil.

Stretch had wrestled the ghost into a back corner of his mind when Blackey entered and sat behind the five pre-flight briefers. He sighed, took out a pad of paper, and began to write. A reinvigorated spirit of Midnight to Noon had waltzed in with his roommate.

Father God, Who art in heaven. You are my help. You are my salvation. In You, I have my being.

Dark and gloom receded, edged aside by a bright, halo glowing entity exuding calm, effusing peace. He wrote:

Dearest Teresa.

Out of the corner of his eye, Stretch caught someone stand by the empty chair next to his. Blackey.

His roommate dropped a sheet of paper atop the award recommendation lying on the seat. Another award recommendation. For Blackey. An Air Medal, a higher award than a Commendation Medal. He'd destroyed a truck.

Stretch was on the Airwing Awards Board.

Blackey said, "You'll take care of that, right, Shithead?"

The phone on the duty officer desk rang. Wiz answered it, listened for a moment, hung up. He glanced around the Ready Room. "Blackey, Stretch, hustle down to the Intel spaces. We've got an add-on mission. They'll brief you there."

"I'm senior to you," Blackey sneered. "I'm leading."

Stretch stuck the papers in the drawer under his seat, stood up, pushed past his roommate, stomped out of the ready room, and joined the flow of bodies moving forward.

In Intel, they found EC waiting for them.

A US Air Force F-4 FAC had been shot down by a SAM in the southeast corner of the DMZ, close to the border with Laos. All the Air Force anti-SAM assets were engaged in missions over North Vietnam. They asked the US Navy for help.

Stretch recalled the incident when the USS Constellation A-7 pilot had been shot down. The air force helped with the rescue of the navy pilot until another air force pilot had been shot down. Then the navy was on its own and all air force assets shifted to save their own.

But a guy needed help, and just then it didn't matter if his color was air force blue or navy blue.

The location of the SAM site was thought to be somewhere within a five-mile diameter circle.

"Okay," Stretch said. "We need at least one TIAS bird. We need two Shrikes and two bombs and take off the bomb racks."

EC said, "I'm going to spare this event. If they have two TIAS birds available, you two can take them."

"No. Blackey doesn't know the mission. If they can put two TIAS birds on this go, put the second one with the spare."

"What the hell? I'm senior. I'm leading the flight."

"No," EC said. "You are not. You will fly wing. You will do what your flight lead says, or I will start the process to remove your wings. You got that?"

Blackey stared at the Maintenance Officer.

"You got that? I require an answer."

"Yes, Sir."

STRETCH LAUNCHED. LANDING GEAR AND flaps up. Immediate turn toward the beach and climb. Power at 95%. So Blackey could catch up. As he leveled at twenty thousand, his wingman pulled into position. On the right wing. He had briefed him to fly off the left. They headed east, south of the DMZ, and from the left wing, his wingman would have been looking north most of the time, better able to detect threats to the formation.

But there he was, flying great formation. Only on the wrong side. Stretch radioed. No response. He pumped his nose up and down. The signal for the wingman to join in close formation. No response.

Blackey!

He should be worried about SAMs, but he had to worry about his wingman. He tried the emergency Guard Frequency. "Warhorse Two, this is One, respond on Guard." Nothing.

This was not the way to go to war with SAM sites. Stretch decided to abort the mission. He banked left, and after forty-five degrees, rolled out to see if Two had followed him in the turn. Nope. Blackey was not much more than a dot, still headed east. He reversed his turn and went to full power to try to catch his wingman. His external fuel tank was empty. He punched it off to reduce his drag.

It was working. He started closing.

What the hell?

Blackey had just jettisoned his fuel tank.

Now he had no room for puzzlement. There was only anger. Blackey was being his horse's butt self.

In spades!

Back to the mission at hand and the hell with Blackey. Stretch checked in with the on-scene commander, Blazer One.

"Warhorse is a flight of two with Shrikes and bombs."

"Roger. Warhorse. The SAM site is north of us, maybe ten miles. He brings his radar up periodically, but he hasn't fired for a couple of hours now."

"Roger, Blazer. We are one minute out, headed for the—"

A blip appeared on the TIAS scope. Five degrees down, five right. He radioed his wingman. "Five right, up twenty-five."

Blackey was in a gradual descent ahead of him. He did turn five degrees to the right. But he did not pull up and launch a Shrike, as Stretch's call had ordered him to do.

Damned Blackey!

Blackey no longer mattered. The downed pilots and killing the SAM site mattered.

Ahead of him, Blackey leveled at ten thousand.

Just what I was going to do. He estimated they were ten miles from the SAM site. Another blip appeared on the TIAS scope. The warning system strobe pointed straight ahead. He was about to pull up and fire a Shrike, when Blackey did.

Deedle, deedle, deedle. SAM launch warning. Dead ahead. Stretch banked left to position himself to better see the missile. He picked it up. Streaking right for him. Reaching up, he turned on his jammer. The nose of the missile kicked up. It would sail over him.

Deedle, deedle, deedle. Ahead and slightly to the right, a cloud of dust rose. They'd fired another one.

Stretch turned, pointed at the dust cloud, and fired a Shrike. The missile whooshed away. Coming at him was another telephone-pole SAM. Jammer already on. Punching out chaff, he banked hard and dove. Reversing the turn, he found the SAM above and correcting down toward him. He punched out more chaff, rolled inverted, and pulled hard on the stick.

Stretch leveled out at three-thousand feet. The SAM had missed, but now, AAA cut loose at him from all over the valley. He banked hard right and started climbing. Passing five thousand, he reversed his turn. He saw the dust cloud, the place where the SAMS had launched from. Secondaries cooked off below him as he flew over the site.

AAA erupted with a new intensity, again, from all over the valley.

"Warhorse One, this is Two. Do you read, over?"

Now he comes up on the radio!

Stretch pressed the microphone button to respond. Something smashed into the bottom of his plane. He said, "This is—" But the radio was dead. The stick in his hand died, too. Hydraulics. He'd been hit by a AAA shell, and the blast had destroyed the hydraulic boost to his flight controls.

He pulled the handle, disconnecting his flight controls from the hydraulics. Manhandling the plane with non-boosted controls, a real bitch, especially at high speed, but it could be done. He was passing through ten thousand. A cloud of AAA tracers rose out of the jungle and floated past him. Muzzle flashes, ten degrees to the right. He muscled the plane upside down, pulled it into a dive, and fired the Shrike. Still in the dive, he selected his two bombs and punched them off. Then he hauled back on the stick. The nose wouldn't move. He tried nose trim, but that didn't work. He deployed his emergency air turbine generator, and tried nose trim again, the nose started coming up. Banking left took all his strength, but he got the plane climbing and heading for the coast.

The radio, dead. Fuel gauge, two thousand pounds, but he couldn't trust it. He would try to find Da Nang and land there. Altimeter and airspeed worked.

He leveled at thirty-five thousand feet and jimmied the throttle to give him a .75 Mach number. Which he figured would give him max miles/gallon.

The coast was visible, and he muscled the plane left. Closer to the coast he could better orient himself.

Visible now, a city on the coast. Hue, he thought. Consulting a map, that'd be helpful, but he had his hands full with the airplane. Da Nang, if he remembered the geography, was sixty miles, give or take, south of Hue.

He passed Hue and started a gradual descent. One option, if he lost power, he'd glide toward the South China Sea and eject. He was making seven miles a minute. Say eight minutes to Da Nang. Arrive there at ten thousand. Altitude meant options and the opportunity to figure out which runway was in use. From thirty, descend twenty thousand in seven minutes. A little less than three thousand feet a minute. His vertical speed indicator, altimeter, and airspeed worked. The clock worked. The engine worked. He had oxygen to breathe. He could still trim his nose, but his right arm ached from muscling the plane around the sky for the last … hours. At least it felt like hours.

For a time, he flew left-handed. As a control stick manipulator, his left was clumsy. His plane probably looked like the bird in the Peanuts cartoon flying erratic as all get out. His right hand took over again. Without saying thanks for the respite to his ham-fisted counterpart.

Stretch wondered about his wingman. That's all he could do, though. Wonder. Blackey!? There weren't enough punctuation marks in English to put after his name.

Time to descend, and it worked out as he'd planned. Level at ten thousand over the airfield, he saw a plane land on the south runway. He started a descent, banked left, and set up to fly down the runway at a thousand feet. Flying at two hundred knots enabled decent control response. Muscling a wing rock as he flew past the tower signaled "I lost my radio."

Hopefully, the tower would see and clear away other planes wanting to land also. Next, turn to set up for landing. Then he put in some nose up trim, which he'd need for landing. The turbine generator might not have the power at low speed to set the trim. That meant he had to fly pushing like hell on the stick to keep from climbing. Then, pull the handle that deployed the landing gear if you lost hydraulic power. He pulled. And waited. Clunk. Which meant one of the landing gear had dropped into place. And locked there, hopefully. If only one gear dropped into place, you had to eject. Clunk.

The second main mount had deployed. Hopefully. If only one main and the nose gear came down, you had to eject. Clunk. And thank, You, God. All three gear down. Hopefully.

He turned left to set up to land.

Flaps?

Word was if you lost hydraulic pressure, if you pushed the flap handle down, there was enough fluid trapped in the system to move the flaps into landing position. Sometimes. He didn't know what damage was done to 510. The flaps would lower his landing speed. Slow crashes were better than fast crashes. He reached for the flap handle and stopped. With the flaps down, he'd need more nose up trim. He fed in nose up trim.

It worked. He dropped the flaps. They came down. He was at 150 knots and needed more nose up trim. It didn't work. He could speed up and try the trim again. But that would cost gas. He had no idea if he had any to spare. His right arm ached from holding back stick to keep the nose up. Before, he'd been pushing forward on the stick. The back of the ejection seat braced him. Now he had to pull back. Hard.

Come on arm. Two more minutes.

The end of the runway was in sight. Just like for a normal landing. Forty-five degrees of turn to go. Piece a' cake.

Traffic?

He rolled out some bank and checked to ensure another plane wasn't trying to land.

Clear.

He lined up with runway centerline, pulled power, and set up a rate of descent.

Oooon glide slope. Oooon centerline. Oooon—

The back stick required to hold the nose up eased.

What the hell?

The flaps were creeping up. Too slow. Add power.

Get it together, Stretch!

Rate of descent. Using power and stick, he got to 500 feet per minute.

The angle of attack indicator worked, and, using power and stick, he forced it to register on speed.

The end of the runway came up to meet 510. Throttle to idle. The nosewheel slammed down. Blam! The nose tire blew. The plane started drifting to the right. He corrected with rudder. Blam! From behind him. The engine fire light was lit. Throttle off. Work the rudders. Keep the damn plane on the concrete!

The back end of his dump truck seemed determined to go down the runway backwards. Working the rudder, trying hard to finesse inputs and not overcorrect. The rudder lost effectiveness when he slowed below eighty. Now it was differential braking.

The left main tire blew. The nose swerved left. He jammed on right brake. That tire blew. The nose skewed around, and he started plowing through the grass beside the runway pointed at the control tower.

⸻ ◈ ⸻

Jennifer and EJ were asleep. As Teresa nursed Ruth on the living room sofa, the grate-your-teeth door buzzer startled the baby, and she lost the nipple. And made an unpleasant noise of her own.

As Teresa covered up and stood, Ruth kicked her protest into high gear. She cooed and patted her little fuss-budget as she made her way to the door and opened it.

In the light from the porchlight, the Catholic chaplain, a navy lieutenant, Sarah Fant, and Amy Allison clustered together on the sidewalk. Their faces all said the same thing.

The CO's wife, the chaplain, a lieutenant, and her neighbor. This was the party that came to notify a spouse that her husband would not be coming home. Their faces said, "Jon is dead."

Jon was dead. She knew that to be true.

The realization stunned her, froze her. Inside herself, she felt as dead as Dearest Jon. He would be classified as KIA. Killed in Action. Death, honorable death, dripped from KIA. Reducing the phrase to an acronym, though, wrung the stink of death from the words.

Thoughts fired. No, please, God. What will happen to the babies and me? Jon—. EJ needs his Daddy. Poor Jon. Father God, *You are my strength, my courage, my refuge. In You I have my being.*

"Mrs. Zachery," the chaplain said. "May we come in, please?"

Teresa squared her sagging shoulders, and said, "No!" And it was not an exclamation of denial of entry, or of despair. It was a declaration of a truth. Jon was not dead. She knew. Her head knew. Her heart knew. Only those people standing on the stoop in front of her door did not know. She knew one other thing. She could not dissuade those people from their version of the truth. They would consider her to be a hysterical female, undone by the sudden loss of her husband.

Amy entered and took Ruth, who stopped fussing. Sarah Fant came in next and led Teresa to the sofa and bade her sit.

Sarah then dragged dining room chairs in for the men, and she joined the women on the sofa.

The priest and the lieutenant took the chairs.

After a pregnant pause, "Mrs. Zachery," the lieutenant said, his young face wearing a mask of grievous burden. "I'm afraid we have bad news. Your husband was on a bombing mission, and he is missing."

"Missing? How can he be missing? Wasn't he flying with someone?"

"Sometimes we only get part of the story with the first notification," Sarah said. "It was the last mission of the line period. Jon didn't come back. Apparently, there was a radio failure. And they're not sure what happened. Only that he never returned to the ship with everyone else."

"No!" Teresa declared. Sarah put her arm around Teresa.

The phone rang. Amy carried Ruth to the kitchen and answered the wall phone.

"A collect call?" Amy said.

Everyone in the living room looked toward the kitchen.

"Teresa," Amy said. "It's Jon."

Teresa jumped up, scurried around the chaplain, hurried to the kitchen, and grabbed the phone from Amy.

"Jon?"

"Teresa!"

She had known he was not dead, but the sound of his voice was a very welcome bit of incontrovertible evidence.

He was calling from an airfield in South Vietnam. He'd been on a bombing mission and his plane had been hit. He lost his radio but made it to Da Nang and landed safely.

She told him about her visitors.

"I am so sorry, Teresa. I called as soon as I could. I hoped I could warn you. I knew the ship didn't know what happened to me."

"Jon Zachery, I knew you were okay. I knew."

"I am so sorry I couldn't get this call through five minutes sooner."

"You're okay. That's all that matters. Now. I will say that when I opened the door and saw who was standing there, and I saw what was on their faces, it took ten years off my life. And for a time, I knew you were dead. But, after a few minutes, after I prayed, I knew that was not true. You are alive, and that is what is true."

"Ah. The sound of your voice Teresa Velmer Zachery. I feel like I have been disconnected from earth, floating above it. But now, I have my feet on the ground again."

They spoke a few more minutes. Then Jon said, "This call is expensive, Sweetheart. How about if we hang up, and I call again from the Philippines? Assuming I can figure out how to get there."

"I don't want to, but I know you are right. One last thing. In this moment of profound joy, for the first time in my life, Jon Zachery, parting from you is sweet sorrow. Goodbye Dearest Jon"

"Goodbye, Dearest Teresa.

Teresa returned to the living room and explained what her husband had told her.

The chaplain said, "I've done a hundred of these notifications, and none of them had a happy ending. Praise be to God."

"Jon asked me to tell you, Chaplain and Lieutenant, that he knows you have tough jobs. He's sorry he couldn't get a call through in time to save you from it."

The chaplain turned to the lieutenant. "It would be a mistake, my son, to expect another notification visit to turn out like this one has."

⋯⟡⟡◉⟡⟡⋯

Jon found a place on the base to make an encrypted voice radio call to the *Solomons.*

"This is Commander Fant, over."

"Zachery, sir. I took a triple A hit to the belly of my plane. Killed the radio and a few other things. I made it to Da Nang. I just called Teresa, Sir, and the your-husband's-been-shot-down team had just arrived and told her I was missing. What did Blackey tell you? Over."

"He, uh, he said a few guns started shooting at you, and you turned tail and ran. Headed for the coast. He thought his priority was killing the SAM site, not flying wing on a coward. He said he killed the SAM."

It was quiet for moment.

"Skipper, if there were two SAM sites, he might have killed one. If there was one site, **he** did not kill it."

"I heard you tell Blackey to shoot a Shrike. He says he never heard you or any of your radio calls, which I heard loud and clear. He did say he saw you pull up and shoot a Shrike. Not long after that, he saw you head for the beach. I had the guys check his radio and his helmet and his oxygen mask. They all worked fine."

"Skipper, Teresa told me the visit from the notification team took ten years off her life. Blackey was my wingman. He should have stayed with me. When I get to the Philippines, I'm going to take years off his life. New subject. My plane suffered significant damage to the belly area. Hydraulic lines were severed. Electrical wires burned. A major hole in the wing. The engine's trashed. I had the guys here take pictures. I'll bring the pics with me, over."

"Okay. I am going to assemble a repair team and fly them to Da Nang, hopefully, this afternoon. If you line up a flight to the Philippines, don't wait for them … over."

17

J ON GOT A RIDE ON an air force cargo plane from Da Nang to Tan Son Nhut Air Base. He had to stay there overnight. To get himself back to the ship, he had a twenty-dollar bill in his wallet. Necessities took a bite out of his cash. Clean underwear and socks. Toothbrush and paste. Cheap razor. Sweatpants. No shaving cream. Paperback book, though.

A William Faulkner title. He'd read a couple of his books. He found them a challenge to slog through because of frequent reading stops to look up a word in the dictionary. Then, after he completed a scene, he'd go back and read the scene again with his new understanding of several key words. A slog, but with the understanding came real mind-engaging storytelling. Besides the Faulkner, the only other paperbacks for sale were westerns and smut books. The westerns, he'd probably finish one of those before he went to sleep that night.

So, Bill, or William, you it is.

The mess hall fed him. For free. Then he checked into the Bachelor Officer's Quarters. Atop one of the beds, luggage. No roommate, thouigh. Which was fine. He had no energy to spend on social interchange with a guy he'd never see again.

In the bathroom, he took an air force shower. A navy shower meant turning the water on, wetting down, turning the water off while you lathered up, turning on the water long enough to rinse away the suds, after which, you promptly turned the water off again. In an air force shower, you turned on the water, stood under the indoor rain and let the hot water cascade over you until your skin wrinkled like a prune.

He set the water hot enough so he'd perspire. When he'd had flights like the one that day, where he expended a bucketful of adrenalin, he considered the extra stink in his sweat the smell of boiled-off fear. The SAMs, the AAA, The *Where the Hell is Blackey*, and *I'm going to die!* All scared the bejeebers out of him, threatening to debilitate him, but then those glands went to work and dumped their juice into his blood. The magic juice focused his mind and magnified his strength so he could have arm-wrestled Goliath and won.

Stretch knew the difference between clean, work-sweat and that scared-as-all-get-out fear sweat. When he jogged, or as a teenager, he worked on a farm and hoisted hay bales onto a wagon in August, he produced clean-smelling work sweat. That perspiration did not smell unpleasant. Unless, of course, you let it ferment before washing it off. Sniffing clean sweat on someone, you were inclined to think: That guy worked hard! However, the stink of fear sweat inspired: What the heck? Did you drink vinegar for breakfast instead of orange juice?

After he sweated himself inside clean, he turned the water to cool to close his sweat pores, soaped up again, and rinsed the suds off again. *Used enough water for a hundred navy showers.*

He dried himself, dressed—in clean underwear, socks, and sweatpants—and took his fear-sweat-stunk-up flight suit to the laundry room. A quarter to use the washer. Another two bits for soap, and yet another for the dryer. With the washing machine running, he returned to the BOQ reception desk. He asked the Vietnamese man for a pad of yellow paper. Back in the laundry room, he sat on a folding metal chair. The chair, and the laundry room, reminded him of the chapel on *Solomons*. As the washing machine agitated the stench from his flight suit, he wasn't wrapped in solemn silence. Rather the swish, swish, the sound of water running into the tub, the sound of the tub spinning to expel the water, created a bubble around him, keeping the world at bay. From inside the bubble, he wrote up a detailed account of the mission he and Blackey had flown.

Back in his room, he wrote three pages to Teresa. At 22:30, exhaustion descended from heaven and invaded every cell of his being. He had just enough strength to pull off his sweatpants and flop onto his pillow.

⸻⬩◉⬩⸻

Five Warhorse wives, Teresa knew, were making the trip to Hong Kong: Sarah Fant, Maryann Toliver, Deborah Wakefield, Monica Newsome, and Lydia Foster. They all had rooms in a hotel in Kowloon. On Hong Kong Island, across Victoria Harbor from Kowloon, hotels, things in general, were more expensive.

Jon was worried about the cost of the trip. Truth be told, she worried, too. But when the Casualty Assistance Calls Officer, the priest, and the CO's wife came to call, from the moment she opened the door, she knew who they were, why they were there, and that Jon was dead. She'd only believed it for a few moments, but she had believed it. Since then, the feeling had been building in her that she needed to go to Hong Kong to see him, even if they couldn't afford it.

The next morning, she called her parents and told them what had happened to Jon. Her father insisted, "Go to Hong Kong. I'll pay for the plane ticket and the hotel."

But was there even time to arrange the trip? As soon as she finished the call with her parents, Teresa phoned the CO's wife.

"Of course, there's enough time," Sarah said. "The Warhorse Wives' Group is shifting into high gear."

⸻⬩◉⬩⸻

Wham! Blinding lights flashed on.

The sudden noise of the BOQ door slamming open, and the light, jerked Stretch from a bottomless pit of blackness into readiness to kill whatever had busted into his room and threatened him.

A tall young man stood in the doorway, his arm around a short young woman, a Vietnamese.

"Sorry," Tall Man slurred. "Di'n mean to wake yuh."

"Next time, try harder," Stretch snapped as he reached for his flight suit.

The girl said, "You wan' be next? Special one-time-for-you-only, five dollah."

Stretch had intended to get dressed, gather his stuff, and go down to the lobby to sleep in a chair. Now, however, a shot of rage blew through his blood. Rage at the woman, rage at both of them.

"Give me your wallet," Stretch snarled. "Roommate."

"The hell you say. Not givin' you nuthin'."

Stretch reached for the man's arm.

Tall Man jerked back and fell, crashing into the lamp table between two easy chairs against the wall opposite the beds. The lamp fell. The porcelain base shattered. Then, from flat on his back, the drunk turned sideways and puked a huge puddle of stomach-lurching stench onto the tiled floor.

Vietnamese Girl wrinkled her nose, hustled to Tall Man, and reached for his wallet.

Stretch grabbed her hand and pulled her back. He took the wallet, extracted a five-dollar bill, and thrust it at her.

Like a cobra striking, she snatched the bill and hurried out the door.

He closed and locked it. Tall Man lay there snoring. Stretch grimaced at the puke stench and turned his head. *As if that would help!*

"You got a nasty job to do, standing there bellyaching and moaning don't get it done." Pop's voice from when he'd been a teenager.

Crap!

He concentrated on mouth breathing. Mistake. His stomach lurched, but he clamped his throat shut and force-swallowed the bilious spit.

The man wore a Barong. It looked new and fancy. Stretch ripped it from him, keeping clear of the vomit. Using the fancy shirt, he mopped up a good bit of the puddle and deposited it in a plastic-lined trash can. Next, he searched Tall Man's travel bag and found a dozen tee shirts. He used half those to finish the clean-up. Then he dragged Tall Man to the bed and hiked one-hundred-eighty pounds of dead, unwieldy weight onto the bed. He arranged the inebriate on his side so that, if he puked again, maybe he wouldn't drown in his own vomit.

With the cleanup job done, Stretch knotted the trash can liner and tossed it out the window onto the lawn at the back of the BOQ.

0400. He'd set the alarm for 0500. That hour would bring him no sleep. He took another air force shower. As the water cascaded over him, a saying from one of the gospels came to mind.

For what shall it profit a man, if he gains the whole world, and loses his own soul?

What does it profit it a people to gain their nation, if in doing so, they lose their souls? *We weren't gaining anything in Vietnam. We were losing the war. The Vietnamese people were losing their souls. With our help.*

"Perhaps," he mumbled, "you ain't in the best frame of mind to be digging for profundities!"

Stretch arrived at Clark Air Force Base in the Philippines at 1000. Outside the passenger terminal, he waited for a bus to take him south to the navy base at Subic Bay. In lieu of a ticket, the air force had given him a voucher to turn over to the driver.

Stretch shook his head over the extent to which so many aspects of the eight-year-old war in Vietnam had become bureaucratized.

Yeah, everything except a way to win it.

But then he recalled the mining of Haiphong Harbor, the resumption of bombing The North. The US Navy committing three and even four aircraft carriers to the battle at a time. During the four-year bombing halt, only one carrier had launched combat sorties from the Gulf.

A bus pulled up to where Jon waited. The vehicle looked like a school bus that had served one full, hard life of service. Now it was serving a second hard life as a passenger conveyance. The roof was jammed full of crates, boxes, and luggage. Inside, he found it jammed full of Filipinos and the smell of chicken poop. Several men and some women held crates on their laps with one or two chickens inside.

When Jon handed over his voucher, the driver hooked a thumb toward the back. He saw no vacant seat but started in that direction. He passed a few rows of two-person bench seats and spotted a vacancy, on his left, on the seat above the rear wheels. There a Filipino sat next to the aisle. A chicken crate took up the other half of the seat. The man made no move to make room. Jon reached across him, lifted the crate, and exposed two black and white pebbles of poop. Chicken Man pushed on Jon's chest.

Jon was sure the man wanted him to take the pooped-on half of the bench. The Filipino's face brought Blackey to mind. He took the man's hand from his chest and shoved the man against the side of the bus; then he placed the crate of chickens on the man's lap, and sat on the butt-warmed, worn, clean, Naugahyde aisle seat.

The flare-up of his rage petered out with the notion that he'd just behaved like *The Ugly American*. He was a guest in the Philippines and should have behaved as such. He felt eyes on him. Those eyes seemed to agree with how he should have behaved.

He recalled 1966. He'd been an ensign of a destroyer. That year, USS *Manfred* made a port visit to Zamboanga on Mindanao. Ensign Zachery and two other junior officers hired a taxi and toured the country. Searching for a place to eat, they wound up at a country club that was hosting a baptismal celebration. The baptismal party welcomed the American interlopers. That was how Jon thought of the Filipino people. Warm. Welcoming. Not as people who would have their guests sit in chicken poop.

I shouldn't have been an Ugly American.

This man next to me should not have tried to make me sit in chicken poop. He started it.

Jon smiled at himself, at the childishness of it all. *He started it.*

He dug through his plastic bag of worldly possessions: clean underwear and socks, toothbrush and paste, a razor, and took out the Faulkner book.

A half-hour later, the bus stopped in a village next to a large, open-air market. Jon's seatmate indicated he wanted out. Jon let him by and sat back down again as the rest of the Chicken coopers also debussed and headed for the market.

The ride to Olongapo, a village outside the US Navy base at Subic Bay, was chicken free. He and William Faulkner appreciated that.

From the bus stop to the main gate into the navy base was but a city block. Jon's ID card passed him through the gate but shunted him aside to speak with a Shore Patrol US Navy lieutenant.

"Why are you out of uniform, Lieutenant?" the SP officer demanded.

Traveling in a foreign country, Jon should have been attired in a dress uniform. But here he was. In a flight suit. Without a hat.

Jon explained.

The SP officer related the Solomons wasn't due until 1700. "Three hours from now. You need a hat. That is at least some semblance of being in uniform, for an aviator anyway. I'll have a driver take you to the exchange."

"I'm broke."

"You are one pathetic son-of-a-bitch."

The SP officer pulled out a wallet, extracted a ten-dollar bill, and thrust it at Jon. "This a loan. I expect to be repaid. No later than tomorrow."

Jon stood, fists clenched, arms at his side, glaring at the SP officer. "Do not," he said in a quiet voice, "say one more word to me. Not one. Right now, I feel like hitting someone." The SP officer's eyes grew big. "Yesterday, I flew with the world's worst wingman. I almost got shot down, but I managed to crash my plane at Da Nang without killing myself or hurting anyone. Last night I spent in a BOQ room mopping up a drunk's puke. This morning I rode three hours in a bus filled with chickens and their shit. Then I come here and run into more chickenshit.

"I am not taking your money. Now, get out of my way."

The SP officer took a step back. He dropped the arm holding out the bill.

Jon stomped past the man and out the door of the SP shack.

"Lieutenant. Lieutenant."

Jon spun around. A second-class petty officer had followed him out the door. The PO2 had an SP band around his arm. "Happy to give you a ride, Sir, to wherever you want to go on base." He held out a navy-blue ball cap with US NAVY in gold letters on it. "We keep these in the shack for people who lose their hats."

"Huh." Jon reached for the hat. "Thanks. Your lieutenant obviously didn't like me. I guess that's why he didn't offer me one of these."

"It's not you personally, Sir. He doesn't like aviators, but I like you guys just fine. How about it, Lieutenant? Can I give you a ride?"

"I'd appreciate a ride to the carrier pier."

"You know Solomons isn't due for—"

"I know. I've got a book."

As the PO2 drove them around the bay to the carrier pier, they talked about books and authors. The petty officer had to read Faulkner in high school. They both liked Hemingway and Steinbeck. They both cited Civil War and World Wars I and II histories they appreciated.

"I'm sure you read The Longest Day," the petty officer said as he stopped the pickup on the empty carrier pier. "Sounds like you had your own longest day over the last twenty-four. That right, Sir?"

"Not a bad way to put it, PO2. I appreciate the lift and, even more, the discussion about books. Been a long time since I had such a conversation. And you've given me a dose of normalcy in … well, in a very long day. Thanks."

"I enjoyed it, too, Sir. Hope the rest of your day takes a turn for the better."

The petty officer saluted. Stretch—he felt like Stretch again—returned it. The SP pickup drove away, and Stretch and William F. found a stack of pallets to sit on and wait for their ship to come in.

18

FOR THE FIRST TIME IN his thirteen years in the US Navy, Stretch watched *his* ship sidle up to the pier. From the pier. What an agonizingly slow process it seemed. Of course, fifty-thousand tons of aircraft carrier, even moving at just one knot of speed carried a lot of momentum. Damage to the pier and the carrier could happen if that momentum got out of control. But, waiting for his ship to inch its way in, aggravating.

He recalled coming into port in San Diego returning from a seven-and-a-half-month cruise—as with many terms, a word in military context connoted something quite different compared to civilian usage—on his destroyer. When the ship had pulled out of port at the start of the deployment, Teresa had stood on the pier holding bundled up three-month-old Jennifer. Such a tiny bundle. But then, after the deployment, the infant—the child—Teresa held seemed so … grown up. And he'd been left with two thoughts. I missed so much in my little girl's life. And I should have been here to help Teresa.

But he hadn't been there, and it was one of those debts for which there was no forgiveness.

Slow, steady, stately, the gray mountain of momentum eased against the dock. A sailor on the pier secured the first line to a bollard. "Moored. The Officer of the Deck is shifting his watch from the bridge to the quarterdeck," blared over the *Solomons'* announcing system. Pent-up organized pandemonium cut loose. The other mooring lines were snugged up, cranes began lifting the forward and after gangways into place. Other cranes hoisted pallets of supplies onto the after-aircraft elevator. From inside the hangar bay, forklifts darted out, lifted the pallets, spun around, and hustled their loads inside as if the aircraft carrier beast were starving and needed tons of sustenance at once.

Stretch was the first to cross the forward gangway, salute the Officer of the Deck, and request permission to come aboard. He felt like he'd returned home after a long absence.

Crossing the hangar just forward of the forklifts ferrying pallets of supplies, he descended a ladder to the second deck and made his way aft to Ready Room Five. Bee was Squadron Duty Officer. As he walked down the aisle between the rows of ready room chairs, the SDO's face lit up. "Good to see you, man. For a while, we thought you'd gotten your ass shot down. A couple of us almost got sad."

"A downright gizzard gripping welcome home! Can't tell you how much I appreciate it."

"Yeah, yeah." Bee picked up the phone and dialed.

"Stretch is here, Sir." A pause for listening before hanging up. "Skipper wants to see you."

Stretch exited Ready Five and joined the bodies moving forward. The second-deck passageway, an artery with blood flowing in both directions at once. Sailors on the starboard side moved forward. Those to port moved aft.

At the Skipper's room, he knocked and entered when told to do so.

The CO sat at his desk. Over his shoulder, penetrating eyes lasered his visitor.

His Adam's apple bobbed as he tried to swallow spit his mouth couldn't manufacture. *Is he mad at me?* "Uh, Skipper," he unzipped the pocket in the left leg of his flight suit, extracted the three-page report he'd written up in the BOQ on Tan Son Nhut, and handed it over.

On the desk, the Skipper smoothed out the lined paper and read. He flipped the page and read the backside.

Stretch watched him scan through the rest of it.

The CO spun his chair, grinned, and shook his head. "You told me once that your XO in the training command said you were a Magnet Ass, that you attracted trouble. I'm thinking he was right, and that maybe we ought to give you a new call sign."

Lieutenant Zachery frowned.

"On the other hand."

Where was this going?

"You brought out into the open something I'd been wrestling with for months. How to deal with Blackey's superior ability versus his asshole demeanor." The Skipper shook his head. "His incorrigible, uncorrectable asshole demeanor."

Some, not all, *some* of the tension holding Stretch in seated attention posture ebbed.

"After your phone call from Da Nang, I convened a review board. Me, the XO, and the department heads. We brought Blackey in and questioned him. He stuck to his story that you'd chickened out of the mission when the North Viets fired SAMs and AAA at you. He insisted he hadn't heard your radio calls, even though I was leading a four-plane to help with the rescue, and I heard your radio calls.

"I had his helmet, mask, and the radio in his aircraft checked and everything worked fine. He still insisted he did not hear your radio transmissions. Then I asked him about him flying on your right wing vice the left as you briefed. He said, 'Everybody knows Zachery doesn't know his ass from a hole in the ground about flying combat, and he proved he doesn't know anything about Shrike when he screwed up the switches and ruined two Shrike missiles. And,' he said, 'I flew on his right so I'd be closer to the North Viets if they shot at us. I'd be better able to do something about it without Dipshit getting in the way.'"

No question, Blackey felt that way about him, but he was surprised to hear that he had said it all out loud in front of all the heavies in the squadron.

"Then, I asked him," the Skipper said, "if he'd seen you pump your nose, signaling him to join in close formation. He replied, 'Sure. But getting the mission done was my priority, and I was sure Dipshit wasn't up to it. I should have been flight lead, but the other dipshit we have in the squadron, East Coast, put Stretch in the lead. Two dipshits supporting each other.'"

"He said that in front of EC. That was it for me. I went to CAG and asked for a Field Naval Aviator Review Board to be appointed from the pilots in the other squadrons. The FNAB convened yesterday. They listened to me present the case for jerking Blackey's wings. They questioned him and every other pilot in the Warhorses, except you, of course.

"Blackey's excuse for his behavior on that flight was that you were incompetent. You couldn't function as a flight lead, and you really didn't know that much about SAMs and Shrikes. If those air force guys on the ground were going to be saved, it had to be him running the show, not Dipshit Stretch.

"When the FNAB interviewed us in the squadron, we all said Blackey was a great stick and throttle jockey. He can land aboard an aircraft carrier. He can bomb. But he is not a team player. He is not for the squadron. In the air, either as flight lead or wingman, he is not for the flight. Blackey is for Blackey.

"New told them he was always badmouthing the heavies in the squadron and the wing. And he badmouthed you, Stretch, all the time. 'Like he was jealous of you,' New said.

"The FNAB also interviewed members of other squadrons, CAG Ops, CAG himself, and everybody said you knew your stuff from enemy anti-aircraft capabilities to how to use our defensive equipment to best advantage.

"After working all day, the Board concluded Blackey's behavior constituted an egregious failure of flight discipline. He ignored radio calls and signals from his flight lead. He abandoned his flight lead after he took a hit. When he returned to the ship, he lied about events during the flight. They recommended Blackey be stripped of his wings and sent back to the US immediately."

Stretch sagged back against his chair. He'd expected to have a battle with his nemesis after he got back to the ship, but here it was. The battle was over. And Blackey lost. Before, he always seemed to slither by no matter what he'd done.

"This morning we sent him ashore via a COD wearing khakis with no wings. He probably passed you heading for Clark Air Force Base as you were coming this way."

The sudden cessation of words from the Skipper hit Stretch like—not a clap of thunder—rather like a slap of silence. He felt like Wile E. Coyote chasing the Road Runner off a cliff. Wile E. hangs there with gravity suspended for a tick and tock; then it grabs Wile by the ankles and jerks him down.

"Nothing to say, Stretch?"

"Well, uh—" He shook his head. "One thing. Blackey's gone. It was like I had had this headache since forever, and I got so used to the pain, I didn't even realize I didn't feel good. Now the headache is gone, and holy crap! I'd forgotten how good it felt to not have a headache."

"Glad to have you back, but there is one more thing."

"Yes, Sir?"

"You smell like chicken shit. Go take a shower."

⸻⸺◉⸺⸻

0700. Teresa stood at the calendar. First, she thanked God for the blessings He'd bestowed on her family the day before; then she asked the Creator to keep Jon and the children safe through this new day.

As she X'ed off yesterday, she wondered where her husband was. The last she knew, he'd been on the airbase at Da Nang, and that, somehow, he needed to get himself to the Philippines. Please, God—

The phone rang and set her heart to pounding. She huffed out a breath and snatched it up. "Hello."

"I love you, Teresa Velmer Zachery!"

"Jon! Where are you?"

"The Philippines. Just got here this afternoon. I waited to call until I knew you'd be awake."

"Daddy!" Jennifer screeched from the breakfast table. Teresa heard the patter of feet racing away from the breakfast table.

Jennifer tugged on her mother's robe. "Can I talk to Daddy. Please?"

"No," EJ insisted. "I talk to Daddy. Please."

"Children. Hush. I need to speak with Daddy first. You will both get a turn." She shooed both back to the breakfast table.

Over the phone, Teresa said, "I'm coming to Hong Kong."

"What? We agreed you wouldn't, that it was too expensive. If the navy boots me out after this cruise, we won't have anything in the bank."

"My father is paying for the plane ticket and the hotel."

"Your father gave us the money!?"

Teresa frowned. A headache was born just behind her forehead. *Do you not want me to come to Hong Kong?*

She asked him that very question. He didn't reply.

"Jon. Jon, did you hear me? I asked if you don't want me to come."

"No, Teresa. No. I mean yes. I want you to come to Hong Kong. I am just so tired. I haven't slept much in two days. I … I guess it seems like every time I think I know and understand where I am, something happens, and — Yes, Teresa. I am happy you're coming, and I will never be able to repay your father."

It was a while before Teresa got in another word.

⸻ ◆ ⸻

Jon told her about his plane being hit, struggling to control the damaged aircraft, and finally getting it to thirty-five thousand feet and headed for Da Nang, and for a second, he felt close to God in heaven up there at altitude. And thanked Him for saving him, for keeping his time on earth with his Dearest Teresa from ending back there in the DMZ.

There was one thing he didn't tell her. He'd also offered a deal to God. A long time on earth with Teresa for eternity in hell. But later, in the basement of the BOQ on Tan Son Nhut, while the washing machine *swish swished* fear stink from his underwear, he'd asked God to forgive him for proposing such a deal, and he submitted himself to God's will.

In the phone booth, Jon spent a couple of minutes crying, producing copious tears and snot, and he, with no handkerchief, used the tail of his shirt.

On the call from the Philippines, Jon hoped he would get away with it costing forty dollars but thought it might require sixty. Actually, the bill totaled a hundred. Every cent he had. But he needed every minute of it, no matter the cost.

After his dollars ran out, he returned to the ship.

That night, there was a squadron party at the O Club. Bachelor pilots all seemed to have plenty of money, but with a wife and three children,

Jon always felt like he had just enough. And for that, *Thank You, God*, was perfectly in order. But just enough did not include trips to the club.

In his room, he paused, probing for the ghost of Blackey, but he was gone. *Thank You, God.* He shucked his uniform and flopped onto the top of the bedding. There was a lot to be thankful for. Halfway through the Thank-You-God litany, his mind went to sleep, with a vision of Teresa in his soul, an entity of purity as sweet as one of her kisses.

While Jennifer and EJ took turns speaking with their father, Teresa held Ruth and got her to giggle, gurgle, and coo. So, all three children communicated with him.

For a phone call that had started like a stab in the heart, it wound up being the most wonderful call ever. In it, she got a glimpse into her husband and his sense of duty she'd never seen before. And she thought the way it happened was probably the only way it could have happened.

Thank You, God.

Then it was time to get on with the day. Jennifer needed to get to kindergarten. She needed to pack. Among the things to pack was a breast pump, so her milk wouldn't dry up during her absence from Ruth. In the planning session Sarah Fant had summoned to prepare Teresa for her trip, the subject of a breast pump came up.

Naomi Engel piped up with, "Oh, she won't need one."

Which inspired the hottest blush Teresa had ever experienced.

The way Sarah Fant had planned the trip, the Warhorse wives arrived in Hong Kong in time to check into their hotel, shower, and dress before meeting their husbands at fleet landing, where the boat from USS *Solomons* would bring them.

Fleet landing. Where navies of the world disembarked their sailors with pockets full of money and picked them up again when those pockets hit empty.

For Teresa, Fleet Landing bookended the week in Hong Kong with Jon. From seeing him, in the middle of a pack of men rushing toward her, but then she saw only him, and not the others. Jon's face alight with love and longing and gilded all over with joy.

From the glorious greeting, the following days blurred past like a movie running at fast forward, like there wasn't time to distinguish night from day, nor time to distinguish one day from another, but everything packaged into one continuous, glorious, beautiful strip of time. There were fleeting glimpses of their time together, making love, and afterward, *talking.* Before, after making love, quite often Jon fell asleep. Sometimes Teresa fell asleep first, but this time they held each other and spoke soul-baring words to each other in a way that was a part of making love, not a thing they engaged in after.

He talked to me after making love. That went into the treasure box in which Teresa stored the memories of Hong Kong.

Together with Jon. In Hong Kong. Heaven on earth. Until it ended. And became Hell on earth.

Before Jon walked away from her at Fleet Landing, his face was full of love and longing and gilded all over with despair. When the boat pulled away, carrying Jon back to *Solomons,* it was as if her heart had gotten so firmly attached to him during their days together, seeing him leave, it was as if it wanted to be with him more than it wanted to do the job for which God had created it.

She put her hand over her heart as if to hold it in there.

Ruthann.

Her six-month-old blasted into the center of her being.

She needed to be with Ruth. Now. Ruth needed her mother. Now.

The wives didn't have to taxi to the airport for hours. There'd be hours of waiting in the terminal. The flight to Japan. More time spent in a terminal. Then the eternal flight across the Pacific. Jon's biggest puddle of water on earth.

"Teresa. Teresa."

Sarah was standing next to her. "We're going back to the hotel and pack."

"Oh," Teresa said.

19

STRETCH SAT ON HIS USUAL back row folding chair in the ship's multi-denominational chapel. He leaned back and gazed at the table draped with a white altar cloth. The sanctuary lamp was unlit, signifying God wasn't home. But He was. Jon had never sensed His presence so intensely in His drab utilitarian house before. Even when consecrated hosts were present and the lamp proclaimed, *Yeah, verily. God is home.*

Also, he'd never felt the presence of Teresa so intensely when he was so far away from her. At that moment, she was on a plane headed from Japan to Los Angeles and moving farther and farther away at more than a mile a minute. But her spirit was with him, and with God.

They'd spent the great majority of their time together in Hong Kong in their hotel room. There was nothing else anywhere near as appealing as being together. Exclusively. There was no ship, no squadron, no friends, no wives' group. There was, in all the universe, just the two of them, with God hovering over and around them.

Stretch smiled. He and Teresa had been in bed. She'd said, "Aren't you hungry?"

"Uh, well, yes, now that you mention it."

He'd been about to kiss her, and she laughed into his mouth and rolled onto her back. "In the entire history of mankind, I bet that's the first time a woman ever had to remind a man he was hungry. I'm going to take a shower."

"We could save time. We could—"

"We'd never get to lunch. Stay."

When he whined like a puppy begging for a treat. Teresa rolled her eyes.

The ship's general announcing system busted into the chapel as if it had no door, no bulkheads. "Lieutenant Zachery, please call Ready Five. Lieutenant Zachery, call Ready Five."

The message grabbed LT Zachery, transported him across the boundary between the physical and spiritual worlds, and plopped him firmly in the former.

Rat snot!

A petty officer manned the duty desk. As soon as Stretch entered the Ready Room, the PO said, "Mr. Z. The Skipper wants you in the intel spaces ASAP."

Out the door and into the always crowded second deck passageway, move forward, climb three ladders, and bust into Intel.

The Skipper studied a map laid out on a table in front of him. He turned. "Stretch. Day after tomorrow, we're flying three strikes against the North. Figure out how to handle the SAMs."

The North! All those times he had moaned about making-toothpick missions, had badmouthed the US for not trying to win the war, all those old notions went through a shredder. Now he was thinking about SAMs and AAA and knowing that, however many of those things he'd seen in over two-hundred combat missions, he was about to see a lot more.

"Stretch, goddammit! Get your head out of your butt and into the game here."

———— ·••••◦•••• ————

Solomons would launch the first Alpha at 0700.

Four anti-SAM Shrike birds, four F-8 MiG protection fighters, and twenty bombers comprised the strike. The target, an underground fuel oil storage area at Vinh. Vinh was about two-hundred miles northwest of the DMZ and sited eighteen miles inland. Eighteen miles amounted to a relatively shallow penetration of North Vietnamese airspace. However, three known SAM sites and a lot of AAA protected the target.

The first thing Stretch did was to find CAG. He leaned over a map spread on a table.

"Sir, have you worked out how you are going to handle your bombers?"

"No. I'm just starting the planning process. Got any ideas?"

Stretch grinned.

"Of course you do, you little shit," CAG said, as he stood up straight, reached out a big paw, and messed up Stretch's hair. Like Tiny liked to do. "Let's hear it."

"Let me show you this drawing."

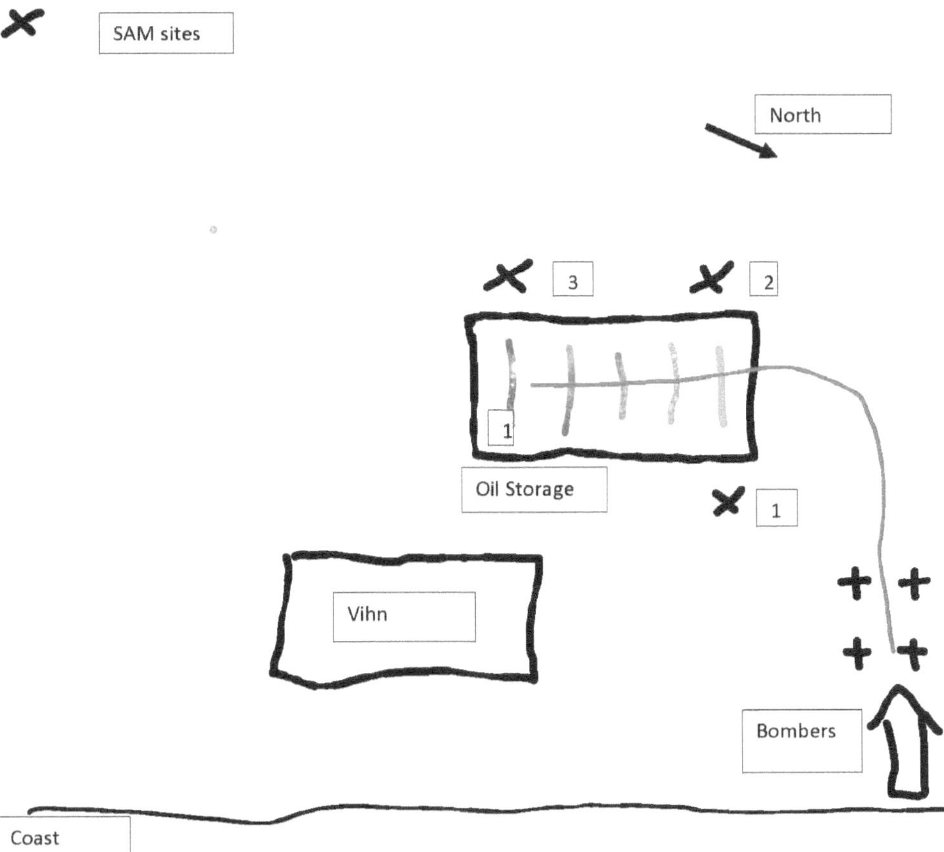

"I think we should coast in north of the target. My suggestion, gaggle up your bomber divisions in a row. Follow the red trace, and, as the lead bomber, aim to drop your bombs on the line marked number one. Each subsequent bomber division aims for the next line. That way, the bomb smoke from your hits won't obscure the target for division number two."

Stretch paused to give CAG space to say something, then he plowed on. "The crosses in front of the bombers are anti-SAM birds." He pointed toward his drawing. "These two will be a mile in front, and these two miles in front, and I'll be one of the *two-milers.*

"If we get SAM radar indications, we'll fire Shrikes. Also, me and my wingman will bomb SAM site number one. Next, we'll proceed through the target area. We'll head for SAM site number three, and we should be out of your way by the time you are ready to roll in."

"I'm going to ask for Alice to fly one mile in front of you, Sir, and he will be assigned SAM two to bomb. What do you think, Sir?"

"I hope like hell you can execute the mission better than you can draw."

"Uh, I can have the Intel guys smooth out the drawing." Stretch frowned. "Or if you don't like the plan—"

"You're so easy, Stretch." CAG laughed. "Excellent plan."

CAG held up an 8x10 black-and-white photo. "I've even got a prominent feature on the ground to show me where to aim my bombs. And it looks to me like the bombers will drop their loads and be back over the water in five minutes. Course you Shrike shooters will be in Indian country twice as long."

CAG placed a new map on the table. "The second and third strikes our first day back won't be so easy. We'll be over the beach for thirty minutes on both of those."

"You started on those?" CAG said.

"We only took a preliminary look at the targets. The Intel guys are going over what we know about SAM sites along possible ingress and egress routes. We are getting together at 0800 tomorrow to lay out detailed plans for the other two targets."

"One more thing," CAG said, "for these first three targets, we've had a couple of days to work out how to attack them. Once we get to the Gulf, we're going to be flying two hops a day, plus the planning team will spend hours working the three strikes for the next day. Watch your ass. Don't run yourself into the ground. Get some sleep. You hear?"

"Loud and clear, Sir."

CAG responded in falsetto. "Loud and clear, Sir." CAG—call sign Bear—and falsetto did not go together. "I'm going to have my eye on you, Stretch. You show up with raccoon eyes, I'll ground you. Then I'll kick your ass."

Stretch said, "Yes, Sir," and got the heck out of there.

The day after the travelers returned to Lemoore, the XO's wife, Laura, hosted a Warhorse Wives' get-together. Teresa was absolutely sure Naomi Engel would ask her if she used the breast pump. She'd prepared an answer. Naomi did ask.

Teresa replied, "I went to all the trouble of packing it and carting it over there. Sure, I used it." She lowered her eyes and blushed demurely.

The wives were stunned quiet for a moment. Teresa was sure they never expected something like that from her.

Naomi patted Teresa on the back and said, "Good girl."

The ladies laughed. For the next three hours, they combined their spirits to hold back the notion that, while the travelers had returned to the States, *Solomons* had returned to the Tonkin Gulf.

The next morning, the Alpha Strike Planning Team worked out the details for bombing a railroad marshaling yard at Nam Dinh. The target was close to Hanoi to the northwest, close to Haiphong to the northeast, and close to the Than Hoa bridge to the south. Formidable defenses surrounded all three places. The team agreed that a direct ingress to the rail yard was not prudent. Getting to the target, minimizing the threat to the bombers, required flying into Vietnam to the west of Nam Dinh, and attacking on an easterly heading.

For the Shrike birds, Stretch saw no better way to deploy the Shrike shooters than the way he laid out the Vinh attack plan. Alice, EC, and Not, members of the planning team as well, agreed.

While the Strike Planning Team was busy in the Intel spaces, the Skipper had the maintenance department check out the warning equipment in their airplanes. On the last hop of the previous cruise, a LT(jg) named Amos Kane had sabotaged the warning systems in the Warhorse airplanes. He'd been clever. He'd broken the connection from the warning system black box to the antennae. The fault would not be detected by the Built In Test (BIT). Following an investigation of that incident of sabotage, the squadron recommended finding a way to test the warning system from the antennae all the way to the warning system display in the cockpit. The US Navy acted on the recommendation and developed a suitcase-sized device that would duplicate the signals emitted by SAM radars and SAM missile guidance. The maintenance techs in all the squadrons were using their test devices to check all their airplanes.

Amos Goddamned Kane's clever sabotage would not bite the airwing in the ass again.

At lunch, Stretch, Alice, Not, and EC ate together.

After they found a table, but before they started eating, EC said, "Not. What's it like? Flying over the North, I mean."

Not scooped a big forkful of lasagna, shoveled it in, took his time chewing, and swallowed. He dabbed his lips with a paper napkin, took a sip from his water glass, set it back down, and looked EC in the eye.

"It's no different than flying over the South, or Laos, really." He forked up another mouthful, took his time chewing, and swallowed.

What in Sam Hill was Not doing?

"Except for two things. One, there's no SAMS in the South or in Laos. In the North, SAMs are all over the goddamned place. Two. Over the South and in Laos, if you get shot at, it'll be in your bombing run. In the North, somebody's always shooting at you. And not just AAA. Picture thousands of farmers lying on their backs on the levees around their rice paddies firing Ak-47s into the sky at the sound of our jets."

With his mouth hanging open, EC stared at Not.

"EC," Stretch said, "eat."

EC was a LCDR, senior to Stretch. He should have said, "Eat, Sir." But he didn't put it that way.

Stretch finished first. "I'll meet you in Intel to plan the third strike." He rose, laid his tray on the conveyer into the scullery, and went to see the Ops O in the Ready Room.

"Simp, I presume we'll all be flying two hops tomorrow."

The Ops O nodded.

"I'd like EC as my wingman on both the hops," Stretch said. "Also, could you put Not on Alice's wing twice? We have to start grooming some other guys to be anti-SAM leads."

He showed Simp his drawing, depicting the placement of the anti-SAM planes and he explained who he wanted flying each anti-SAM position on each of the three strikes.

"Is all that okay with you, Sir?"

Simp shrugged. "Okay by me."

He thanked the Ops O and returned to Intel to plan the third strike.

Planning for that mission only took an hour. "Practice makes perfect," L'il Lord said. He was leading the third strike but had observed the other two being planned.

Probably right. Probably mostly right,

It boiled down to getting the bombers to their target. MiGs and SAMs were the major threats. Once they arrived at the target, finding it, finding an aimpoint, that was the bomber's problem. Stretch could only contribute to suppressing or killing SAMs. The MiGs, that's where the F-8s were needed. Finding the target was a matter for the Intel guys and what photos they had, and, of course, the strike lead. They had plenty of good pictures for this third strike of their first day back in the Gulf.

With the planning done, Stretch had time to write another long letter to Teresa. The one he'd written the night before would require extra stamps, but in the Tonkin Gulf, postage was free. Tomorrow he'd mail both his post-Hong Kong compositions.

That night, he wrote about how their two souls loved each other, and how God had been with them, there in the hotel room in Kowloon.

As he wrote, he felt so spiritually connected to Teresa all the way around the world, it triggered memories in his mind, which triggered muscle memories in his body, and also engendered a fierce aching, longing for her. The body, it seemed, had no ability to find gratification in sweet memories, only intense need for what had been, but could not be again for a long, long time.

He sealed the envelope and was about to write SWAMLAAK on the back. Sealed With All My Love And All My Kisses. Instead, he wrote SWAMSAMMBAAMK—Sealed With All My Soul All My Mind All My Body And All My Kisses.

He smiled, giving Teresa a thirty-seven percent chance of figuring it out.

As he was about to stand up and turn on the overhead light, a thought entered his bubble of illumination.

Did God give us Hong Kong because there will never be another together time for Jon and Teresa Zachery—until heaven, of course?

Jon rose from the desk, turned on the overhead light, and stood there for a moment, feeling a remnant of Blackey's spirit in the room. He left and headed for the chapel. On the way he recalled Jesus in the Garden, on that Thursday night. Jesus had prayed, "Let this cup pass from me," before He prayed, "But not My will, Thine be done."

He arrived at the chapel and took his rear row seat, looked at the folding table altar, and prayed, "Thy will be done."

Jon waited to feel some acknowledgement from God the father. But he felt nothing.

Wait! God, did you think I was trying to one-up Jesus? You know, not ask to have the cup pass from me but jumped straight to Thy will be done part? I wasn't trying to do that. You know that, right?

Jon hung his head. He'd just screwed up the most important prayer he'd ever prayed in his whole life. Something touched his head, like when he'd been a kid and was sick in bed with the flu, and his mother had come into the room, took his temperature, and before she left, she'd kissed the top of his head. From the top of his head, warmth, peace cascaded down through him as if his head had been touched by a sunbeam and absorbed it, not just felt it on his skin.

He felt hungry, said goodbye to God, and hustled to the Dirty Shirt Dining Room to grab chow.

After, he went to the Ready Room to watch the movie. But it was *The Bridges at Toko Ri.* In it, the hero, played by William Holden, winds up getting shot down and dying in a ditch in North Korea. Jon did not want to watch that movie and returned to his stateroom. After brushing his teeth, he climbed up onto his bunk and turned out the light. And heard Blackey sniggering.

Jon took in a deep breath and let it out. Inhale, and *Thy will be done* rode on the exhale. Inhale, *Thy will be done.* Inhale, *Thy will be—*

Teresa stared at the calendar and worried and prayed. "Please, Father God in heaven, keep Jon safe." Teresa sensed that a lot of the Warhorse wives were praying to their calendars, too. She walked into the dining room and sat at the table. She reached out a hand to Ruth in her infant seat, and the baby grasped her finger. Then she asked EJ to take her hand, and for him to hold hands with Jennifer, also.

EJ frowned, and said, "Breftus."

"EJ, I want us to say a prayer for Daddy."

"We already said the prayer."

"EJ, I want to say a prayer to keep Daddy safe. Will you do that with me?"

The boy thought about it, then nodded.

"Take my hand."

He took it.

"Now take Jennifer's hand."

He took it, and Jennifer reached out to the baby. She grabbed onto her finger.

"Father God Who art in heaven," Teresa said.

"Father God Who art in heaven," Jennifer and EJ repeated.

"Please watch over Daddy."

"Please watch over Daddy."

"And all the men on the *Solomons*"

Jennifer: "And all the men on the *Solomons.*"

EJ: "And all the men on the *Sah mens*,"

"Sol oh mons," Jennifer enunciated.

"Sah mens," EJ said.

"Amen," Teresa said.

Which both repeated quite accurately. Ruth smiled hers.

20

ALPHA STRIKE #1. AGAINST THE North.

CAG was strike lead and the number one bomber. He used Stretch's crude diagram to brief the mission and wrung no small number of laughs from the packed briefing room with his opening remarks. Then he put on his serious face. Frivolity fled like a lizard sunning on rock spying a hawk circling. The rest of the brief proceeded with CAG's imputed pay-the-hell-attention-or-you're-going-to-die.

The Shrike guys used the call sign Baron. Stretch was Baron One, EC Baron Two, Alice Three, and Not Four.

As per his plan, Baron One flew two miles in front of CAG. CAG's wingman had his TACAN set to air-to-air mode to enable the Shrike shooters to maintain proper distance ahead of the strike lead.

Before launching, white-capped waves around the carrier indicated fifteen knots of wind. From twenty thousand feet, the sea looked smooth and blue. As if there were a sky above and another three miles below.

Ahead, the coast. *The North.* Stretch's hearted kick out a thump-thump in place of a single beat. He checked his TACAN: 2.0 miles. He checked on EC. A couple of degrees ahead of abeam. Just where Baron Two was supposed to be.

Click, click, sounded over the radio. CAG signaling, he was descending to cross the beach at ten thousand. Baron One pushed over. EC stayed with him.

Passing fifteen thousand, a blip appeared on Stretch's TIAS scope. Strobe on his warning system, too. A SAM radar had locked onto to him. He pulled back on the stick and leveled. The blip was six degrees down. He keyed his mic: "Baron Two. Five left, up twenty-five."

EC pulled up hard. Ahead, no SAM. Yet. Wingman check. His Shrike streaked away. The strobe and TIAS dot had disappeared. He resumed his descent. And waited.

"Tally ho," Baron Two called.

Good. That meant Baron One did not have to waste time and position to get his two-plane back together again.

From ten-thousand feet, waves breaking on the beach manifested as a strip of white. The town of Vinh stood out prominently to the southwest. From the town, the target area was easy to find.

A TIAS dot appeared. Ten degrees down. Stretch yanked back on the stick, parked the nose at ten up, and punched the pickle. The Shrike *whooshed* away. He rolled upside down and pulled back to level. His warning system showed a strobe pointed straight ahead. The SAM radar still had him locked up. *Deedle, deedle,* the SAM launch signal sounded in his earphones.

A SAM streaked toward him. He turned left and dove for a couple of seconds, then rolled upright. He picked up the missile above but arcing down toward him again. "Baron Two. Jammer."

He switched on his own jammer, and the missile broke lock and pitched up and away.

Baron Three radioed, "Baron Four, up fifteen."

Probably shooting at SAM#2.

Stretch was at seven thousand feet. He started a gentle climb and checked on EC. Right where he was supposed to be. The TIAS scope showed a dot, probably SAM #2. Before he ripped his eyes away, the scope showed another dot. This one down fifteen degrees. *Close. SAM #1 again.* He mashed the pickle and a Shrike *whooshed* away. He banked left, pulled hard for two seconds, then leveled his wings, so he could see if a missile was coming at him. There was. Coming right at him. No time to think, talk, or pray.

He rolled into a forty-five-degree dive, banked left, and pulled hard.

Keeping the diving turn going, he was blind on the missile. *Reverse the turn. See what the missile is doing.* The thought formed, but before he could act, he heard, "Keep it going, Baron One!" from EC. Completing the barrel roll maneuver brought him upright again. He spotted the SAM contrail above him. Bottoming at three thousand feet, he put the nose at five degrees up and searched for EC.

Deedle, deedle. SAM launch warning. Ahead, above, and slightly right, Stretch saw a missile contrail form and streak toward the ground. EC had fired a Shrike. Behind the start of the Shrike contrail, he expected to see a fireball and his wingman's flaming wreck of an airplane plummeting toward earth trailing smoke.

Stretch! The SAM site.

If the SAM was going to hit EC, it would have done so by now. Switching his eyes ahead, he spotted smoke and dust rising from the ground. From the SAM launches. He banked left, keeping his climb going, and he checked his ordnance switches to make sure he was ready to drop his cluster bombs. He was. Passing seven thousand, he rolled upside down and pulled hard. Ideal roll-in altitude would have been ten thousand, but no time for that. He shallowed his dive a degree, and at five thousand, *Pickle, pickle.* His two cluster bombs thumped away. 37- and 57-millimeter tracers flew by his cockpit. He hauled back on the stick, got his aircraft climbing, and banked hard left. He rolled out heading 225 degrees, the heading he'd figured from SAM #1 to SAM #3. Stretch turned on his fuel dump switch for a second. He'd been at full power for … eternity, it seemed, and jet engines at full power were big-bellied dragons who never got enough to eat. But a spurt of fuel would enable EC to pick him up visually.

"At your six. Tally."

He executed an S-turn around the base heading and found his wingman moving into position. He rolled out on the 225 heading and had to force himself to reduce power to 95%, to enable Baron Two to stay in position. Power, speed, those were life itself. But he did it. Then he took stock. He had a single Shrike left. EC had his two cluster bombs. Fuel state, 4000 pounds. EC probably about the same amount of gas. No warn—

Deedle, deedle.

Left bank to clear under his nose, Stretch picked up the SAM. No. Two of them in trail. Streaking toward them.

"Baron Two, two SAMs dead ahead."

No time to shoot his Shrike, Stretch banked hard left and entered into a repeat of the barrel roll maneuver he'd used earlier. His arm was heavy from the G's, but he reached up and turned his jammer on again. He punched chaff. *Nothing else to do but complete the maneuver—and hope like hell it worked on two SAMs as it had on one.* When he rolled upright with the world, he looked above and found two puffs of smoke, maybe three thousand feet above him. He was at five thousand and climbing. A blip appeared on the TIAS. Dead ahead. Twenty degrees down.

His Shrike *whooshed* off the rail and streaked straight ahead for a second; then it cut sharply down. Stretch rolled left again and entered yet another barrel roll. *What the hell else was there to do?* He hadn't seen a SAM, but he knew, *he knew,* one was there.

He radioed, "Baron Two?"

"With yuh!"

A grin form under his oxygen mask. *EC. I could kiss you on the lips!*

Stretch rolled upright at three thousand. Ahead of him, a carpet of flak bursts covered the way ahead. He jerked back on the stick.

"Baron Two?"

"Here."

"Climb."

With a good climb going, he rolled upside down, pulled into a ten-degree dive, and rolled upright. There it was, right in front of him. SAM site #3. All he had left was twenty- millimeter machinegun ammo. He turned on the gun and squeezed the trigger. *Brrrrp.* Pulling gently on the stick he eased the nose up to lay his bullets in a swath across the SAM site. A lot of guns were firing at him. His machine gun abruptly stopped. *Out of ammo.* He hauled back on the stick and climbed away from the AAA.

"Baron Two, you got it?"

"Tally. I'm rolling in."

Stretch leveled at eight thousand headed south. He picked up EC in his bomb run passing his altitude. Hopefully, the guns that had fired at him weren't able to readjust their aim to his wingman.

From the target area, huge balls of fire and black smoke billowed skyward. The bombers were blowing the hell out of the target.

EC pulled out of his bomb run headed north.

"Baron Two, off left." That was to keep EC from flying through where the bombs were falling.

Click, click. EC acknowledging.

Stretch banked hard left to keep his eyes on EC. Baron Two rolled left and turned hard. He stayed with him. EC rolled wings level, headed for the beach and flying over Vinh.

He punched his radio mic button twice. That meant "I've got you in sight. You have the lead." It also meant pull your power back to 98% so I can keep up.

EC had established a gradual climb, and the beach flashed under them as they were passing seven thousand.

And, *Lord God of heaven and earth, being alive, it's just the greatest thing, You know?*

And Lord God, flying with a wingman like EC, that's dad burned great, too.

After landing on *Solomons*, Stretch pulled open the door to Intel, and unholy pandemonium blared out at him. The room was packed with pilots. Every single one of them was talking, and they did not appear to care if anyone was listening.

A hand shoved Stretch aside. He spun around. CAG.

The Airwing Commander hollered, "Shut the goddamned hell up!" His voice as loud as an F-8 in afterburner.

Silence swallowed every voice.

"Flight leads," CAG's voice now down a few decibels, "Huddle up your guys and write up what you saw. You write it up. Don't have the Intel guy do it. Mind. If anyone, anyone starts bellowing like a bull next to a corral of cows in heat, I will grab your sorry ass and toss it out into the passageway. One more thing. Do. Not. Dawdle. This space is needed to brief the next Alpha Strike in forty-five minutes. Now. Hop the hell to it!"

By the time Stretch finished writing up the Shrike shooter report, there was no time to eat. He had to rush back to the Ready Room, write up the paperwork for the plane he'd flown and get back to Intel for the second go briefing. He and EC also flew on the second strike.

Strike #2 target: a large railroad marshalling yard near the town of Nam Dinh. The Strike Planning Team laid out a route to the target that kept the bombers ten miles away from any known SAM site.

"Known SAM sites," Stretch told his Shrike shooters. "That's a key phrase. Expect them to have snuck in a missile site we don't know about." He had changed the weapon load out for the second go: three Shrikes and one cluster bomb per aircraft. He figured that, unless they encountered a surprise site, they'd be shooting Shrikes from long range to suppress the firing of SAMs at the bombers.

It turned out that, compared to the first mission, the second was a piece of cake. On the first, the Shrike shooters dodged ten SAMs. On the second, not a single missile was fired at the strike. No surprise SAM sites popped up, either.

Skipper Fant flew Strike Lead. In the debrief, he said, "Man, I felt it on the ingress. The air was electric with threat. I could almost see the Gomers working themselves up to fire SAMs at us, and as soon as I got that feeling, the Shrike shooters shot first, and the tingle in the nape of my deck died down. It was like that all the way to the target."

With the debrief room full of pilots, Skipper Fant lased his eyes at Stretch. "Shrike Shooters, what you did out there, it was, you know, halfways to, sort of, kinda, almost semi-satisfactory."

Most of the pilots laughed. One wrote on his knee board what the Skipper had said, and he wanted to get it right. He asked L'il Lord to repeat it. Which elicited more guffaws.

One thing on Stretch's second Alpha Strike had **not** gone *halfways to, sort of, kinda, almost semi-satisfactory*. After the mission, as he led his four-plane up the side of the ship prior to landing, exhaustion flooded his arteries, which carried *just-let-me-sleep* to every cell in his body.

Not a good thing to happen right before a carrier landing, even on a clear-to-the-moon daylight day. Even daylight landings required an on-your toes performance from the stick and throttle jockey. *Even Blackie—*

Blackie! A spike of molten hot anger torched the weariness from his body and got him through the landing. By the time the crew had chained his aircraft and he'd shut down the engine, he had no energy to climb out of the cockpit. For a moment. In that moment, he knew what he'd done wrong. He hadn't taken the time to eat between flights. That would not happen again.

On the second day of the three Alpha Strikes per day schedule, EC and Not flew as #3 Shrike Shooters. On the third day, EC and Not both flew as Shrike Shooter lead. They both performed halfway to sort of, etc.

On the fourth day on the line, the ship shifted to noon-to-midnight operations with no Alpha Strikes on the schedule. The missions involved scouting the main roads leading to South Vietnam and bombing any worthwhile target. Results from the missions continued to include trucks destroyed, secondary explosions, and even a locomotive belching steam and hightailing it toward a place to hide.

Stretch and Nose happened onto the train north of Vinh. Stretch rolled in and dropped his bombs in front of the engine and blew up the rails. The locomotive plowed off the tracks and into the trees. Nose dropped his bombs on the rear car, which was a fuel tanker. When his bombs hit, the tank car exploded, and the top careened off to the side, sailing like a giant frisbee. Secondaries started cooking off from the boxcars in front of the fuel tanker.

After the flight, he put his wingman in for an Air Medal.

Night flights all carried flares. Stretch, with Nose as his regular wingman of late, briefed him on the dangers of vertigo. He had dropped bombs under flares back when the ship operated off Hawaii. "I got all the respect in the world for the vertigo monster," he told his flight lead.

"The other thing is managing ordnance switches. We both need to pay close attention to that."

The ship liked to have one section of Shrike shooter airplanes over the beach for all missions. The load out for Shrike Shooters was one Shrike and three bombs, except at night. Then it was one Shrike, one flare pod, and two bombs.

"Over the beach," Stretch said, "we have the Shrike selected and the Master Arm Switch on. So, if you want to bomb, or drop flares, turn the Shrike off."

"Yeah, yeah," Nose said. "Got it."

Their assigned route coasted in just south of Vinh and followed the main highway leading toward South Vietnam. Stretch got them headed south; then he had his wingman punch out two flares. As soon as the flares were away, Nose, as per the briefing, turned right to begin a three-hundred-sixty-degree turn to see if they could spot something from the light of flares. With the first two flares, they observed nothing. They flew farther south, and Stretch radioed his wingman to drop his last two flares. The same turn produced the same result. The manufactured sunlight disclosed nothing but trees and an empty highway.

As they proceeded south, Stretch turned his Shrike station off and his flares on. He dropped two, and in the circle, he spotted what looked like a road worn into the jungle alongside the highway and into the trees.

"Nose, I've got a place where they might be hiding trucks. I'll bomb it. I'll tell you where to aim from my hit."

He selected his bomb stations, made sure the Shrike was off, and rolled in. The flares off to his left tried to convince him **up** was in a different place than where he knew it was. He gritted his teeth, fought it off, and concentrated on aiming his bombs. At five thousand, he hit the pickle twice, pulled up to wings level, and turned right.

"You got secondaries," his wingman reported.

"Okay, Two, try to drop just to the west of my hit."

"Roger. I'm in."

Stretch leveled at seven thousand, turned back toward the target, and watched for Nose's bomb hits.

Suddenly, from where Nose's aircraft should be, a bright streak of light blossomed. At first, he thought a SAM or AAA had nailed his wingman.

"Shit," Nose radioed.

The Shrike! He'd fired the Shrike! The missile would have blinded him! As he dove toward the earth at 450 knots.

"Nose! Pull back on the stick! Pull back on the stick!"

With his lights out for the bombing run, Stretch couldn't tell if Nose pulled out of his dive or not. "Warhorse Two, you okay?"

No response. For a long heart chilling moment. Then, "In a way, yeah. In another way, hell no."

After they landed aboard *Solomons,* Nose thanked Stretch for his call to put in backstick. "Shit man, I'd have busted my ass tonight without that call."

"Okay, as soon as we're done in Intel, we're going to the Skipper and tell him what happened."

"Why the hell do we have to do that? Can't we—"

"We can't drop it. You're going to tell him."

In the Skipper's room, after Nose confessed his *switchology* mistake, the Skipper said, "Thanks for telling me, Nose. There're big lessons for all of us here. One. Flying Shrike Shooter missions, keeping your switches straight is important as all get out. And all of us can get caught up in things and forget. And two, Stretch understood the Shrike rocket motor would scorch your eyeballs blind. He had the presence of mind to call for back stick.

"This is what you're going to do, Nose. Write up what happened here at my desk. Make sure you write pretty, so folks can read it. Tomorrow, every pilot in the squadron will read and initial your paper. And, Nose, this is embarrassing. But the absolute worst thing is after something like this happens, the guy who makes the mistake says nothing, and the next night, another goober pilot kills himself making that same mistake. Understand?"

"Crystal clear, Sir."

That night, on the launch after the one Stretch and Nose had flown, a LCDR from a Warhorse sister squadron, the Raiders, failed to call off from his bombing run. His wingman spotted a fire on the ground and presumed it was his flight leader's crashed plane. He presumed the vertigo monster bit his flight lead on the ass.

⋯⋯●━●━●⋯⋯

Word of the loss of LCDR Farley from the Raiders flashed around the base. Teresa learned of it from the wives' calling tree. That night, at the dining room table, she tried to come up with words to write to Jon. What screamed inside her was, "Come home, Jon Zachery. Come home!"

But from his first few letters since the ship returned to the line, she knew he was feeling a sense of accomplishment, that they were finally doing something useful, that they might now be on a path to win the war. And she sensed how much he wanted to be a part of winning it. So, she launched that plea to Father God in heaven. Once that was done, she could write.

> Every day, I think about being together in Hong Kong. Today, it reminded me of the "for better or for worse" part of our vows. Before, considering the vows, I almost always dwelt on some "for worse" thing. Now I see Hong Kong as <u>the</u> for better thing. And if we never better that "for better," I will not be disappointed. I will always see it as a most special blessing."

And the most special blessing kept the loss of LCDR Farley at bay. Until her head touched her pillow.

21

A
FTER TEN DAYS OF NOON to midnight, *Solomons* got a day off. Planning three Alpha Strikes for the next day took up the morning. The first strike targeted a railroad bridge at the northeast corner of Hanoi. This would be the highest pucker factor mission the *Solomons* had been assigned. Nine known SAM sites sat along the ingress route. AAA ringed the target. MiGs also posed a threat. Stretch planned to fly Shrike Shooter #1 with Alice as Three.

Second and third Alphas would attack other bridges near the first one. Alice would fly Shrike One of the second, and Stretch would take the lead again on the last mission.

With planning complete, the Shrike Shooter team ate lunch. After eating, Stretch and Alice walked back to the Ready Room. When they entered, the enlisted duty officer said, "Mr. Zachery. Ops O just called. The ship wants us to launch a two-plane to check out the minefield outside Haiphong harbor. They want to know if the North Viets are trying to sweep the mines."

"I'll go," Stretch said.

"Me, too," echoed Alice.

In Intel, Stretch asked the briefing officer if it wasn't a waste of time. "Surely, if the North Viets are sweeping the mines, they'll do it at night, won't they?"

"They've been doing it at night, but we sent A-6s from the other carriers, and they've blown the hell out of the North Viet's minesweepers.

The North Viets may be desperate enough to try it in daylight. Any rate, you need to check it out."

On the flight deck, Stretch found his plane parked on Catapult #2. A TIAS bird. Alice also had a TIAS bird, and his was spotted behind the JBD, jet blast deflector. Both aircraft carried three bombs and a Shrike.

An F-8 sat on Cat #1. Alert Five. If a threat appeared, the alert had to start engines and launch within five minutes.

Stretch completed his preflight and looked around the JBD. Alice gave him a thumbs up. Climbing into the cockpit, Stretch buckled his lap belt and shoulder parachute connections. He tugged on the TIAS scope. That display screen had come out of the instrument panel on a cat shot before and jammed the stick back. The pilot managed to get the scope back in its hole and avoided flying into the water. Almost killed him though, and, it was surmised, it probably killed a couple of pilots who inexplicably flew into the water immediately after a cat shot. As he often did, he mentally saluted all those guys who died to teach subsequent generations of pilots how to avoid dying. He checked the rest of the cockpit. *Good to go,* and thought, *Huh! This is the first time I ever launched off a carrier when **I** was ready to go, not when the ship was ready to shoot me.*

Stretch started his engine and checked the instruments: Good. He gave a thumb up to the crew outside. A director inched him forward into final position on the cat. From outside, *thunks* and *clunks* told him he was being hooked to the cat. The Cat Officer signaled full power. He rammed the throttle forward. The engine roared. The plane vibrated and squatted a bit. The catapult had him in tension, ready to blast his thirteen tons from a standing start to 160 knots in little more than a hundred feet.

A cat shot. Such a commonplace occurrence, yet at the same time, brand-spanking new each and every time. Another lesson from all those dead pilots.

Engine instruments: *good.* Sweep the control stick in a circle: *no binding in the flight controls.* Salute the Cat Officer and press your head against the headrest.

Wham!

The cat fires and forces you against the seat so hard you can't breathe, and just when you think this G force is going to go on for a while, it lets you go. For a second, you are just hanging there in the air, and you wonder if you are flying. Or are you going to drop like a rock into the ocean? Then the wings bite air. *All right. Flying!*

Landing gear up. Slight turn to clear the bow. In case you do go in the water, the ship won't run over you. Two hundred and twenty knots. Raise the flaps. Now you really accelerate. Three hundred knots, turn left to north and start a climb. Set the power to 95% to enable his wingman to catch up. Wingie just launched. Head back inside the cockpit. Two hundred ninety knots. Too slow. Climb at three hundred knots, whatever climb rate 95% power will give you. That's what he'd briefed Alice, and he was obligated to give what he promised.

Below, white caps frothed lacey frilling on the blue sea. Above, milky cirrus was smeared over the sky, muting the blue a bit.

Alice pulled into position off his right wing. Stretch squeaked the power up to 96% and watched to see if Wingie stayed with him. He did. Stretch added another percent. At 99%, he started dropping behind. Stretch set the power to 98% for their climb to twenty-seven thousand.

Stretch thought it was funny how, today, he noted every detail of flying. On other days, all this mundane stuff sat in the background, taken care of by thought he didn't have to think. *Or something.* Maybe because he flew with Alice. The two of them knew each other in an airplane. Maybe it was being free of the requirement to teach somebody something, like he'd been doing with EC and Nose for weeks.

Stretch leveled the flight and set the power to give them the best cruise speed, max miles per gallon of gas burned. Check on Alice. Right where he was supposed to be.

Maybe flying was ... *fun?* ... because Blackey was really gone, in the States, now. Two nights ago, Stretch moved down to the bottom bunk. By that act, the lingering ghost of his erstwhile roommate evaporated. He'd worried the ghost would invade his sleep, keep him awake, and that he'd have to retreat up to the top one. Though he was sure if he retreated, he'd make the ghost stronger. But that hadn't happened, and he slept like Ruth with a full tummy and a dry diaper and no phone ringing.

And he was flying. *Flying!* And savoring every little detail. Having his hand move the throttle. Having the other one moving the stick ever so slightly. A tweak to correct a degree to maintain heading. Another tweak to descend fifty feet to return to twenty-seven thou. That afternoon it seemed important to savor those details. On almost every other hop he flew, those details were taken care of by a part of his brain that didn't involve conscious thought. Like breathing.

Off to his left, Hon Me Island. The North Viets had fortified the island with heavy AAA. Intel said there were no SAMS there, but maybe the godless commies snuck a site on when Intel wasn't looking. *At any rate, if we don't spend all our gas on blowing up mine sweepers, we'll check out Hon Me on the return trip.*

Stretch set up a gradual descent. He wanted to arrive at the edge of the minefield at five-thousand feet, going 450. He wanted speed flying over that patch of water, just as he'd have wanted speed if he were flying Over North Nam.

Alice anticipated the power reduction. He stayed locked into position, looking past Stretch toward the coast, where the Bad Guys lived.

Stretch crossed the edge of the minefield and leveled. Below, no whitecaps on the surface. Light winds. No boats or wakes of boats visible. Halfway across the minefield, his TIAS showed a blip on the left edge of his scope. His threat warning system also showed a strobe. Rolling sharply left and pulling hard, he turned through forty degrees and rolled out with the warning system strobe dead ahead. The TIAS blip showed five degrees right and slightly down. The nearest known SAM site would be twenty miles away.

"Twenty-five," Stretch radioed.

To the right and behind him, Alice pulled up abruptly. His Shrike blasted off the rail.

"Right," Stretch radioed, rolled hard right, and pulled back to his original heading.

"Tally." Wingie had him in sight.

Stretch, still at five thousand, checked and found the warning strobe gone. He also looked for evidence of sweeping and found none. He could see several merchant ships at anchor and trapped inside the mines. Word was one or more of those were British. Our buds, the Brits. *Couldn't resist making a buck—or a pound—I guess.*

Besides checking out Hon Me on the return, Stretch wanted to check out Cam Pha, a town northeast of Haiphong. On the first strike the next day, the Alpha would coast in at Cam Pha and turn west-northwest, heading for a bridge on the northeast corner of Hanoi. There was a SAM site at Cam Pha. He hoped the site would come up, like the one at Haiphong, and he could fire his Shrike at it.

He set his power at 95%. Alice was still behind but catching up.

They crossed the northern boundary of the minefield. Twenty-some miles from Cam Pha. Stretch noted no minesweepers anchored below him.

A blip bloomed on his TIAS. Dead ahead. He jammed on full power, jerked back on the stick, pulled to twenty degrees nose up, parked the nose, and fired his Shrike. It *whooshed* off the rail and streaked away. Stretch punched the button to start the stopwatch feature on his instrument panel clock, rolled upside down, dove back to five thousand. He set his power to 95% and checked on Alice. Right where he should be.

Blip on the TIAS scope? Still there. And a strobe on his SAM warning system. Pointing dead ahead. No launch warning though.

Time of flight of the Shrike, about ninety seconds. He was making seven miles a minute toward the coast. If he kept going on the present heading, he'd be six miles from the coast when the Shrike hit. He didn't want to be that close, but he also wanted to see if the blip disappeared when the second hand passed ninety seconds.

Stretch banked hard left for a couple of seconds, then he reversed and pulled to his original heading. He still had the TIAS blip. Still had the warning strobe. Now he got a launch warning. He held steady. The blip extinguished. The *deedle, deedle* launch warning quit. Ninety-two seconds.

Gotcha! Though it wasn't certain, still, it was sure enough to warrant the *gotcha.*

Mission accomplished. Time to get the … heck out of Dodge. Full power. Hard, right-climbing turn to the heading for home. And the next objective. Hon Me.

After rolling out, Stretch pulled power to 95%, and adjusted his climb to maintain three hundred knots.

"At your six," Alice radioed.

Good. He'd catch up. Stretch checked his fuel. They'd both gotten rid of their Shrikes. They still had the three bombs. Fuel. He and Alice should land with two thousand pounds. Above bingo fuel to Da Nang. Working out just as he'd planned. By all rights, he and Alice should just dump their bombs into the South China Sea. Cut the weight and drag and save a sip of fuel. But he did not want to waste the bombs. Thus, the visit to Hon Me. If he could get some AAA reaction, the bombs would not be wasted.

He leveled at thirty. There was Alice. Just where he was supposed to be.

Stretch had briefed him about poking at Cam Pha and Hon Me. "You got a problem with either of these?"

"Nope."

They were passing Thanh Hoa. Home to a famous bridge. USAF and USN bombers had tried mightily to drop the thing prior to the bombing halt in '68. The obstinate thing still stood though. Like a sing-song schoolyard taunt: *Nyah nyah nan nyan nyah. You can't catch me.*

Besides being one sturdy sucker of a bridge, it was heavily defended by AAA and SAMS. Hon Me was one thing. The Thanh Hoa Bridge was another.

Time to start a gradual descent. He wanted to be at five thousand at five miles from the island. By all rights, he should stay a few miles away from Hon Me, but he knew he wouldn't get a reaction unless he got close.

Are the Solomons' *radar controllers tracking me? Maybe. Probably.*

If they asked, he planned to say he'd gotten a TIAS indication of a SAM located there, and he thought he should check it out.

Descent rate set. He looked for Alice.

Not there! Not on his other side, either. *Where in Sam—*

Deedle, deedle! SAM launch warning. He was twelve miles off the coast. No SAM radar strobe. The nose of his plane was pointed in the wrong direction for TIAS to see a SAM at Than Hoa.

Stretch banked hard right and hauled his nose around to point at the bridge and leveled his wings. A blip about eight degrees down. *Crap! No Shrike.*

The *deedle* quit. The strobe on his warning system disappeared. The TIAS blip was gone.

Stretch crossed the beach at full power and at twenty thousand.

"Warhorse Two?" Stretch radioed.

"Evacuating the premises."

Evacuating the premises? What the hell kind of call was that?

Hopefully, it meant his crazy wingman was heading for the coast and away from the bridge.

Stretch knew there was a North Vietnamese military barracks somewhere beneath him. The Alpha Strike planning team had taken a look at how they might attack the bridge and other military targets near Thanh Hoa. Passing seventeen thousand, he banked right, then left. And saw the barracks. *Maybe. Pretty sure.*

Setting up for a normal roll-in from ten thousand feet would take too much time. Reaching to his instrument panel ordnance switches, he turned on his CP-741 bombing computer. The Skipper had prohibited using the unreliable piece of junk, but just then, it seemed like a good idea to Stretch. He set his bomb site to zero degrees, rolled upside down and pulled his gunsight dot onto the barracks, rolled upright, finessed the dot back onto the target, hit the pickle, and pulled four Gs.

He pulled up, and up, and began to think the bombs wouldn't come off. Then, *thump, thump, thump.*

Stretch leveled, banked hard left, and pointed his aircraft at the Tonkin Gulf.

"Warhorse Two?" This was a please-tell-me-you're-still-alive check.

Stretch crossed the beach.

"Feet wet in one," Alice radioed. He'd be over the water in a minute.

"Twenty thousand. Five miles. Left orbit."

His wingman would know he'd be five miles off the beach. Or, he would have known before he went berserk and attacked the *fribble frapping* Thanh Hoa Bridge by his *fribble frapping* lonesome! *Judas Priest! What the Sam Hill was he thinking?*

Stretch hit what he figured was five miles from the beach, pulled the power back, and started slowing to three hundred. Banking thirty-degrees left, he entered his rendezvous orbit. He was about to ask himself about his wingman again, and about how foolish he'd been. Instead, he examined his own conscience.

To his simple minefield recon, he'd added the attack on Cam Pha.

But that made sense. Alpha Strike #1 was flying over that very town tomorrow. It made all kinds of sense. The attack on Hon Me he'd planned, though, not so different from what Alice did. Except Thanh fribble frapping *Hoa!*

The other thing was fuel. Stretch had burned six-hundred pounds of his fuel margin. Wingmen always burned more than the leader, plus he'd attacked the bridge.

"Feet wet," Alice radioed. "Short count."

His wingman was over the South China Sea and wanted Stretch to key his radio so his direction finder equipment could get him on the proper heading to rendezvous.

Stretch radioed a five, four, three, two, one count.

"Tally ho."

Stretch's aircraft pointed at the beach. He picked up a dot against the blue. The rendezvous would work out just right. If he tightened his turn. Which he did, then rolled wings level to check on his wingie. He turned harder and rolled out headed for the ship.

Alice slid into position slicker than snot, slipped beneath his lead to check him for damage, emerged on the right wing, assumed flight lead, and Stretch checked him for damage. Clean. When he emerged on his wing, he signaled passing the lead to Stretch. Stretch shook his head.

He nodded, assuming the lead. Then he pushed the power up and started a climb. Stretch stayed with him, glued into position.

Alice switched the flight to the *Solomon's* check-in frequency and asked the ship to launch the alert tanker.

The flight lead leveled them at thirty-seven thousand as they passed Hon Me, the pile of rocks island Stretch had intended to provoke.

Alice was doing just what Stretch would have done. Squeeze max miles out of the gas they had left.

Stretch wrestled with himself over what to do about what both of them had done. The Shrike fired near Haiphong: totally justified. The one he had fired at Cam Pha, not justified. Except by himself. On the first Alpha Strike the next day, he'd be flying over that very SAM site. Attacking the site today to minimize the threat tomorrow, looking at it that way, it made sense. He recalled ratting on Nose to the Skipper. By all rights, he should first rat on himself, and then he should rat on Alice. What the two of them had done was much further out of bounds than what Nose had done.

Furthermore, he had concocted a story as to why he fired a Shrike at Cam Pha. He had another as to why they bombed Hon Me. What he did not have was a story about Thanh Hoa.

Stretch was going to have to think about what to report to Intel. *No time.*

Forty miles from the ship, they rendezvoused on the tanker.

Once flight lead stuck his refueling probe in the basket strung behind the tanker aircraft and was receiving fuel, the tanker pilot headed for the ship and set up a gradual descent. At this stage in a cruise, everyone knew the right way to do things. Pass the gas while leading the bomber guys to the ship. So they could land with little time and gas wasted.

When it was his turn to refuel, Stretch took on fuel until his gauge registered twenty-four hundred pounds. Max fuel load for landing on a carrier was twenty-two hundred. His jet would burn the extra pounds getting into position to land. He disengaged from the basket. The tanker reeled in the hose. Stretch joined on his lead's wing.

They were at three-thousand-five-hundred feet flying behind and perpendicular to the ship's wake. Alice signaled speed brakes, and the two of them deployed theirs at lead's head nod. Lead turned left and descended to eight hundred feet, signaled retracting speed brakes, and flew along the starboard side of *Solomons.*

That feeling Stretch had at the start of the flight, marveling at how he and Alice performed the mundane tasks of flying, how well they could anticipate what the other would do, and the blue sky above the blue water frothed with whitecaps, and how they got to fly through that glorious sky blossomed anew.

Alice gave him the kiss-off signal—which meant he was leaving the formation—and broke hard left over the bow of the carrier. Breaking into the carrier landing pattern over the bow put the pilot in a tight spot. Slowing down, deploying the landing gear, doing the landing check list, and rolling out behind the carrier exactly on altitude and airspeed. All those things had to be performed precisely. There was enough time to perform those functions if the pilot performed each item perfectly. There was no room to goon up even one of the steps.

Stretch flew straight ahead, counting, one-potato, two-potato until he hit the right potato; then he broke into the landing pattern, slowed, deployed gear and flaps, did the landing checklist, and turned to line up behind the ship.

Alice's tailhook snagged an arresting cable. Not a concern of Stretch's. Fly the landing pattern precisely. Line up behind the carrier precisely. Be precisely on speed.

He rolled wings level behind the carrier. The yellow light, the meatball, right where it was supposed to be, centered between the rows of green lights. Lined up with the centerline of the landing area. On speed. He called, "Five One Four, ball, two point two." He was flying side number 514. He saw the meatball. His fuel state was two thousand two hundred pounds.

In his peripheral vision, he caught sight of Alice beginning to clear the landing area. Not his concern. Meatball, lineup, airspeed. Those three things were all that mattered for the next handful of seconds. If Alice did not clear the landing area, the LSO would wave him off. Meatball, lineup, airspeed. Meatball, lineup, airspeed.

Then he was three seconds from landing. Two of the vital items disappeared, and it was meatball, meatball, meatball. Keeping the ball centered on the green lights. That was all that mattered. Until, *Wham!* 514 slammed onto the deck. Power to full and prepare to take off again if you missed all the wires. But he was flung forward against his shoulder restraints, and the plane went from one hundred-twenty-five knots to rolling backwards quicker than you could think it.

Then, off to his right the flight deck controller was signaling "Power idle. Power idle. Raise the tailhook. Raise the tailhook. Now taxi forward. Taxi forward. Hustle it the hell up."

He felt his face smile under his oxygen mask. *God, I love this stuff!*

Following his directors, he taxied to the bow, where he stopped. He felt a clunk from under the nose. That was one of the flight deck crew sticking a nosewheel steering bar into place. Then a mob of green shirted sailors assembled in front of his plane, and they started pushing him backwards. Stretch glued his eyes on his yellow shirted controller.

With 514's tail over the water, Yellow Shirt signaled, "Stop!"

Stretch jammed on the brakes, locking the wheels, and 514 rocked nose up and down again.

Clunks from outside. Wheel chocks were dropped into place. Chocks were never set on the deck to block the wheels. Chocks were dropped. The plane captain was off to his left. He had tie-down chains draped over his shoulders. Twelve of them. He walked toward the plane and started unloading chains at the points where the chains would secure 514 to the flight deck. Others in the crew started securing the chains to padeyes in deck and to tiedown points on the aircraft.

And like that, the whole process from catching a wire, taxiing clear, being pushed into position, being chocked and chained, all completed with practiced precision and alacrity.

God, I love this stuff!

"Shut down," Yellow Shirt signaled.

Stretch moved the throttle outboard and back, and the engine whined as the RPM coasted toward zero.

Stretch safe-d his ejection seat, undid his shoulder and lap belts, and opened the canopy. As happened sometimes, he sat there for a couple of seconds, bringing himself back to earth.

Crap! He hadn't figured out what to tell the Intel weenies about Thanh Hoa.

His plane captain climbed up the ladder to beside the cockpit. Stretch handed him his helmet bag.

"Mr. Z.", the PC said, "I'm supposed to tell you to hustle your butt down to the ready room, Sir. The Skipper wants to see you, chop chop."

Thanh Hoa!

Father God, Who art in heaven, forgive me for calling on You only when I am in trouble. But, here I am again.

22

TERESA LAY IN BED. 2:30 a.m. She'd changed and nursed Ruthann. The baby slept, but she could not.

A thought was chiseled into the front of her mind. Just like the one that proclaimed she had to go to Hong Kong to be with Jon. She had to.

This new message chiseled into mind-stone shouted: *Bring Jon home. Father God, Who art in heaven, hallowed be Thy name, bring him home. Please. Bring him home.*

He had written to her once that, at times, he prayed to God only when he was in trouble. Try as he might to remember to pray at other times, he forgot and woke up to fact that here he was. In trouble again, and he hadn't prayed since the last time he was in trouble.

He'd also written that he made better, more proper confessions to her than he did to priests in the confessional. He'd written:

Thank you, Father Teresa.

He had also called her Saint Teresa several times.

She wrote back saying it made her feel uncomfortable when he called her those things she was not: Saint and priest.

He wrote back:

I want you to know how important you are to me. I know the Son of God died so I could be saved. All I have to do is to reach out my hands, accept the salvation He offers, and take it inside me. The thing is, I know that, but I am such that I did not reach out and take *my* salvation that God held out to me, until I fell in love with you. You, Teresa Velmer Zachery, guided my hand to reach out and accept the salvation He held out to me, to accept it, bring it back, and press it into my soul.

Her husband wrote such wonderful letters. Sometimes she wondered if she loved him in his letters more than she loved him in person. She knew, though, that was part of examining the love they had for each other. No. She loved him in person. And Love-letter Jon helped her love In-person Jon that much more.

Father God, Who art in heaven, bring him home. Please, bring him home.

Prior to falling asleep, a thought crept into her head. He would consider it his duty to stay with the squadron, with Alice, with all of them. But he'd get over it. He'd be happy to be back with the children. *And maybe even me.*

But I won't write about praying for God to bring you home, Jon Zachery.

⸺⸺◦━◦━◦⸺⸺

Jon's flight boots thundered down the ladders—stairs—to the second deck, and he joined the flow of bodies headed aft. There was no passing lane, and the bodies could not be hurried.

At Ready Five, he pushed open the door, stepped inside, and strode down the aisle between the pilot seats.

Nose stood behind the SDO desk. "Let's all say goodbye to Stretch," he shouted.

"Goodbye, Asshole!" the Warhorse pilots responded with great gusto.

Goodbye? Stretch frowned.

The Skipper stood up from his front row chair. He turned. "Congratulations, Stretch. You just flew your last hop of this cruise."

"What? I'm on the schedule for two Alpha Strikes tomorrow. I didn't turn in my wings."

"Your orders to post grad school came in while you were flying. There's a COD taking off in a half hour. You're going to be on it."

"Like hell. I refuse the orders. I need to fly on those strikes tomorrow."

"Here's the thing. You are a lieutenant. I am a commander and your commanding officer. And I am telling you, you have flown your last flight this cruise. And you will be on the COD."

He was thinking, but had just enough sense to not say, "You need me. You can't do the anti-SAM mission without me. But he felt worse than he ever had when he used to get seasick.

I'm leaving the guys at the time when the threat will be the worst we've seen to date. This is exactly what all the studying, all the training, all the preparation had been for. I have to be on those strikes tomorrow.

"You want me to go to school while you guys go up north, to Hanoi?"

The Skipper grinned. "Yeah. It's a kick in the butt, ain't it?"

Tiny was sitting in his chair. "Tell Teresa hi."

"Stretch," the Skipper snapped. "Times a wasting. COD leaves in half an hour. Grab something to eat, change into khakis, and get on that plane. Oh, and you might want to take a shower. You stink."

Tiny went with him to the Dirty Shirt dining room. They hustled through the serving line, found a table with two seats available, plonked down, and began to shovel in the grub from his aluminum tray. He felt eyes on him and looked up. A young guy sat across from him, staring. Probably a new guy, maybe from one of the other squadrons. A clean-cut looking guy, close-cropped dirty blond hair, about his own height and build. The new guy shook his head.

"Stretch, this is Mike Falcon. He's a newbie in your squadron. He came aboard in the COD that's going to take you off. By the look on his face, I'd say he's thinking, 'Lord God, how long before I turn into an animal eating like that?' So, see, Stretch, that's another reason you have to leave. We can't have you grossing out the newbies."

Jon said hi to Mike and returned to scarfing his food. Then hustle to his room, hustle through a shower, hustle up to the flight deck. Tiny hustled up to the flight deck with him. Stretch boarded the COD with five minutes to spare. He strapped into a seat as the engines started and coughed to life. The plane was only half full, but still, he was not the only one abandoning his shipmates when the going was getting rough.

Cat shots were high pucker factor events. Night cat shots were the worst, though. Except for cat shots in a COD. In the passenger plane, he was in control of nothing. If something went wrong, he'd be able to do not one blinking thing to fix it. Except die of course. God, he hated COD cat shots.

That, too, passed. The copilot raised the gear, and they were on their way.

Jon felt much as he had when he'd said goodbye to Teresa on the pier in Hong Kong, and the ferryboat started taking him away from her. It was as if he had a fishhook in his heart, and the line was tied to Teresa. As the distance between them increased, a chunk of heart meat ripped out stayed with his wife.

Now in a COD, flying ultimately toward home, toward Teresa, another hunk of heart meat ripped out of his chest and stayed there, on the *Solomons*, with the Warhorses. Leaving them felt like he'd just committed the biggest sin he'd ever committed. This was desertion in the face of the enemy.

He thought about the chapel on the ship and felt another chunk of heart meat rip out in his longing for that sanctuary. But that could not be. The drone of the engines and props. He sank into those and anguish diminished.

Just before he boarded the plane, Tiny had given him an envelope from the Skipper. He opened it and pulled out a note.

> Stretch, I know you feel a sense of duty to be here with
> us, to lead our SAM fighting efforts. But, this endless
> war is going to end. Someday, and not too far into the
> future. When it is over and done, our navy will have some
> rebuilding to do. Go to school, get even smarter than
> you already are, and help put our service together again
> in much better shape than it is now. You have taught us
> all a lot about fighting SAMs and using our equipment

to best advantage. We will miss you in the friendly skies
Up North, but you need to go to school. Study hard and
don't you flunk out.

Li'l Lord

*You know, Li'l Lord, I've grown sorta, halfways, kinda, well, almost
fond of you.*

He took in a deep breath, huffed it out, and pulled his letter-writing
material out of his bag.

Dearest Teresa.

Out of the blue, a blessing straight from heaven. I am
coming home. Nobody can even guess when this cruise
will end. Except for me, and it ends now. And I have to
admit, I feel some guilt over my joy coming at the cost of
my shipmates continued service in the Gulf.

But, my anticipation of seeing you, holding you, loving
you obliterates my guilt. At least most of it.

He owed her putting it that way.

23

ON THE COD FLIGHT TO Da Nang, LT Zachery—he wasn't Stretch anymore, just a plain, ordinary, common, US Navy lieutenant—realized he was alone. No longer assigned to a squadron. Cut off from them. Cast off from them. As rejected as Blackie had been.

He pictured Nose standing in front of the packed Ready Room saying, "Here's how it shakes out Lieutenant Zachery. We got important stuff to do, you know? Fact is, we can do it better without you. So, so long, *auf wiedersehen*, *sayonara*, *adieu*, and don't let the doorknob hit you."

It hadn't happened that way, but he couldn't feel worse if it had. The sense of having lost something priceless and irreplaceable and irretrievable was overwhelming. The Skipper's letter had no power to fill the cold hole in his soul.

For the first time, he wondered what thoughts occupied Blackie as he flew home. Did he feel disgraced, despondent, depressed? Angry? Maybe revenge boiled in that raptor brain of his.

Get a grip Str—Lieutenant.

He sucked in a lungful, huffed it out, and pulled his orders out of his helmet bag, which he was using as a briefcase.

Holy crap! He had to check in to the US Navy's Postgraduate School in Monterey, California, in ten days. In a week and a half, he had to travel around half the globe. Using government transportation! As soon as he got home, he had to arrange for his household goods to be packed up and shipped to Monterey.

There won't even be time to kiss Teresa and hug the kids!

He tried to remember if you gained a day or lost a day crossing the International Date Line moving from east to west.

Probably lose a day!

That last thought dripped pessimism. It sounded as if it had come from Eeyore.

Father, God, Who art in heaven, into your hands I commend my … our future.

The COD landed in Da Nang and disgorged its passengers at the Air Operations Building/terminal. Jon got in line at the check-in desk and was assigned a hop to Tan Son Nhut that evening.

He thought about calling Teresa but did not want to terrorize Ruth with the phone jangling in the middle of the night.

At Tan Son Nhut, the passenger check-in desk there, the BOQ, both familiar territory. But, thankfully, no puke to mop up. That night, his roommate was a USAF second lieutenant, a kid really, alone and scared. But he didn't drink.

Stretch—Jon considered saying something, like, "We're all scared when we first get over here, but you get over it." But he kept his mouth shut. The kid was going to have to work it out on his own.

Jon set his alarm for 3 a.m. He wanted to call Teresa before boarding his 7 a.m. ride to Clark AFB in the PI.

He slept well and woke to punch off the alarm five minutes before it rang. Nine days until classes started at Navy Post Graduate School.

Rip through the bathroom business. Snag a ride to the phone center. Place the call. Teresa didn't answer. He tried Amy Allison. She didn't pick up either. He didn't know the phone numbers of the other wives. When he got to the PI, he'd try Teresa again, even though it was the middle of the night for her and the air-raid siren.

Jon landed at Clark AFB in the PI at 1005. At 1015, LT Zachery joined an officer's queue for assignment to a flight back to the US. At 1045, he was assigned to ride on a C-5 cargo plane with the capability to transport one hundred passengers above the cargo hold. Scheduled departure time was 1400. Passenger check-in time: 1200.

Call Teresa. Still no answer. *Where the heck are you?* It was the middle of the night back home, so he didn't try Amy Allison.

At 1145, he checked in. At 1215 he and ninety-nine others, mostly air force enlisted men, boarded the behemoth jet with its cargo hold filled with jet engines on the way back home for overhaul. The upper deck passenger accommodations resembled a civilian airliner. To a certain extent. Except for the flight attendant. An air force enlisted man who obviously resented having to be a servant to several men who were junior in rank to himself.

Jon settled into his seat and pulled a book from his helmet bag/ briefcase. He read two chapters and checked his watch. 1430. They hadn't even started engines yet!

Reluctant Male Stewardess announced that the aircraft had a tire that needed to be changed. The passengers should deplane and remain in the passenger terminal. They'd re-board once the aircraft repair was completed. Which happened at 1800. After sitting on the plane for twenty minutes, Reluctant Male Stewardess announced that the trip to Guam for that day had to be canceled because the crew's maximum time in flight status for a day would be exceeded before the plane landed. They were now scheduled to take off at 0700. But, if all went well, the plane would make it to Hawaii the next day.

All did not go well the next morning. With all the passengers in the seats, with engines started, the crew discovered low oil pressure on one engine. Again, the passengers disembarked for the terminal.

After the repair and re-boarding, Jon wound up in the second row of seats. RMS, Reluctant Male Stewardess, started into the safety brief.

A US Air Force enlisted man in the front row said, "Yeah, yeah, yeah. We've heard that brief so many times I could give it. Put a sock in it."

"The regs say I have to give the brief. They also say you have to listen to it. If I think you are not listening, I can have you put off the plane. If that happens, you probably won't get manifested on another flight for a week." RMS glared at the interrupter. "Anything else to say?"

"I'm all ears."

When the safety brief concluded, Interrupter said, "Must be a pain in the butt. Working on a piece of crap airplane like this."

"It's not a piece of crap airplane," RMS snapped. "The C-5 is an amazing aircraft. It can carry huge loads of cargo. We've even carried tanks. It is a complex piece of equipment, though, and, on occasion, some part breaks. Now buckle your damned seatbelt."

Jon expected Interrupter to make a comment about, "*on occasion, some part breaks*" but the RMS glare shut down further questions and comments.

The C-5 arrived in Guam but had to remain overnight because of aircrew-flight-day limitations.

Jon tried calling both Teresa and Amy Allison. Still no answer from either. He also used Information to get the number for Sarah Fant, but there was no answer at the CO's residence either.

At 0800 Lemoore, California, time, and using the government phone system, he called the Catholic chaplain's office. An enlisted yeoman answered the phone. The priest was not available. He was celebrating daily Mass. The yeoman took a message.

Jon returned to his BOQ room and shaved, showered, and Shinola-ed his shoes. Then he called the chaplain's office at Lemoore again. The chaplain was in.

"Lieutenant Zachery, your wife is fine. I just spoke with her."

"Where is she?" Jon said.

"She's in your quarters on base here."

"Chaplain, would it be possible to patch me to my wife?"

"My yeoman knows how to do that. Hang on?"

While Jon waited, precious seconds ticked away. He had to be at the terminal soon to check-in for the flight to Hawaii. Plus, he fretted and fumed over Teresa's absence. *Where in Sam Hill had she been?* Didn't she know how worried he'd been?

Then her voice, "Jon, where are you?"

"Where have you been?"

"Uh, Jon, are you mad at me?"

Here I am, Lord. In trouble again. And I need Your help.

"No. I'm not mad at you. I've been trying to call you and got no answer. I was worried. That's all. I am *not* mad at you. I could *never* be mad at you."

"It sounded like you were mad at me."

"Forgive me. And I don't want to make this worse, but I am in Guam, and I need to get to the passenger terminal, so I don't miss my flight. Teresa, I love you more than my own life. Please kiss our babies for me. I'll call from Hawaii."

"Just another minute. Sarah Fant helped me get our move set up. Our things have all been packed and moved to Monterey. And our furniture and everything are already set up in our new apartment there."

"Dear God in heaven!"

They talked for three more minutes. Their marriage was in good shape when Jon hung up.

En route to Hawaii, Jon wrote a long letter to Teresa. As he wrote, his soul filled with peace. As if an angel poured a bucketful of the holy substance into a hole in his spirit head. For the first time since the tender and touching farewell in Ready Room Five, soul salve oozed into every corner of his being. It felt pretty darned close to almost sort of good.

⸻◈⸻

In Hawaii, another critical part on the C-5 failed. The air force located replacement parts at Tan Son Nhut and on the east coast of the US. It would take two days for the part to arrive. Jon explained the time crunch he faced and asked for reassignment to a different flight. He was manifested on the C-5 all the way to the US. He could not be reassigned. He would have to be patient.

Jon carried his pay records with him. He went to the paymaster on base, drew a month's advance pay, and bought a ticket on a redeye to Los Angeles. He didn't sleep much. Someone, other than himself, flew the plane. That didn't seem right.

In LA, he found a bench near luggage claim, sat and promptly fell asleep.

A voice called his name in a dark, fog-filled room. "Jon. Jon."

Amy Allison had watched the Zachery children. Monica Newsome drove Teresa to LA. They departed Lemoore at midnight.

At 0700, Teresa found Jon asleep on a bench near Luggage Claim. She said, "Jon," and touched his shoulder.

His eyes popped open, and he smiled. Then he shook his head and a serious look slipped over his face. "You're not a dream. You're real."

"You're sort of close to almost real, yourself, Stretch." It was Monica Newsome.

The two ladies were exhausted after their all-night drive. Jon was tired, too, but he figured he had more experience with the midnight to noon schedule, so he drove them back north.

North! That word, so packed with concern for Alice, Not, EC, Nose, and the others. The Skipper. CAG. All of them. The guys on the flight deck. The thousands working below deck. As he navigated Monica's car out of the terminal parking lot and away from the LA airport, The North boiled and bubbled in a witch's cauldron of worry in one of his minds. Another mind drove.

The two ladies slept. He drove and worried.

His worry mind flew the route to the first target near Hanoi the day after he left *Solomons.* He hoped they let Alice fly as Baron One. But perhaps EC or Not pulled rank and took lead Shrike shooter. Alice knew the mission better than those two. Would the Ops O or the Skipper appreciate that?

There was no comfort to be found anywhere in that line of worry.

Maybe, though, he had killed the SAM site at Cam Pha. Maybe that made a difference on that first strike. Maybe all of them on that first strike made it back to *Solomons.*

Maybe! There's a word packed with an ephemeron of hope based on self-deluded wishful thinking.

Jon jerked awake to find himself going eighty-five miles an hour down the north side of the mountains and about to hit the flat floor of the San Joaquin Valley south of Bakersfield. The other traffic on I-5 that morning was light. *Thank You, Father God in heaven.*

Maybe, Jon Zachery. You should get your head out of your butt and pay attention to driving and not killing Not's wife. And your own!

And maybe, Jon Zachery, you should work on not sandwiching prayer to God between lost hope and despair and crude sailor talk.

For the second half of the drive to Naval Air Station Lemoore, Jon shrank his worry mind to the size of a walnut. His driving mind filled the rest of his head. They arrived safely. At 1100. In the driveway of Amy Allison's house. The Zachery's car was parked in the carport of what had been their now empty quarters. Teresa and Monica stirred and stretched.

Jon turned off the engine, stepped out of the car, and walked around it to open the passenger door for Teresa. The front door of the Allison's home flew open, and Jennifer and EJ spilled out onto the sidewalk and ran to the car, with, "Daddy, Daddy," preceding their crash into kneeling Jon Zachery.

"Oof! You are so grown up, both of you. You almost knocked me over." Jon stood with a grown-up child in each arm.

Back-seat Monica said, "Wonder where Amy is?"

"She's probably got babies to take care of," Teresa said.

"EJ woke them up," Jennifer reported.

"I saw wee."

"Today is a happy day, Edgar Jon," Daddy said. "No need to be saw wee."

Teresa stepped out of the passenger side and held the seat forward to allow Monica to exit.

Amy stepped onto her front porch with a baby in each arm. "Hi!"

Jon and Teresa both hurried toward her. Jon reached for the baby, stopped, stepped back, and said, "Sorry."

"Today is a happy day, Jon Zachery. No need to be saw wee. Go ahead. Take her."

Jon eased his daughter from his neighbor's arm and cooed, "You are such a big girl."

Ruthann fussed and waved her arms.

"She says it's lunchtime," Teresa said.

"She's right." From Amy. "Come on in, you all. Lunch is on the table."

They filed into Amy's home. In the dining room, apron-wearing Deborah Wakefield waited. A warm and welcome smile lit her face.

"Welcome home, Jon Zachery. Before we get caught up in eating, I wanted to say thank you."

"Thank me?"

"Yes, Mark—

Mark? Oh. EC. Her husband.

—wrote how much he learned from flying with you. He said he owes you a lot."

"Ah, Mrs. Wakefield—

"Deborah."

Jon shifted his weight from one foot to the other. He held Jennifer's and EJ's hands and both his palms generated sweat. "Deborah. EC … Mark is a good stick and throttle jockey. Flying over Vietnam, though, it's different. There are a few things he needed to know he couldn't learn flying from the east coast. But, he listened and learned fast. I didn't do anything for him RT, he was maintenance officer last cruise, did for me."

"I meant to thank you, too, Stretch," Monica piped in. She was the only Warhorse spouse who used the men's call signs rather than given names. "But I slept all the way back up here. Nose wrote that you saved his life one night."

Jon wiped a sweaty palm on his trousers. "When's lunch?"

They all took places around Amy's table. Except Teresa. She nursed Ruthann.

Amy invited Jon to say Grace, which he did.

Jennifer then sliced the "men" off "Amen" with, "Daddy, I read big-girl books now."

EJ: "I take fwimmin' lessons."

Teresa walked into the dining room as she patted Ruthann on the back, searching for a burp. "Jennifer, EJ, eat your sandwiches."

"Jon," Amy said. "I almost forgot to tell you. Sarah Fant is hosting a farewell party for you and Teresa tonight."

"A farewell party! After all you've done for our family, I should be hosting a thanksgiving party for all of you."

"That's true," Monica, Mrs. Nose, said. "But you're a male, and we understand the limitations attached to that half of the species, so we females put together the event."

24

A BABYSITTER TENDED JENNIFER AND EJ at Amy Allison's house. Teresa and Amy brought their babies to the function.

Jon felt as out of place as a fan dancer in a nunnery. The Warhorse wives all made an effort to include him in conversation. How it worked, though, one of them would approach him, and exert the effort to say something to him, which he'd respond to, and then, bereft of possible further words to say, the wife would rejoin the nearest female conversation.

Each of these interventions drove home ever more forcefully, that here he was, safe at home, while their husbands were on the other side of the world dodging SAMs.

One thing, though, impressed the heck out of him. The pot-organized supper. Each of the heavies' wives organized some part of the meal. Laura Davison, Mrs. XO, was in charge of Sarah Fant's double oven, and she made sure what the ladies brought did not exceed the oven capacity. Working closely with Laura, Maryann Toliver, Mrs. Ops O, approved the menu. Deborah Wakefield organized a set-the-table detail from the junior wives. Not's wife Naomi would organize the clean-up.

Could have used the wives to organize a couple of our Alpha Strike planning sessions.

At seven, with everyone assembled in the living room, Sarah said a before meal blessing. Then, she invited Jon and Teresa to pick up their plates from the dining room table and proceed to the kitchen, where all the elements of the pot-organized were laid out on the kitchen island. After loading their plates, the guests of honor returned to the table where they sat across from each other next to the hostess' place at the head.

The other guests filed past the serving station in order of husband's rank.

Laura Davison sat next to Jon. "I'm sure your children were happy to see you."

"Yes, Ma'am—"

"Laura."

"Yes, Ma'am. Laura. Almost as happy as I was to see them. It was amazing how they took turns telling me about school, books, toys, friends. Almost as well-orchestrated as your pot-organized dinner."

Maryann Toliver sat across from Laura. "I don't know how many potlucks I've been to over the years where half the people brought salad and the other half brought dessert. A boatload of times, though."

Deborah Wakefield took the chair next to Laura. She leaned forward. "Jon, I don't know how busy things will get tonight, but I wanted to be sure and thank you. I've gotten a couple of letters from Mike where he told me about how much you helped him when he was going through a rough time. He is most grateful for what you did for him. And so am I."

She already told me that.

"Ma'am—

"Deborah."

Oh! She wanted to say it in front of the others.

"I only did for your husband what RT, he was our Maintenance Officer last year, did for me. There're things you need to learn about flying over Nam that you can only learn by flying over Nam. We all went through what Mike did. He was a quick study, and I liked flying with him."

The other ladies took their places, and Sarah arrived at hers. She picked up a glass of white wine, raised it, and said, "To the Zacherys. A great Warhorse couple."

"The Zacherys!" rolled around the table.

The CO's wife took a bite of enchilada, chewed, swallowed, dabbed a napkin to her lips, raised her glass, and said, "To Main Course Wanda Mason. A blue-ribbon creation."

The Warhorse Wives responded, "To Wanda, To Main Course Mason." and a few other variations.

Jon lifted his glass. "To the War—"

"Ah, ah," Mrs. Skipper said. "Later, Lieutenant Zachery. Now we eat. Eat."

He blushed. Teresa smiled at his discomfit. He squirmed in his seat. "Eat."

He ate.

"I understand you had an interesting journey home," Sarah stated.

Jon swallowed a half-chewed mouthful, wondering whether that had been a question.

She looked at him expectantly. *Alright. A question.* "Yes, Ma'am. Sarah."

I got to come home. Nobody else's husband did. She—Sarah is putting me in my place.

"Sarah. Invite me back another hundred-and-eleven times, and I may pick up the rules here."

The hostess permitted the ensuing hush to prevail for a moment, and said, "I understand you had an interesting journey home."

In that moment, he saw the aura of authority and command in her, as he had seen it in her husband and CAG. He swallowed a sip of water and replaced his glass on the table and looked at his interrogator.

"Yes. Sarah. Interesting. And a few other *ing* adjectives come to mind. Annoying, for instance. I had no problem getting out of Vietnam. But then I arrived at Clark Air Force Base."

"In the PI, right? And you tried to call Teresa, but she wasn't home. And you found that annoying, right?"

"Well, no. I found that interesting."

Sarah smiled at Jon as if he were her son and had finally brought home a decent report card from second grade.

She orchestrated this whole thing! The wives would have resented him being home, and their own husbands still over there. And thank You, God, I, with Your help, pulled it off. I earned my way to being considered an honorary Warhorse Wife. Now don't screw it up, Zachery.

He related the litany of aircraft malfunctions that delayed his departure from Clark AFB. Reluctant Male Stewardess was mentioned.

"So, it took a day longer than it should have to make Guam, and there, more problems with the airplane. But I was able to use the military Autovon phone system to call the Catholic chaplain on base here at Lemoore, and I connected with Teresa and found out what all of you did to help her. And us."

Jon picked up his wine glass and glanced at Sarah. She smiled. "To the greatest wives' group in the universe. The Warhorse Wives."

The phone rang and dumped a bucketful of chill on every heart at the table.

Sarah inhaled a deep breath, let it out, and hurried to the kitchen to answer it.

Jon's eyes followed her. He was sure every eye at the table did likewise. It also grew quiet. Not the solemn peace-giving silence he'd found in the *Solomon's* chapel. This was like waking up to a strange sound and listening intently for another to give a clue as to what evil threatened from the concealing blackness.

"Hello," came to the dining room. Sarah had tried to subdue her voice, but that menacing silence magnified it.

"Oh. Yes. I'll bring her." She hung up. "Jon, would you come here, please?"

When he arrived in the kitchen, Sarah was writing a note on the counter next to the sink. She turned and her eyes burned with intense hurt and an equal measure of determination.

Jon took the note she thrust at him.

EC has been shot down. He's MIA.
Please leave. Now.

It hit him like a baseball bat in the chest. The news would stab Deborah in the heart. His being there would twist the blade.

He closed the rear door softly behind him, walked around the house, and stood at the end of the driveway. For a moment, he couldn't remember where he'd parked the car.

Maybe I should walk the seven miles to base. Leave the car for Teresa.

There was punishment and sacrificial atonement embedded in that choice. Both appealed. But no. He needed to remove himself from the scene. Quickly.

Jennifer and EJ slept soundly in the other double bed in their Navy Lodge room. Ruth slept in a playpen, provided by the Lodge.

In their bed, Teresa had her arm across Jon's chest. "I know it hurts you to be the cause of pain and grief to Deborah and the other wives. Sarah got a message from the CO. He told her you wanted to refuse the orders to Post Grad School and to stay with guys on *Solomons*, but the Skipper wouldn't let you. She said the Skipper told you the Navy needed for you to go, get another degree, and help the service figure out what to do after the endless war in Vietnam ends. Is that what happened?"

He just lay there.

She needed to get him talking, to unburden himself. "Talk to me," though, was the worst possible thing she could say to him. Those three words, he'd written to her once, *rip the tongue out of my mouth.*

"When you left Sarah's, did you come directly here after picking up Jennifer and EJ from the sitter?"

He just lay there. She puzzled over what to try next.

"No. First I stopped at the chaplain's house here on base. Told him I needed to go to confession."

She waited for more. *Men!* "What happened?"

"I confessed. Father told me he could not absolve me because I had not sinned, and that survivor's remorse is not a sin."

Jon took in a big breath and Teresa's arm rose on his rising chest. He sighed it out.

"Father said, 'Survivor's Remorse comes from a strong sense of duty and a loving heart. Pray to the Father for help in bearing this grief you feel over your sense of letting your buddies down. Pray to Him. Ask and you shall receive.'"

Teresa rolled off him and took his hand. "Hail, Mary, full of grace. Say it with me, Jon Zachery."

He said it with her, and the Our Father which followed.

Then she prayed, "Father God of heaven and earth, rest your healing hand on Deborah's broken heart. Help her to mend. Help her cope. Help her.

"And this good man beside me, please heal him as well. Help him bear the burden of grief he has taken upon himself. Help him see he has not failed in his duty, rather that he has discharged it well. And please watch over all the Warhorse wives. Amen."

"Amen." He squeezed her hand.

She climbed on top of him and kissed him. With fervor. After a time, she pulled back to look at him in the dim from the night light.

"I was going to say something," he whispered.

"Sometimes," she whispered, "you talk too much, Jon Zachery."

Jon snorted. Teresa giggled. They laughed.

Jennifer said, "Mommy?"

"Sorry I woke you, dear. Daddy told a funny, and I laughed too loud."

"Can he say the funny to me?"

"Um," Jon said.

"It was just a stupid grown up thing. Go back to sleep dear. We'll be quiet."

"Okay. Night, mommy. Night, daddy."

"Nighty-night, dear," they responded as one.

And they were sort of, almost, kind of quiet.

⸺⊱❦⊰⸺

The next morning, Jon awoke at five. He slipped out of bed. Jennifer and EJ were still zonked in their bed. Ruthann slept in her playpen. Teresa lay on her back, her brown hair splayed around her head like an earth halo. *Thank you, God, for bringing her and me together.*

His heart and soul felt better than they had since he walked into Ready Room 5 and all the Warhorses shouted, Goodbye, A— Well, what they always shouted.

Looking down on his Dearest, the urge to kiss her awake, to hold her, to love her mounted to the point where he could barely contain it. But he did. After drinking in another helping of her image lying there, he entered the head and did his business. As he would have on the *Solomons*. Complete *his* business before reveille rousted the hordes to do theirs.

When he reentered the room, Ruthann was fussing, at well below air-raid siren level.

Teresa stretched her arms above her head.

"Shhh, Roofann," EJ whispered.

Jon smiled. Pandemonium lurked just around the corner, but, Lord, God in heaven, it was a glorious feeling to be there in the middle of it.

"I'll change Little Miss Fuss-budget," he whispered.

She wrinkled her nose. "It could be a two-person job."

"I got it."

Teresa slipped out of bed, kissed him, and used the … well, bathroom civilians called it.

We she returned, Jon was bathing Ruth in the kitchenette sink. Jennifer and EJ were eating cereal

Teresa fixed herself a bowl of Corn Chex and ate while her husband finished with the baby. Then she returned to bed and nursed the little one while he orchestrated their crew through bathroom visits and began the kitchen clean-up.

"You mind burping Ruthann?" Teresa said.

He draped a spit-up diaper across his shoulder, arranged his daughter, and began patting her back.

"My turn," Teresa said and headed for the bathroom.

Jon patted and paced.

> *Do you not see, Jon Zachery? There is duty in this, too. And*
> *it is every bit as sacred as that duty you felt, and feel, for*
> *those on the* Solomons.

He had not seen it. He should have but had not. Instead, it had to come at him like a thunderclap from a sunny sky.

Sometimes, Jon Zachery, you can be so stupid.

After nine o'clock Mass at the base chapel, Jon drove them back to the Navy Lodge. When he parked, Deborah Wakefield stepped out of her car and walked toward them. "I am so glad I didn't miss you."

She wore no makeup. Her face was pale. She wore a frown. And a little smile.

"How are you?" Teresa said.

"Happy. That I didn't miss seeing you before you left."

"Would you like to come up to the room? We can make a pot of coffee."

"I don't want to hold you up if you need to get on the road."

"Not at all. Come."

In their second-floor room, Teresa had the children change out of their church clothes. Then she settled Jennifer and EJ on the sofa with books.

Jon placed a mug of coffee in front of Deborah. "Milk? Sugar?"

"Milk, please."

He got the half full half gallon from the mini-fridge and set it in front of her.

She poured and stirred.

He sat across from Deborah. Teresa took the chair next to his, and she unbuttoned and started to nurse the baby.

Deborah wrapped her hands around the mug, staring at it. She appeared to be struggling with where to start. Or maybe emotions roiled hot and heavy inside her, and she was trying to get control.

She looked up.

It was as if the grief Jon saw in her eyes jabbed out in a fist and smacked him in the chest. In the next instant, her eyes brimmed with compassion and concern, and these smacked him as well. So surprising after the grief.

"Jon, last night, when Sarah shooed you out of the house, I … I was glad I didn't have to see you. Sarah couldn't tell me what had happened, only that she had to get me home because the CACO and a chaplain needed to talk to me. So, I knew Mike was dead or, please, God, a POW. And seeing you would have been hard. That was last night."

She took a sip.

"Oh. I should have asked how you like it. I make it strong for myself."

"Mike does—" She stopped. He wondered if she'd amend her sentence to past tense.

She raised her chin. "Mike does, too." Her smile brightened by a lumen or two. "I wanted to tell you that Mike wanted to fly combat in Vietnam for years. He was so afraid the war would end before he got into it."

Jon considered mentioning that he'd had the same worry when LBJ announced the bombing halt in 1968, but he kept his mouth shut.

"When he joined the Warhorses and you all deployed, he thought he was older and more experienced than you snot-nosed lieutenants and JGs. What did any of you possibly have to teach him? He especially detested Blackie."

Again, he kept his lips zipped.

"But then, after his first real combat hops, he found out the snot-nosed JOs had learned some things he hadn't picked up. He wrote that the things they knew, they learned by flying in combat. Flying in combat was the only way to learn those things." Her eyes met his. "Just the way you said it. Anyway, all his age, his flight hours, his seniority earned him was sitting in a corner wearing a dunce cap. He was discouraged and ready to turn in his wings."

She sipped, and he did, too. "Want me to warm it up?"

Deborah shook her head. "Mike said that you took him under your wing and showed him how to approach flying in combat."

"He paid attention, and he learned fast. All he needed was to step back a bit and understand that the expectations he had of himself were a smidge too exalted."

"Comparable to a hummingbird thinking he's an eagle, Mike put it."

Stretch—he felt like Stretch again—smiled.

"Anyway, I wanted to tell you Mike considered it his duty to serve in Vietnam. Because of you, he was able to fulfill that sense of duty, of purpose. And I wanted to thank you for what you did for him?"

Deborah stood. "Teresa, request permission to hug your husband?"

She was in the process of shifting sides, and the baby was worried lunch was over, not just half over. Once Ruth was settled again, Teresa said, "Not too long and not too enthusiastically."

Deborah motioned for Jon to stand. She hugged him. Hard. Then she let him go. "Hopefully, that wasn't too long."

Jon piloted their red, two-door Impala west down Highway 198 toward I-5. Cotton fields lined both sides of highway 198. Ahead of them, the coastal range rose brown out of the haze. The children were quiet on the back seat.

"Funny," he said. "It took the wife of an east coast puke whose husband was just shot down to show me how to understand the Vietnam War and my sense of duty."

Teresa undid her seat belt and slid across the seat of their two-door Impala next to him and hugged his arm. "The Lord works in mysterious ways. I've told you that often enough."

"Yes, you have, Father Teresa."

"I have to go potty," EJ said.

"From profound to potty in the blink of an eye," Teresa said.

"Things went that way in the Tonkin Gulf, too, Sweetheart."

"I have to go potty!"

"Welcome home, Jon Zachery."

"There's nowhere on earth I'd rather be."

No traffic behind them. Jon pulled off onto the shoulder, stopped the car, and did his duty.

After, with the Impala breezing down the highway again, with Teresa against the passenger side door, with the children quiet in back, Jon recalled LBJ making his big bombing halt announcement in 1968. He'd been in flight training. He'd prayed, *Please, God, don't let the war be over until I get in it.* The prayer was answered. He thought about saying the prayer anew. *Please, God, don't let the war end until I get **back** in it.*

But he only thought about saying it.

VA–92 WARHORSE OFFICERS

Commanding Officer	CDR Leroy Fant	Little Lord, CO, Skipper
Spouse, Sarah		
Executive Officer	LCDR Dave Davison	Double D, XO, the exec.
Spouse, Laura		
Operations Officer	LCDR Simon Toliver	Simp
Spouse, Maryann		
Maintenance Officer	LCDR Mark Wakefield	EC (East Coast)
Spouse, Deborah		
Administrative Officer	LT Harvey Engel	Not (Not an Angel)
Spouse, Naomi		
Assistant Maintenance	LT Howie Wisdom	Wiz
Spouse, Tara		
Flight Schedule Officer	LT Rob White	Blackey
Former Spouse, Carolyn		
Weapons Training	LT Jon Zachery	Stretch
Spouse, Teresa		
LTJG Mike Allison	Spouse, Amy	Alice
Personnel Officer	LTJG Nat Newsome	Nose
Spouse, Monica		
Line Division Officer	LTJG Terry Foster	Nooner
	Lydia	
	LTJG Oliver Mason	Skippy
	Spouse, Wanda	
	LTJG Cal Mudd	Mudder
	LTJG Walt Short	Stump
	LTJG Eli Banks	Bee (Newbie)

NAVY RANK ABBREVIATIONS

Officer

Captain, O-6	CAPT
Commander, O-5	CDR
Lieutenant Commander, O-4	LCDR
Lieutenant, O-3	LT
Lieutenant (Junior Grade), O-2	JG
Ensign, O-1	ENS

Enlisted

Seaman Recruit, E-1	SR
Seaman Apprentice, E-2	SA
Seaman, E-3	SN
Petty Officer Third Class, E-4	PO3
Petty Officer Second Class, E-5	PO2
Petty Officer First Class, E-6	PO1
Chief Petty Officer	CPO

GLOSSARY OF TERMS AND ACRONYMS

AAA	Antiaircraft artillery, also called triple A and flak.
AFB	Air Force Base
airdales	On an aircraft carrier, the sailors assigned to the airwing.
airwing	Squadrons assigned to an aircraft carrier grouped and commanded by a senior officer.
Alpha strike	In a low-threat environment, targets could be attacked by flights of two to four aircraft. In a high-threat environment, sixteen to twenty-four bombers would gaggle together while other planes protected the gaggle from MiGs and SAMs.
AOM	All officers meeting. Pilots and ground officers.
APM	All pilots meeting.
bingo	To divert ashore due to a problem with the carrier, with the airplane, or reaching a critical fuel state.
BIT	Built-in test.
Boatload	As used in the story, sailor talk for a lot, or a large number
BOQ	Bachelor officer's quarters.

CACO	Casualty Assistance Calls Officer
CAG	Commander of the airwing.
Cat	Catapult
Click	A thousand meters
CMC	Classified material custodian.
CO	Commanding officer, also called the skipper.
COD	Carrier Onboard Delivery. Plane equipped to ferry personnel and supplies to an aircraft carrier.
COS	Chief of staff.
CPO	Chief petty officer, an E-7.
Det	Detachment
Division	Formation of four aircraft
DMZ	Demilitarized zone.
EW	Early Warning
FAC	Forward air controller, generally in a small propeller-driven plane, whose job was to spot targets on the ground and direct bombers onto the targets.
Feet wet	Refers to a pilot who had been flying over land and leaves the land behind and is now over water
FENAB	Field Naval Aviator Evaluation Board. Pronounced *fee nab*. A board constituted to evaluate the performance of an aviator after a mishap to determine if the aviator was at fault, and if so, to make a recommendation as to whether, or not, he should continue on flight status.
Freq.	Frequency
FUBAR	Fouled up beyond all recognition.
Fuel State	Given in pounds, A gallon of jet fuel weighs approximately 7 pounds
Go	As in "1030 to noon go." The sorties that launch from a carrier at 1030 and return to land at 1200.
Ground Pounder	Maintenance officer, not a pilot.
Head	On a ship, a bathroom

Heavies	Senior officers, typically O-4 and above
Intel	Intelligence
Ironhand	The anti-SAM mission. Ironhand aircraft equipped with Shrike protected a group of bombers from surface-to-air missiles.
JBD	Jet blast deflector, a slab of steel raised from the flight deck behind an aircraft on the catapult. It is slanted and deflects the blast from a jet engine up and away from planes behind the cat.
JG	Junior grade appended to the navy rank of lieutenant. A lieutenant (JG) wore one silver bar; a full lieutenant wore two.
JO	Junior officer.
JOB	Junior officer bunkroom.
JOPA	Junior Officer Protective Association, a fictious organization incapable of protecting anyone but affording junior officers an opportunity to gripe about the capricious orders issued by senior officers.
KIA	Killed in action.
MIA	Missing in action.
Morted	Killed
NAS	Naval Air Station
nighter	Night flight.
OCS	Officer candidate school.
OINC	Officer in Charge
OOD	Officer of the Deck
OP	Observation post.
Ops	Operations.
Ops, or Ops O	Operations officer.
PI	Philippine Islands
Pickle	As a noun, the bomb release button on the control stick As a verb, to pickle, to press the bomb release button

PO	Petty officer (navy-enlisted rank).
PC	Postal clerk.
QA	Quality assurance.
Recce	Reconnaissance
Rockeye	Cluster bomb. A bomb-like canister containing a large number of bomblets. The bomblets covered hundreds of feet with lethal shrapnel, as compared to a regular bomb whose shrapnel extended perhaps thirty-five feet.
SAM	Surface-to-air missile.
SDO	Squadron duty officer.
Section	Formation of two aircraft
Shrike	An air-to-ground missile carried by US aircraft designed to home on the radars guiding SAMs or AAA fire against US planes.
Skipper	A term for a squadron commanding officer, generally denoting respect and admiration
Skyspot	A bombing technique used in bad weather. A radar controller directs a flight of bombers, above the clouds, over a target area, known to be free of friendly forces. When the radar controller orders, the pilots pickle off their bombs and return to base.
SOP	Standard operating procedure.
TACAN	An electronic navigation aid. In a cockpit, the device displayed range and bearing to a TACAN ground station or an aircraft carrier.
Tech Rep	Technical Representative from a company responsible for manufacturing a navy aircraft or components.
Thou.	Thousand
TIAS	Target Identification and Acquisition System.
TS	Top secret.
VC	Viet Cong.
Ville	Village
XO	Executive officer.